I0724115

RAGE Issues

Anne Louise Bannon

Healcroft House, Publishers

Altadena, California

Copyright 2021 Anne Louise Bannon
Published by Healcroft House, Publishers
2591 N. Fair Oaks Ave., #408
Altadena, CA 91001
626-502-7416
annelouisebannon.com
Library of Congress Control Number: 2021912848
ISBN: 978-1-948616-18-8

Cover design by Tatiana Vila, www.viladesign.net

Acknowledgments

Many thanks go out, as always, to my wonderful editor, Carol Louise Wilde. I also want to thank my new cover designer, Tatiana Vila.

On the support side, thanks go to my husband, Michael, Holland, and my daughter, Cornelia Ann Klarner. In addition, I want to thank all my friends from the Lady Sings the Clues Author Pod: Sheila Lowe, AJ Llewellyn, Peg Brantley, Saralyn Jacobson Richard, GP Gottlieb (who had the whole crazy idea in the first place), AE Wasserman, Ilene Schneider, Carolyn Pouncy, Maryann Spencer, and P.K. Adams. You ladies are amazing.

Dedication

To Analyn Revilla, Phoenix Smith, Bennie Thomas, and Bri Webber, my journaling friends. You were the best blessing of the Pandemic.

Chapter One

It started because I snapped. I was working at a domestic abuse shelter in the northern part of L.A. I'd been there almost eighteen months, which was pretty good for that job. I was technically the secretary for the group. There was a lot of handholding involved as well and not just the hands of the clients. The caseworkers needed their fair share of propping up, although, to be fair, they were always available when I needed to whine and weep.

Martina Rivera was in my office, a miserable puddle. For months, the poor woman had been calling, trying to find a way to get away from her husband, an exceptional son of a bitch, even among the bastards we usually dealt with.

Now, I know how incredibly hard it is for an abused woman to break away from her abuser. The stats say seven tries, on average, before she finally gets out, and that's about right. It's even harder for Latinas, who face tremendous cultural and family pressure to stay with the louts. If the woman is an immigrant and her husband is here legally and she's not, such as was Martina's case, the bastard has even more power over her.

However, Juan Rivera had seriously injured one of the kids. The cops got called in, Children's Services had removed the rest of the children, and the D.A.'s office was talking about prosecuting Martina as an accessory because she didn't stop her husband. Great idea, punishing her when she was just as much a victim.

Only that's exactly what I wanted to do. Cripes, the woman had been calling and calling. We'd given her option after option. She still didn't leave.

That's when I snapped and walked out. The caseworkers took care of Martina. A week later, I went to lunch.

"I wanted to ask her why the hell didn't she get out?" I told my friend Berto Esparza, who was buying. "Of course, I didn't. I got her caseworker and got out the lawyer list." I shook my head and blinked back tears. "Berto, I just couldn't take it anymore. I was building up a shell just to keep from caving in from all the sadness. Anyway, that's why I quit. Merrilee gave me all the vacation time I've accrued, like they can afford it. She was pretty grateful, actually. I held out longer than most people do there. I just have no idea what I'm going to do now."

Berto opened his mouth and I glared.

"Don't say it," I said.

I knew what Berto was about to suggest. We've been close friends for a lot of years and have had a few of the same conversations more than once.

He's about medium height, with gray flecks shot through his thick, dark hair. His build is stocky and muscular – he's built like a cement block and his face is almost as square. For somebody who's spent as much time as he has dealing with the dregs of humanity, he's pretty cheerful.

"I wasn't going to," he replied with a big, shit-eating grin on his face.

He's a private investigator with fancy offices next to Beverly Hills and a nice house in the Valley. What he was going to do was ask me to formally join his firm, never mind that he'd just said he wasn't.

I met Berto back in the days when he was mostly process serving. In fact, that's how I met him. He tried to serve a subpoena on a partner of mine. Berto tipped me off that the son of a bitch was embezzling the entire budget of a play we were producing. What's really ridiculous is that the show was run on a freaking shoestring even for the cheap house we were in.

Since that time, Berto has periodically asked me to become his associate. You see, as a theatre producer in Los Angeles, I was making a living, but not a great one. I had resisted because I still had some residuals coming in from various acting jobs I'd done. Since I'd turned forty, however, the acting jobs weren't all that plentiful, and I was pretty much done with The Industry, anyway. Yes, I capitalized that correctly. It's an L.A. thing that says a lot about our local economy.

"Berto, I really don't want to work for you," I groaned, stabbing my salad with more force than necessary.

Berto laughed. He was in full dress uniform that afternoon, as in a custom-tailored dark wool suit and a snowy white Egyptian cotton shirt with French cuffs. His tie was more colorful, but still a subdued mélange of dark greens and grays. He had taken me to one of those hotshot places in Pasadena, a brass rail and wood sort of place with a trendy menu featuring currant emulsions, for crying out loud, and beautifully tender meat.

"Daria, you damned near already do," he said.

"There's a huge-ass difference between serving the occasional summons and being a full-on associate," I said. "You know, like people shooting at you."

"As if they don't shoot when you serve a summons."

"Just because it hasn't happened yet," I grumbled.

Berto chuckled again. "I got shot at more often process serving than anything I do now."

He had a point. Berto's specialty is tracking down the stalkers behind various and sundry threatening emails and letters that celebrities get, preferably before the stalker does something that requires police intervention. Thanks to social media and the access it gives fans to their faves, business is booming. Pretty tawdry stuff, by and large, but he's probably saved a life or two and he gets paid very well for it. His other cases are usually runaways or digging up evidence on behalf of the law firm next door. So, while the folks he's chasing can be pretty icky, they aren't usually violent.

That didn't mean I was ready to concede. I waited while the waiter came by to take our salad plates away. Okay, I was trying to find some new way to wriggle out of working for Berto.

"Berto, I really appreciate the offer, but I really don't want to be a charity case."

Berto laughed loudly as the waiter placed a beautifully scented rib-eye in front of me and half a roasted chicken with perfectly golden-brown skin in front of him.

"Like I'm going to risk my business to help you pay your bills." Still chuckling, he dug into his bird. "Come on, Daria. I want you because you're good. You've got great instincts. We work well together. All you need is some training, which I expect you to take. You'll also have to work under my license for a couple years, then you'll get your own."

I winced at that part and Berto nodded.

"I see what's going on," he said.

"See what?" I took a bite of my steak.

It was heavenly, cooked with just the right amount of red in the middle, juicy, with a little bit of spice and some lovely pan juices, and, yes, I was desperately trying to avoid what Berto thought was going on.

"You forget I really know you," Berto went on without mercy. "And I know what you really want."

"Seriously, Berto?" I rolled my eyes. "I don't even know what I want."

"Aha!" Berto gleefully slapped the table. "It is now my turn to call bullshit on you, *hermanita*. You know damn well what you really want to be doing with your life, and I know why it's scaring you. After what happened, I don't blame you. But you know that, more than anything, you want to get back to producing plays."

"Well, duh. Of course, I want to. But I can't. I can't make enough money to survive on."

"But you can working for me." Berto sat back, utterly satisfied with himself. "The whole reason you're pushing back is that you're afraid that working for me means that you're giving up on theatre."

"I am not!" Okay, I was, and I knew damned well I was.

"That's what you're not getting, Daria," Berto chewed on some more chicken, then grinned. "Did I ever say you had to work full-time?"

"Huh?"

"Trust me, Daria. This is how we're going to get you back to the theatre. You work part-time for me, for the money, then you work theatre the rest of the time. I can't promise there won't be times when I'll need you to put the extra time in. You know that's going to happen."

"And probably at the worst possible time, too." I glared at my almost gone steak.

"Probably." He shrugged. "I need you. I need someone I can trust."

"Great way to put a few extra nails in the coffin." I sighed.

Berto had good reason to worry. When his last associate had left, the asshole had tried to take all Berto's clients with him.

"There's still the potential for getting shot at," I said. "That really does scare me."

"It should," Berto said. "But you have a gun and know how to use it."

I made a face. I hated that gun, but fortunately, I had yet to do more than wave it around.

"Come on. I've got a big case coming in, and I think you'll find it interesting. Come with me to the meeting this afternoon."

I tried to glare at him and couldn't. "I'm not saying I'm going for it. But I'll go to the meeting."

"Good. It'll be fine."

"I don't know, Berto. This is, like, way outside my wheelhouse."

He grinned again. "Good. It's the cocky assholes who get into trouble."

Like that was reassuring. Still, I'd done errands and even served a few summonses for Berto before. He was right. There was no reason I couldn't work with him and do a play at the same time.

We rode back to the Westside in Berto's BMW sedan. It's a fairly discreet car, given that they're everywhere in L.A. Berto loves it because the paint job is such that the car changes color depending on how the sun hits it.

I spent most of the ride bracing myself. It was one of those wet, drizzly February days, varying between mists, dry spots, and downpours, with an occasional break of sun just to throw things off. Like most Angelenos, Berto doesn't slow down just because the freeways are wet. We skidded a little as he got off the 134 freeway onto Forest Lawn Drive.

We wriggled around on surface streets and a quick patch on the Hollywood Freeway, then Franklin until we got to Sunset. Past the Chateau Marmont, where John Belushi took his last trip. We were waiting for the light at Doheny when I looked up.

All along the side of this tall, narrow building, a mural-type ad had been painted. The building was at least ten stories tall. On a dark, navy-blue background was the figure of a man surrounded by a halo of white light. It was a three-quarter back view, from about his hips up. His shirt was dark blue with white stripes, and it was one of those cowboy styles - you could see the curved edge of the yoke. He wore a white cowboy hat and held a microphone to his face. His free hand was raised over his head, either in blessing or to greet the unseen fans he faced.

"Luke Winston, Live in the U.S., in stores now!" read the banner underneath.

I tried to think of something sufficiently sardonic to say that would note that a country western star was as big as Springsteen. Of course, Luke Winston had been that for some time and had one huge crossover following.

"Aren't you curious about your first case?" Berto teased, as he made the turn into the building's garage.

"Assuming it is my first case. Isn't it the usual celebrity getting threatening letters?"

"Somehow, I think this one's going to be a little bit different. Hal Watkins is bringing the client over himself, and he didn't say anything about letters."

Hal Watkins is one of the partners next door at the law firm. He refers a lot of Berto's clients.

Like all the offices on his floor, Berto's outer office wall is glass, letting you see into the antechamber as you walk up from the elevator. Berto's wife, Marisol, decorated the office because, frankly, Berto would have put up Super Bowl posters and his kids' latest school projects. Instead, Marisol chose a couple Frieda Kahlo prints for the outer office.

The rest is done in a soothing blue and soft gold palette, to accent Franny's cherry wood desk, which faces out onto the corridor. There's an overstuffed leather couch facing her desk, with its back up against the glass, and another on the wall furthest from the door, which has the filing and copy room on the other side.

Hanging around Berto as long as I have, I know most of the players around him by name, though not by sight. As we walked up to the office, I could see Franny, Berto's administrative assistant, smiling and shaking hands with five strangers. Franny's an African American woman, with rich, dark skin who is... Well, she's not fat by any means, but hardly thin, either. She's tall and carries her weight well. She generally wears her hair straightened and in a more conservative turned under do, although, at that moment, she was in one of her periods when she experiments with braids. She always dresses in nice suits. Nobody in their right mind messes with Franny, least of all Berto, who is completely dependent on her.

Of the five strangers, Hal Watkins was easy to peg - he was the White guy in light gray Armani and no topcoat. Okay, the other strangers were White, too. Two other men and the one woman were all wearing Burberry raincoats of varying shades of tan. The last man was wearing a discreet black and white twill woolen topcoat buttoned all the way up. He had dusty straw-colored hair that was decidedly thinning on top, a straw-colored mustache that wasn't anywhere near thinning, and he wore wire-rimmed glasses that he constantly pushed up his nose with a black-leather-gloved hand.

He did look vaguely familiar. That wouldn't have made any difference, except that it suddenly hit me what Berto had been talking about when he'd asked me if I was curious about the new client. Berto's new client was the guy on the side of the building, country star Luke Winston.

I hitched my beat-up navy pea coat around my shoulders. I'd dressed up for lunch, well, for me anyway. I was wearing a white oxford shirt over a dark green turtleneck, and my best jeans and cross trainers. I was a little under-dressed for this crowd.

I ran a hand over the curly dark blond mass I call hair. I wear it down to my shoulders because if it gets too short, I look like a poodle. Too long, and it becomes a real pain in the ass to deal with. I have the kind of hair most women I know covet and then some. Except on rainy days, when it all goes psycho, like that day.

I'm pretty much average height, and while I've added some padding over the years, I can still legitimately zip up a pair of size eight jeans without lying down.

The group in the office had seen us coming because they all turned as one toward us. Berto grinned as he ushered me in.

"Hal, good to see you again," Berto said, quickly shaking Hal's hand and sliding out of his own Burberry.

"Good to see you," Hal replied quickly, then turned to the man in the black and white topcoat. "Mr. Winston, this Mr. Berto Esparza."

"It's a real pleasure to meet you, sir." Mr. Luke Winston's voice was firmly planted in the deep South, and for all the ritual was professional, I got the sense that Winston was utterly sincere at the same time.

"Same here, Mr. Winston." Berto smiled warmly as he shook Winston's hand.

I saw a flicker of surprise in Berto as Winston melted back and Hal introduced the entourage. As Berto later explained, most celebrities introduce their helpers in passing, and they certainly don't step aside.

There was Leo McKesson, Winston's manager, a thinnish, serious man with a perfectly tanned face and broad shoulders. His voice pegged him as also coming from the South. Jenny Richards' voice had no distinguishable accent. She was in her early thirties, pleasant and professional, and head of Winston's mail department. Jay Swanson looked like he was fresh out of college. Tall and broad-shouldered, he had that kind of jovial, eager to please puppy look.

Then Berto pushed me forward.

"I'd like to present my new associate, Daria Barnes," he announced as I smiled reluctantly. "Let's get your coats, and we'll talk in my office."

"I've got them," Franny said, and indeed, she already had McKesson's raincoat in her arms.

Winston had slid off his gloves and pocketed them and his long, pale fingers quickly unbuttoned his coat. He noticed that I was watching him and grinned.

"Expecting something different?" he asked softly as I took his coat.

He was dressed in an exquisitely tailored dark gray suit of the prettiest worsted wool I had ever seen. The cut was more English, although it emphasized his slim form nicely without the showiness of an Italian cut. His shirt was sky blue silk broadcloth with a matching tie. His shoes were Italian, though, and black business pumps that laced.

"Not quite your concert image," I replied.

"Well, it's a more discreet way of getting around. I don't get recognized as much." His soft brown eyes twinkled impishly. "I got my cowboy shorts on underneath."

He was a lot shorter than I'd expected, building murals notwithstanding. Up next to him, I could see that he was almost six feet tall, but he didn't seem tall, if you know what I mean.

Franny relieved me of Winston's coat and my own and I found myself swept into Berto's office.

It's a large room, with the same cherry and soft gold accents played this time against a deep, rich green. Berto's huge desk, which is always a mess, is flanked by rows of filled bookshelves behind him on the walls. Two tan leather wingback chairs face the desk, and to the side is a corner group of two black overstuffed couches with a glass coffee table.

Hal had excused himself, so while the client settled himself on a couch, I dragged over the wing backs. Winston had landed next to the corner. Berto, who was getting his notepad from the desk and some other papers, said that he'd sit next to Winston on the other couch. McKesson sat next to where Berto was going, and I was waved into the place on Winston's other side. Richards and Swanson took the wing backs.

Winston leaned over and picked up a framed photograph.

"Mr. Esparza, is this your family?" he asked.

"Yes, it is." Berto rooted around the desk some more, then picked up his phone. "Franny, the contract, please."

I pointed out the children as I named them. "That's Sarah, she's ten, then Jesse, five and Ruben, three, and that's Marisol, his wife." All had cowboy hats and western wear on.

Winston nodded at the photo. "They wouldn't happen to be country western fans?"

I rolled my eyes. "And how."

"Let me guess, you're not." Winston's eyes were teasing, as opposed to peeved.

"With all due respect, Mr. Winston, I'm afraid not."

"Who is your favorite group?"

"The Chicago Symphony." I smiled, slightly uncomfortable with where I stood.

He laughed, loud and hard. "That's the best answer I've heard yet."

"Chicago Symphony?" snorted Berto from his desk. "Everybody's heard of them."

I rolled my eyes. "I was on the spot." I smiled weakly at Winston. "I'm sorry, Mr. Winston. I really don't have a favorite group. Classical music is as close as I get to a favorite genre, but I listen to almost everything that isn't on a major label."

"The more obscure the better," teased Berto. "If you've heard of them, Daria's not listening to them."

"Well, nobody's heard of me." Winston winked at me. "Don't worry about it. Got fans enough. Now, Mr. Esparza, about my case."

Berto was finally sitting down. "Yes. How can I help you?"

Winston shifted. "It's about Larry Ochoa."

Somewhere in the back of my mind, I remembered a report from the eleven o'clock news that Winston's drummer had died in an accident at a rehearsal.

Winston's face had suddenly become unreadable.

Richards and Swanson both fidgeted uncomfortably while McKesson glared. He was obviously pissed off at something, what, I had no clue.

Berto nodded.

"I don't know how much you know about the case," Winston continued. "It was a week ago today. The police have decided it was an accident. It was the fall from the catwalk that actually killed Larry, they told me."

"You see," said McKesson, "the autopsy turned up Vicodin in his system. You know, the pain killer?"

"He'd been injured recently?" Berto asked.

Winston sighed. "Well, yes. I, uh, don't think we need to go into that."

"They need to know," McKesson told him softly, then turned to us. "The problem is, Larry used to be hooked on heroin and probably other stuff, years back. He's been clean for six years and playing for us for a little over four years now. The police figured he got strung out on the Vicodin, climbed up the catwalk and fell off."

"I know he hasn't gone back to using," Luke said emphatically.

"If he wasn't using, how did the Vicodin get in his system?" Berto asked.

"We don't know," said McKesson quickly. "He may have been taking it for some back pain he was having."

Winston groaned. "Leo, he wasn't using. I couldn't even talk him into taking an aspirin." He looked at Berto. "We've been friends for a lot of years, you know. Since he got clean, Larry was real careful about taking anything. I know the cops meant well, but they got it wrong about Larry taking the Vicodin because he was using again. I let it go until Jenny here came to me the other day."

Richards recognized her cue and opened a leather padded folder. "Obviously, Mr. Winston gets so much mail, he couldn't possibly look at it all. Ninety-nine percent of it is fan mail, and my staff handles it. Of the remaining one percent, half are gifts, which are also handled by my staff. The other half is the nasty stuff. We get an occasional death threat, but most of it's just hate mail. I keep an eye on that and track it. So far, there hasn't been anything to be terribly worried about. The day after Mr. Ochoa died, this came through."

She handed Berto a postcard. He read it and passed it on to me.

"MAKE SURE YOU GET THE RIGHT DRUMMER THIS TIME," the message read. It had been done on a computer, in a basic block letter font which filled most of the one side. The other side had the address and no return address. It also had been printed on a computer, in a smaller version of the same font, only with upper and lower case. It had been date stamped on the address side, presumably by a Winston staffer.

"The timing just seemed really bad," Richards continued. "Then I heard Mr. Winston talking about his suspicions about Mr. Ochoa's death. I don't normally show Mr. Winston the hate mail, but this, I kind of had to." She paused and looked at Winston and McKesson. "That's when I strongly suggested we hire a private investigator and, fortunately, Mr. Winston agreed."

Berto took the postcard back from me and slid it into his notebook. "It could be just a coincidence."

"I s'pose," Winston said with a slight sigh. "Mr. Esparza, I just don't think so. When you spend as much time working with a band as I have, you get to know your guys, and Larry and I were already tight. I'd know if he was using, and he wasn't. I just can't figure out why someone would dump him off a catwalk."

"How high up did the catwalk go?" Berto asked.

"About two stories-worth," Winston replied. "It's a sound stage near Culver City that I rent. That way we can get all the set pieces inside for a concert and check lighting and all that. The catwalk is up pretty near the ceiling, at the far end of the stage, which we don't use. In fact, there's a black cyc hanging between where my stage ends and where Larry fell."

Cyc is short for cyclorama, which is one of those huge backdrop things used on stages as background.

"If Mr. Ochoa didn't just go up to the catwalk and fall,

then how did he get there?" Berto asked. "Was he dragged or walked up? And how would you get the drugs into him in the first place?"

"Well, that's what I hope you'll find out," Winston said.

I had a thought. "Do you have coffee on the stage?"

"Sure," Swanson said. "We've got the whole craft services table, with hot water, regular and decaf. Even got a soda machine."

"What kind of coffee cups do you use?" I asked. "Paper, regular mugs?"

"Oh, everybody has their own mug," Swanson said. "If we didn't have the same crew all the time, it'd make more sense to use paper or something like that. But since it's the same guys, why add to the whole trash problem? It's cheaper, too."

"So, each person's mug is distinctive?" I asked, ignoring Berto, who had the biggest, ugliest I-told-you-so smirk on his face I'd ever seen.

"We all have our names on them," Winston replied, frowning. I think he had an idea where I was going with this.

I nodded. "I'd be willing to bet that the day of Mr. Ochoa's death, he was complaining that the coffee tasted burnt or bad."

Mr. Swanson bounced excitedly. "Mr. Winston, Larry did! He was pouring a whole bunch of sugar into his cup and joking about how bad the coffee was."

"Jay, everybody complains about the coffee," Mr. McKesson said. He turned to me and chuckled. "I can get the best beans in the state, keep it fresh, and they still complain."

"I think Jay's onto something," Winston said, shaking his head, as if he didn't want to agree, but had to. "I saw Larry adding cream and he doesn't usually do that unless the coffee's really bad." Winston turned to me. "What does bad coffee have to do with Mr. Ochoa's passing?"

"A lot," I said. "Vicodin, like most drugs, has a very bitter taste, which makes it pretty hard to spike something with it because the bitterness will tip off whoever tastes it. Coffee, on the other hand, is naturally bitter, especially if it's been sitting in the pot too long. If your coffee tasted unusually harsh, you wouldn't assume it was spiked. You'd assume it had burnt and toss it or doctor it up."

McKesson nodded. "That would explain how the Vicodin got into Larry's system."

"It does not explain why or how somebody got him up to a catwalk two stories up," Berto said. "Unless they walked him up after he was doped up. I think I also have to point out, Mr. Winston, that if Mr. Ochoa did get the Vicodin this way, it points to someone on your staff. Who else would know what to do and who else would have access to the craft services table?"

Swanson snorted. "Lots of people would. It's so easy to get on that sound stage. I'm surprised we don't get more fans bugging us. There's always tons of people hanging around."

"What you do for Mr. Winston, Mr. Swanson?" Berto asked with that direct way that sounds like an accusation.

Swanson gulped. "I— I'm Mr. Winston's personal assistant."

"He's a glorified gofer," Winston chuckled. "Fresh out of college and just starting out. I always make my new hires do assistant duty before moving them up in the organization. I get a better sense of what all they can do that way."

And a sense of a few other things, I decided. For all that Winston was sweet and gentlemanly, I began to realize he was one savvy bastard. I also suspected security on his sound stage was a lot tighter than it looked. Still, it was within the realm of possibility that someone who knew Ochoa could have gotten in and observed, then found the right opportunity.

Berto apparently had decided the same thing.

"Well, Mr. Winston," he said. "I'm not sure about the catwalk scenario, but there are a few interesting possibilities. Tell me about Mr. Ochoa. What kind of enemies did he have?"

"That's a good question because as far as I know, he didn't have any," Winston replied. "Assuming he was murdered, there must have been somebody. Maybe it was somebody from his past. I really can't tell you."

"He used to use drugs," Berto mused. "Was there an ex-wife, family members that he may have hurt?"

Winston frowned. "He didn't talk much about his family. They weren't close. I believe he has an ex somewhere. He didn't talk much about his past, and his family wasn't too big on talking about him. Jay's got his family's phone numbers and addresses."

Jay pulled two sheets of papers stapled together from his padded leather folder and handed them to Berto.

"It's someplace to start," Berto said. "Do you know the name of the detective who worked this case? Even if it was an accident, somebody wrote the case up."

"That was, uh, Detective Isabel Lancaster. Jay, you got a copy of her card for Mr. Esparza?"

I bit my tongue as Berto covered. It was a beautiful thing. If I hadn't known, it would have gone right past me, and I know Berto like the back of my hand. You see, Isabel Lancaster is not exactly on Berto's list of favorite people. They have nothing but respect for each other. They just don't get along very well. If Isabel was saying Ochoa's death was an accident, it probably was. That wouldn't stop Berto from trying to show her up.

Berto was busy explaining his terms and getting the contract signed. Swanson produced a check, which Winston filled out and handed over. Then we all trooped out to the outer office, coats were collected, and everyone said good-bye.

As soon as everyone was safely off down the hallway, Berto started laughing as Franny tried to push a message slip into his hand.

"You nosy bitch!" Berto thumped my back as Franny glared. She does not like foul language. "Sorry, Franny. Seriously, Daria, where, in heaven's name, did you come up with that Vicodin and the coffee sh—, uh, stuff?"

I shrugged. "I worked with Jeffrey Bates for all those years."

Bates was a playwright who specialized in murder mysteries and psychological thrillers. Not terribly deep, still, they pulled in the audience. For about eight years, he was the in-house playwright at the little company I was running, and during that time, I had him revise more than a couple improbable scenarios.

"And you say snooping is not your style," Berto continued. "Daria, you're a natural."

I shook my head. "I don't know. I've done enough time with the dregs of humanity."

"Yes, but with me, you get to do something about them." Berto threw his hands up in the air. "At least think it over tonight, will you?" He sighed. "I could really use you, Daria. You've got good instincts and you're one tough cookie."

"I'll think about it, *hermano*. I'll see you tomorrow, I guess."

I grabbed my pea coat as Berto turned to Franny.

"So, what does Reisner want?" he asked Franny.

"To interview you. She's doing some report on celebrity stalkers."

I turned. "Reisner? Wasn't she that anchorwoman who got all teed off at you because you investigated her last summer?"

Berto shrugged. "We made up."

That didn't surprise me.

"Okay. *Hasta manana*," I said and zipped out to the floor foyer.

There was an elevator right there, which Winston and company had just boarded. Winston held the door for me.

"The elevators are so slow in this building," I remarked as I got on.

"They're not so bad," Winston replied, reaching for the buttons. "Which level did you park on?"

I groaned. The doors had already closed, and we were moving down. "I didn't. Berto drove me here. I'll have to get off on the next floor and see if he can set me up with a Lyft."

"Where are you headed?" Winston asked.

"I live over in Eagle Rock," I said, then for some reason, kept babbling. "We had lunch in Pasadena. Berto was meeting with a client in South Pas and the Parkway Grill isn't that far from my place."

"I'm headed in that direction myself," Winston said.

I caught the slight frown on Swanson's face and figured Winston was fibbing. "Why don't I drop you off? It'll save you an Uber or Lyft."

"It's too much trouble."

"It's no trouble at all. I've got an appointment in Pasadena. Eagle Rock's on the way."

Swanson was just uncomfortable enough. I didn't know if I could get anything out of him, but a ride in a car with him might yield something. Besides, even Uber or Lyft fare to Eagle Rock was no small chunk of change.

"If you're sure it's no trouble," I said, "then thank you very much."

Chapter Two

There was a limousine waiting on the street for us as we came out of the building.

"My car is back at the office," Winston explained. "We'll drop these folks off then head out from there."

McKesson didn't seem too thrilled about that option but didn't say anything. For all those stretch cars seem huge, it was still a bit of a squeeze, with us five adults in the back.

"How long have you been Mr. Esparza's associate?" Winston asked as we pulled out.

"Uh…" I smiled, trying to buy a little time to explain why I wasn't necessarily going to be working for Berto without getting Berto into trouble for including me in the meeting. "I've actually been running errands and stuff for Berto for years. We're in the process of working out how the associate thing is going to happen. Paperwork and all that."

McKesson grunted as if he wanted to comment on that but knew he shouldn't.

"You seem pretty good at it," Winston chuckled.

"I'm not as good as Berto," I said. "Berto is great. He's the best around, believe me."

Winston nodded, then changed the subject to the weather and other trivia. His office was in a restored 1920s bungalow just off Fountain. There wasn't much of a driveway, just two cement strips to the back building, which had been converted from a small garage to McKesson's office. The rest of the two-story building had been turned into several smaller offices and a conference room from which was run the entire Luke Winston empire. At least that was Swanson's terminology. Winston, himself, just gently shook his head and grinned. Swanson offered to show me around. I demurred.

"I don't want to make Mr. Winston late for his appointment," I said.

"Oh, that," Winston said suddenly. "Nah. I got a call or two to make anyway."

There really wasn't that much to see. Winston, of course, had a prime corner office upstairs, with windows looking onto the backyard and driveway. The entire backyard, oddly enough, had been turned into a vegetable garden. Richards was the gardener, Swanson explained. Winston had invited her to put the garden in when he overheard her grumbling about not being able to grow things at her apartment. The staff was welcome, indeed, encouraged to take home the produce. The house's original kitchen was more or less intact, and Swanson told me that Winston had hired a chef to feed the staff every day.

Tour completed, I cooled my heels for a few minutes longer until Winston got off the phone and came downstairs. He had changed clothes to a bland yellow t-shirt, jeans, and running shoes, and was putting on a beat-up brown leather bomber jacket. He led me out to the dark Mercedes SUV parked in the driveway and opened the passenger door for me. He got the directions to my place as we pulled out.

"That a house or an apartment?" he asked, casually.

"A house. I bought it during the last recession," I said. "I'd had a really good couple years with a recurring role in a series, and then my great aunt died and left me some money. I was able to pay cash. It's small, but it's home."

"You're an actor."

"Very rarely." I snorted. "I prefer producing."

"Really now."

"Mostly theatre. I've been out of the game for a couple of years now. It's an awfully tight way to make a living."

"So, what are you doing now?"

"Looking for work. That's why Berto wants me to work for him." I gazed out the window down La Brea, which we were crossing at the moment. "I don't know. It's a pretty good gig."

"Nothing like a steady paycheck," Winston said, almost wistfully.

"What's your meeting in Pasadena?" I asked suddenly.

"I'm just getting together with a friend. I've got to find another drummer, and he might have some leads. You don't know any drummers, do you?"

I shook my head. "Not any that would match your kind of music. Most the musicians I know play solid blues and some even play acid."

"Acid's a bit much." A soft grin crept across his face. His eyes were riveted to the street, but his mind was only marginally on the task at hand. "Blues drummers work real well."

"You're kidding."

He glanced at me and chuckled. "You don't know much about country, do you?"

"Not really." I squirmed because it was really tempting to get snarky and Winston was being nice enough to give me a ride. "It's, uh, not an interest."

"That's 'cause you're thinking about twang, twang. I won't say that isn't a large part of it. I do some more traditional stuff, myself. You ever hear Lyle Lovett?"

"He's a little too popular for me."

Winston chuckled. "Lyle is as much blues as he is country. Blues may have been appropriated from the African American culture, but it does share some of the same roots as country, namely American folk music."

"Huh." I looked at him. "I didn't know that."

"Mm-hmm. My music is as much old ballad and bluegrass as it is what you call country."

"No kidding. I like bluegrass. That's fun stuff." I grinned myself. "You are seriously mainstream, but maybe I will have to check out one of your CDs."

"Don't do it on my account. You get in my position, it ain't easy staying grounded. I put my pants on one leg at a time, just like everyone else."

An odd sadness seemed to fill him.

"You were close to Mr. Ochoa?" I asked softly.

"Oh yeah. Went to Julliard together."

That sat me up. "Julliard? You?"

"Why not me? I'm classically trained. Got my degree in

violin and trumpet." Winston chuckled. "Well, truth be told, I only went to make my parents happy. I couldn't wait to get to Nashville. Larry was more interested in the jazz scene. We stayed in touch, even while he was lost in the drugs. I was so proud of him when he went into rehab. I told him, when he was ready, he'd have a job with me. He was doing really well, too."

"Yeah. I know how that goes." I thought. "It's one of those diseases that leaves a trail of enemies. It won't likely be hop heads because they're too messed up to plan something like this. Probably somebody Ochoa hurt while he was using, a girlfriend or a grown-up child or something like that."

Winston shrugged. "I think you were right the first time and it's someone working for me."

"It still could be the abandoned child. What with stagehands and all, you've got like, what, a hundred people working for you?"

"Something like that."

"That's a lot of people to keep track of." I looked at him. "You're thinking of somebody specific."

"Two of them, except they couldn't have done it." He sighed again, and again focused on the road. "The thing is, when you hire people, you're looking at the work they can do for you. You don't ask about politics or how they treat their families and hope that they ain't bigots or beating their wives."

"Except you've got a bigot and a wife beater working for you."

"Rick Kemper is easily one of the best lead guitarists in country music today, not to mention banjo, steel guitar. I found out sometime after I took Larry on that Rick is also a white supremacist. In fact, I'm pretty sure he's the one that sent that card. He's sent me stuff like that before, just not to the office."

"Why haven't you fired him?"

"He's one of the best lead guitarists in country music today, and, well, hell. I thought maybe that by keeping him around, I could help re-educate him. In fact, he and Larry roomed together on tour. Rick wasn't happy about it but came around, and as far as I knew, the two were good friends. Besides, he couldn't have killed Larry, because he and I spent the entire morning together working out an arrangement."

"Didn't go to the head? Didn't step away for a smoke?"

"Nope. We were pretty focused in."

"Okay, so that lets the bigot out. What about the wife beater?"

Winston took a deep breath. "Leo McKesson."

"He seemed pretty angry to me."

"He's got the motive, too. I'd known about him hitting Candy for years. I thought about dumping him, but Candy begged me not to. It would just make the hitting worse, not that she would admit he was doing it. He was just as hard on his two girls, too, especially as they got older. The last straw for Candy was when Susan, her oldest, came home from a date with fresh bruises."

"And not from her dad."

"Nope. She'd gotten tangled up with an abuser. That's when Candy called me at the office and said she needed help. I talked to Larry about it because he knew some friend who'd had to leave a beater and he knew who to contact. Then around the end of last month, I kept Leo in a late meeting and Larry got Candy and the girls out."

"Right, and abusers are at their most dangerous after their victims leave."

"Yeah, that's what the shelter told me." Winston was bemused. "We haven't seen hide nor hair of Candy and have no clue where she is. Hell, the girls aren't even going to their normal school."

I nodded. "If it's been that recent, they're probably getting intensive counseling, and they probably will be sent to a new school when it's time."

Winston looked at me and grinned. "You sure know an awful lot about this."

"I just left a secretarial job at a shelter. You know, I see at least one problem with McKesson as a suspect. He got the wrong victim."

"Well, he doesn't know where Candy is."

"If he's turning his rage on those who helped her, he should have gone after you. I mean, would he have known that Ochoa was helping his wife?"

"Come to think of it, no. Besides, I know for a fact that he was in his office the whole morning Larry was killed. His secretary vouched for him, and she's in that little garage, too."

"Could the secretary be in on something with him?"

"No. Agnes is pretty straight."

I had to interrupt to fine tune my earlier directions, and a minute later, the Mercedes pulled up in front of my house.

"Well, Mr. Winston, I don't know what to tell you." I put my hand on the door handle and paused. "You know, it's entirely possible that the Vicodin was a sick joke and Larry's fall off the catwalk was an accident. I know the cop involved, and she's pretty smart."

Winston nodded. "Yep. Still, sometimes you just got to go with your gut, and my gut is telling me that Larry was murdered. I'm looking forward to working with you."

I opened the door. "Uh, thanks. I'll pass on what you told me to Berto." I got out, then turned back toward him. "It was nice talking to you, and it was very, very sweet of you to drop me off. Thank you. I really appreciate it."

As I shut the door, I heard him holler, "I'll see you tomorrow."

I just got my keys out of my pants pocket and waved.

"Was that who I think that was?" asked a cranky voice from the garden next door.

Amanda Hitchens is almost an anomaly in Los Angeles - a real, live nosy neighbor. She could be fifty, she could be one hundred. She keeps herself up well, despite her wrinkled face. Her hair is frosted, and she wears it in a pageboy cut with perfectly straight bangs. She wears expensive, drapey boutique-style clothes, even when she's working in her garden, which she usually is. It's a patch the size of a sandbox but looks like the gardens of Versailles in miniature.

Amanda doesn't smoke and disapproves of people who do. She also disapproves of sex and people who have sex, Republicans, Democrats, ecologists, people who wear fur, daytime television talks shows - although she can tell you all about what happened on any one of them on any given day - and pretty much everything I say and do. The woman is a walking guilt machine.

I try to stay on her good side because the one time we had a burglary on the cul de sac, Amanda saw what was going on and called the cops and, thanks to her description of the getaway car, the victims actually got their stuff back.

"A client of Berto's," I said, answering her question without thinking.

Amanda knew all about Berto. I'd had to tell her because she'd once tried to get Berto arrested when he'd been waiting for me to come home one time so we could get some lunch.

"Really?" Amanda sounded far too eager. "That looked an awful like Luke Winston, that country singer? Is he hiring Berto to find out the truth about his fiancée's little flings?"

"What?" I turned on her in shock.

"It's been on the cover of People, Us, even Newsweek is covering the big break-up."

I rolled my eyes. "Amanda, you know I don't pay any attention to that kind of stuff."

"Of course, I don't, either. It was in Newsweek." She looked wistfully after where the Mercedes had been. "Poor man. First, he loses his fiancée over her fooling around, then his drummer gets killed. He's not having a good month."

"I guess not," I said. "Listen, Amanda, I've got to get inside. I've got a shit-load of resumes to get out."

"Daria, do you have to use such language? And the mail's already come."

"I see that. I'd better go check it out."

"Looks like you got another check from that commercial company. I don't know why you don't try harder to get a better agent. You haven't been out on an audition in years."

"Because I don't like acting that much."

"Everyone uses that excuse. You're not that old. You

could still get cast."

"If I really wanted to and I don't." I grabbed the stack of envelopes and flyers from my curbside box, which was right next to Amanda's. The box was the standard shape and size but formed the huge head of a very small cow, complete with udder underneath. My mom, who's an artist, had made it for me. Amanda hated it, and I always felt a twinge of guilt because that's the only reason I kept the mailbox up. "Catch you later, Amanda."

Her cranky voice followed me to the front door, moving from my lack of interest in my career to complaining about my front yard again. My house was built in the early teens, then rebuilt in the 60s, and looks like your basic ranch style from the outside, with clapboard painted steel blue, and white trim. Only it was built on the edge of a hill. The front yard is postage stamp small with a huge, very old pine tree, under which almost nothing will grow. I've seeded a fair amount of clover and planted rosemary, and while it's doing better, it still looks mostly wild.

There is a tiny, attached garage with driveway - part of the 60s remodel. That's where my CRV was. When I drive in, I go into the house through the garage door, because I'm already crammed into the garage. That afternoon, I was walking and went through the front door. The first thing you see from the front door is across the living room to the picture window and through that to the hill on the other side of my back yard. What you don't see is the back yard because that goes straight down for almost 50 feet.

My house is solidly anchored onto the side of a hill, with a bottom floor that you can't see from the street. Upstairs is the living room, kitchen, utility room, and dining room, all of which are distinct rooms that had individual doors before the remodel. Downstairs is my bedroom, the only bathroom in the place, and my study.

I dropped my coat on the couch, petted Macavity, the older of my two cats, then headed, with my little stack of mail, to my study to work on my resume. My natural frugality having been honed to a fine point by years of work in shoebox theatres, I hadn't splurged much in that brief time I'd had a steady paycheck. First, I'd had some debts to pay, then it's just not my style. I had saved and managed to buy a used Honda CRV, and I'd upgraded my computer just after Christmas when they all went on sale. I'd also gotten a smartphone earlier that fall, assuming there'd be an income to support it.

But there I was, out of work again. I thumbed through my mail. There was, indeed, a residual check from a commercial I'd done over three years before that for some reason still aired every so often. It was a whole $5.32. I had money saved, but not a lot, and while I don't have rent to pay, I do have to pay taxes, and upkeep on the house isn't exactly cheap. I did have a job offer, though, and I kept my promise to Berto and thought it over. I thought about it all evening, as I nuked a frozen pizza for dinner, then vegged in front of the tube. By the time I turned the tube off and staggered downstairs to bed, I had pretty much made my mind up. A sleuth I was not and did not want to be.

Why I didn't just call Berto the next morning, I don't know. Actually, I do know. I just wanted to enjoy my denial a little longer. I rationalized all the way out to the other side of West Hollywood that it was only fair to Berto to tell him in person that I would not be joining the firm. It was the only kind and decent thing to do.

I was mildly miffed when I arrived at a little after ten-thirty and Berto still wasn't in. Franny, on the other hand, was seriously miffed because Berto hadn't called. Worse yet, no one had picked up at his house.

"He does it all the time," she sighed. "I keep telling him that I can't schedule clients if I don't know when he's going to be in the office. By the way, this arrived for you."

She handed me a medium-sized basket wrapped in cellophane.

"Huh?" I asked stupidly.

"It's from Mr. Winston," she said. "He sent one for me, another for Berto, and one for his family, too. You should see that one. It's loaded with CDs and signed pictures for each of the kids."

"Oh, geez, they'll go nuts." I laughed as I looked through

the cellophane on my basket. There was a bottle of red wine, a jar of garlic-stuffed olives, a pretty wine glass, and several CDs of works by the Chicago Symphony. I love wine and olives, especially garlic-stuffed ones. "Nothing like good swag. What did you get?"

Franny smirked a little. My eyebrows rose.

"Wow. It must have been really good."

"In the interest of client confidentiality, I will not divulge."

My ass, she wouldn't. She was dying to show off, but the phone interrupted. I started tearing at the ribbon on my basket while Franny picked up the line.

"Esparza Investigations," she told the caller, then gasped. "Oh my god... Is he all right...? You poor thing... Where is he...? All right, we'll be right down... Daria's here. She'll want to come... I don't care if he'd want me to keep the office open. You both need support and we'll be there for you. I'll see you in a few... Bye then."

Franny put the phone down slowly and with considerable difficulty, composed herself.

"That was Marisol," she said slowly. "Berto was hit by a car yesterday. He's down at Cedars in ICU."

"Oh my god." I gulped. "Let's go."

Franny insisted on driving since she had the key card to get out of the building's garage.

"Was it an accident?" I asked as she sped down Doheny to get to Beverly Boulevard.

"I don't know," Franny said, her eyes glued to the road ahead of us. "Marisol didn't say."

I hoped upon hope that it had been an accident but couldn't explain to Franny just then why that was so important to me.

We pulled into the visitor parking garage at Cedars Sinai hospital in record time and hurried up to the ICU ward. There were signs all over insisting that only family members were to be allowed in to see patients, but we went right in anyway. We found Marisol in Berto's darkened room standing at the foot of his bed, staring at him.

Berto's head was wrapped in gauze and a plastic tube

ran under his nose, providing oxygen. Marisol looked up as Franny and I slid in. Wordlessly, she motioned us out, then joined us. I reached out to her, and she fell into my arms and began sobbing.

"They said somebody backed out on top of him," she said, slowly gaining control. "It was in the garage at his office. It may even have been on purpose. The police were here last night. That's when it happened. When he was coming down to his car to go home. He'd been working late. I was so mad. I'm so tired of him working late, and now…"

She sobbed again as I held her, and Franny laid her hand on her back as she cried. Slowly, Marisol got her grip again. I wasn't surprised. In contrast to Berto's strong, squared-off features, Marisol is small and thin with lightened hair that she wears long. She has the traditional Latina curves and some of the traditional attitudes about woman's role. Which means she's one tough broad, certainly an even match for Berto, who's not exactly a pussycat, himself.

"You know, Marisol, the police have to check out every accident," I said softly. "It wasn't necessarily related to anything Berto's worked on."

"I know." She sniffed.

"The kids okay?" Franny asked.

"They're at Mom's. Sarah's worried to death. Jesse and Ruben just know Daddy's hurt, and everyone's upset and so they're acting out." She shook her head.

"How's Berto doing?" I asked.

She shrugged. "It's hard to say. His legs are both broken, his ribs are cracked and there may be a fracture in one of his arms or his shoulder. The worst is the skull fracture. He's sort of in a coma, or he's in a coma but it's not a bad one. Anyway, the doctor said that he's responding to my voice, which is good. There's still a lot of swelling and he needs to stay on the oxygen just in case. The doctor thinks there's a good chance he'll be okay. We just have to wait to find out what's going on with his brain." She fiddled with a crumpled piece of tissue. "I just don't know what to do. I talk to him, but I can't tell if he hears me. He just got that big case and what's going to happen to his business? Oh, Daria, you've got to help him now. He told me he asked you to come be his partner again. Daria, Franny, we've got to keep the business."

My gut froze. I knew I had to be there for Marisol and Berto, but at the same time, my nightmare was coming to life.

"You don't worry about that," Franny said gently. "You just take care of Berto and the kids. We'll see to the rest. Won't we, Daria?"

"Are you kidding? Of course, we will," I said, in spite of my terror. "It'll be fine, Marisol, and if you need to scream or cry or get things off your chest, we'll be here for you."

Marisol nodded with a sniff.

"Can we see him now?" Franny asked.

Marisol nodded, then led us into the room. It was not an easy visit. I mean, what do you say to somebody who's unconscious? Franny and I each told Berto that we were looking out for things and to just concentrate on getting well.

Franny grumbled something as we stepped into the hall.

"What?" I asked.

"I was just thinking I saw a cop hanging around near the garage elevator this morning," Franny said.

"Well, yeah," I said. "It'd be a crime scene because of the hit and run, even if the driver didn't hit Berto on purpose. I wouldn't have seen it because I parked in the visitors' section. Why didn't you?"

"Probably because the team was really busy last night and made a point of clearing that scene by one a.m.," said a woman's voice from around the corner.

Isabel Lancaster walked into the hallway, a look of vague disgust on her face.

The scary thing about L.A.P.D Detective Isabel Lancaster is that she doesn't look like anything she is. If you had to take a guess, she looks like a mom with three kids, a doctor husband, a nice house in Brentwood and a successful business. She's tall, white, rail thin and wears the most interesting suits I've ever seen, most of them silk. People have suggested that Isabel supplements her income illegally, but the suits came from Isabel's wife, who was a fashion designer. Good thing for Isabel, who's the most honest cop on the force.

I'd first met Isabel several years ago. Berto and I had been doing lunch again when he got paged to a client's house. Turned out a stalker had gotten violent and had attacked the client. Berto decided he didn't have time to drop me back at the theatre where I was working then, so he dragged me along with him. Isabel, a newly minted detective, was on the scene and trying to prove herself. Needless to say, things got ugly quickly and I found myself playing go-between for the rest of the case.

Since then, unbeknownst to Berto, Isabel and I had kept up a casual buddy-type relationship. We'd sometimes go bar hopping when her wife was out of town. A couple times when I needed an off-duty cop for an event, I'd call her. Although, truth be told, I hadn't seen her in a couple years, ever since I dropped the whole theatre thing. A steady job will do that to your social life.

That morning, Isabel was wearing a dark green suit with a straight skirt and a jacket with lapels that were kind of stuck through the shawl collar. Her dark, shoulder-length hair was loose but out of her face.

"There was a shooting on Fairfax with multiple bodies," she explained. "Kind of beats a measly hit and run." Her tone softened. "How are you two doing?"

"Holding on," Franny said. She sniffed. "Marisol's doing as well as can be expected."

"That's his wife, right?" Isabel looked around us into Berto's room.

"Yeah," said Franny.

Isabel touched my arm. She knew how close I am to Berto, and Isabel's always been one of those touchy-feely types, never mind that she can back down a linebacker in full rage with just a stare.

"How are you holding up?" she asked.

I had to stop and think. "I don't know yet. You here to say hi?"

She shook her head. "Police business." She looked over

at the room. "I probably will anyway."

I closed my eyes. It was exactly what I'd been most worried about.

Isabel took a deep breath. "We found burnt rubber tracks in the parking space next to where Esparza was hit. That may be why he's still with us, just enough warning so he didn't get the full impact." She looked back at the room again. "You know, he can be a real pain in the ass at times, but I'm told he was a damn good cop."

Like most P.I.s, Berto had started out doing police work. He left after six years, mostly because he hated the prejudice and bullshit from many of his fellow cops and was afraid he was going start hitting people.

Isabel pulled a notepad and pen from her purse and flipped the pad open.

"Anyway, Franny, do you know if Esparza had been getting any threats lately?" Isabel was all business as she clicked her pen.

Franny shook her head. "It's been pretty quiet, actually."

"What about any cases he's currently working?"

"Well, we just got the Ochoa case yesterday."

"I know." Isabel looked at me. "Esparza told me you were going to work that one with him."

I caught my breath. "That presumptuous bastard. I was just going in this morning to tell him I wasn't. I don't know what I'll do now. It's not like I know what I'm doing."

Isabel smirked, which surprised me.

"Trust your gut," she said, which surprised me even more. If there's one thing Isabel hates, it's people playing amateur cop, which means she cleans up the mess afterward. She turned back to Franny. "Any other cases?"

"We just cleared the Kramer case last Wednesday," Franny said thoughtfully. "They put the kid in rehab. I could check and see where and see if he's still there. We only have two other open cases and both of those are just waiting to see if the perp pops up again."

"Do you have anybody fingered in either of those?" Isabel asked.

"Nope. In the one, I think we just flushed the perp

underground. The other hasn't been open that long."

Isabel glanced back at the room. "You think Mrs. Esparza's up to talking?"

I nodded, then went and got Marisol. Isabel was business-like and asked the same basic questions about enemies and any threats. Marisol said that there'd been nothing like that. She looked at Isabel.

"Detective Lancaster, someone did this on purpose, didn't they?" Marisol asked.

"It looks that way."

Marisol nodded. "I'm glad you're on the case. I know you and Berto didn't get along real well, but he always says you're the smartest cop on the force. We got three kids and they need their daddy. Please get this person. I don't want someone else hurting like this."

"We'll do our best, Mrs. Esparza. Um, may I see him? To say hi?"

Marisol smiled. "Oh, please. He'd like that."

We followed her back into the room as Marisol explained Berto's condition again. Isabel touched the back of Berto's hand and told him to hang in there. She, Franny, and I left the room together.

We hadn't even gotten to the end of the hall when Marisol's screams stopped us.

Chapter Three

"**G**et the doctor! Get the doctor!" Marisol came running out the door as a nurse hurried up from the nurses' station.

Franny, Isabel, and I were outside the room in an instant.

"Doctor's on his way," said the nurse as she checked Berto.

"It's his eyes," Marisol sobbed. "They fluttered."

An African American doctor wearing scrubs came running up the hallway. Marisol grabbed him.

"Doctor, it's his eyes!" she repeated. "They fluttered. I made sure. They fluttered."

"All right," said the doctor brusquely as he pushed into the room. He, too, checked Berto and waved Marisol in. Franny, Isabel, and I crowded the doorway. "It looks like he's coming around."

"Thank God," I sighed, as Franny sniffed.

Sure enough, another minute later Berto groaned and opened his eyes. He smiled weakly as he saw Marisol and whispered to her in Spanish. Sobbing, she whispered back, grabbing his hand, and holding it to her chest.

"Can you tell us your name?" the doctor asked Berto.

"Heriberto Esparza," Berto gasped.

"Can you tell us what month it is?"

"February. Am I in the hospital?"

"Yes, Mr. Esparza. You were in an accident."

Berto let out a weak chuckle. "I sure as hell feel like I was. Did a truck hit me?"

"Just a car, we believe. Can you tell us what happened?"

Berto couldn't quite shake his head. He frowned, though. "I don't know. The last thing I remember…" His eyes fell on me. "We were having lunch. Today?"

"Yesterday," I said softly.

"I don't remember anything else. Aw shit, I was supposed to meet with Luke Winston on a case!"

"You did, Berto," I said.

Marisol was starting to look panicked. "Dr. Fellows, he did have that meeting. He called me right after it. Yesterday."

"This is not unusual," Dr. Fellows said calmly. "Mr. Esparza, you have a fractured skull. Obviously, it joggled your short-term memory a little. It's nothing to worry about. We'll check your long-term memory later when you're feeling better. You're coherent now, and that's a good sign. The most important thing to do now is rest and let yourself heal."

"I've got cases," Berto grumbled as Dr. Fellows made a note on his chart and left, mumbling to the nurse.

I looked out at the nurses' station. Isabel had followed the doctor and was giving him her card. Clearly, she'd realized that if Berto saw her, he'd know it wasn't an accident that had landed him there, and apparently had decided he didn't need to know that just yet.

"We're on it," Franny told him, coming up to the bed. "Daria and I will keep things floating until you can get back to work. The MacElroy perp isn't coming back, and you've done everything you can so far for Bachner. It's just a matter of waiting for the creep to send something new. The most we're going to have to do is send the boys out for that, anyway."

"Oh." Berto sighed. "We didn't get the Winston case."

"We got the Winston case," I said.

"I filed it under Ochoa," Franny said. "He's the victim."

"Anyway, Mr. Winston gave me some information," I continued, not at all sure I wasn't lying through my teeth. "I guess I can ask a few questions here and there. Just enough to keep things rolling. Lucky for us, these things take time, so we can stall Mr. Winston 'til he comes back from his next tour. So, don't worry about rushing back to work. We can handle things."

"Good." Berto didn't look convinced.

"They can handle it, Berto," Marisol insisted.

"Oh, yeah." He sighed. "I just want to be there."

Marisol rolled her eyes and chided him softly in affectionate Spanish. Franny and I took off shortly after and were met by Isabel at the doors to the unit.

"It looks like I'm going to have to put off questioning him," Isabel told us. "It's not going to do any good if he doesn't remember what happened. Will you two make sure Mrs. Esparza knows to call me the instant he remembers anything?"

Franny nodded. "If she doesn't think of it on her own."

"Well, she's got other things on her mind right now." Isabel sighed deeply, then snapped out of it and looked at me. "So, are you taking over the Ochoa case?"

"Uh, sort of," I said. Trust me, it was at the tippy top of the list of things I did not want to be doing. "I'm just going to do enough to keep Luke Winston stalled."

"Well, if it's any help, I'll let you look at the police report."

"You're kidding."

Isabel shrugged. "A basic police report is public information. I can't really stop you if you wanted to look at it. Come on, I'll walk with you guys to the garage."

"I thought they'd decided Ochoa's death was an accident," I said, scrambling after her to the elevators. Okay. My curiosity had gotten the better of me again.

"That's the official conclusion." Isabel paused as an elevator opened and we got on. She waited until the doors had closed. "The coroner's report backs up Winston's statement that Ochoa had been clean for years. The Vicodin left in his system was the only trace of any drug use, and there wasn't enough to have killed him."

"That's right," I said. "Winston said he'd been told it was the fall that actually killed Ochoa."

"Yes. Technically, which is why the lieutenant decided that Ochoa had gone back to using. It's not like we haven't seen it before. We see it too damned often. Still, even if there aren't any additional drugs in a body's system, there are degenerative changes that can indicate recent drug use. It's not conclusive enough for the courts, but Dr. Cho said he would stake some solid money that Ochoa hadn't been using for a long, long time. And the first time he gets hopped up again, he manages to fall off a catwalk?" Isabel shook her head. "I know stranger things happen every day, still something just doesn't feel right about this. There are a couple other things, especially some odd bruising, but nothing conclusive. I don't have a shred of evidence to go on."

The elevator door opened, and we got off. Isabel's eyes swept the hospital lobby.

"The lieutenant is getting a lot of pressure to bring up our clearance rate," she said, finally. "You know what that means. Sloppy arrests, sloppy cases for the DA's office and some bad convictions."

I sniffed. "Smells like somebody's getting a little singed around the edges."

Isabel laughed bitterly. "Oh, you have no idea. Let's go bar hopping soon. You, too, Franny."

"I don't think so, Isabel," Franny chuckled. "I've got a life."

Meaning two boys, a great husband, and a house. Franny will do just about anything to keep Berto's business running, except work overtime.

"Good for you," Isabel said. "Daria? I'm off on Friday. Can you make it Thursday night, or are you still on the Monday to Friday grind?"

"Not at the moment," I said. "What time do you get off on Thursday?"

"Supposedly at six. Have you still got that old landline of yours?" She dove into her purse for her notepad and pen.

"Yes, but I finally got a smartphone last fall. Do I have your mobile?"

We exchanged numbers and then I followed Franny to the garage.

Franny was frowning as she started the car.

"Isabel's a smart lady," she said finally.

"I wonder why she's getting pressure to back off on Ochoa," I replied.

Franny shrugged. "Probably what she said. Damn."

Franny's brother was in jail for a rape he swears was really consensual sex. Berto had dug up a witness that cast some serious doubt on the girl's story, but the jury believed her. Franny and I both knew damn well if he'd been a White boy, if the jury still hadn't believed him, he'd have gotten a slap on the wrist and time served.

If the cops were looking to bring up the case clearance rate, then the targets would mostly be Black and Latino kids and they'd get the highest conviction rates and the toughest sentences. Justice is not color-blind by a long shot.

There really wasn't much to say on the way back. Franny talked me into coming up to the office to get my parking validated, which cost Berto something, however Franny pointed out that he still had an income, and I didn't.

"I'm going to do a print-out on all of Berto's cases for the last five years," she announced. "Maybe one of the stalkers got sprung and went after him."

"That's not a bad idea," I said.

Franny's eyes fixed on me. "You going to check them out for us?"

"Me? I'm only supposed to ask a few questions to keep the Ochoa case going."

"You're not working."

"I've got to find a job, and not this one. I don't have an income, remember?"

"What about Berto? You gonna tell him you don't have the time to find out who did this to him so he can have some peace of mind and heal? What makes you so sure this crazy person won't try again?"

"Why do you think I don't want to do this?" I said, almost crying. "I don't want to end up mangled or dead. Why can't you do this? You know more about it than I do!"

"I've got to keep the business going. I'm going to have my hands full leaning on clients and making sure the checks come in because Berto's going to need that money. ICU ain't cheap, honey."

I flopped onto the outer office couch. "You bitch. You tricked me into coming up here."

"I'll do whatever it takes." Franny folded her arms and glared at me. "Berto isn't doing as well as you think. Things picked up pretty well this fall, but last summer he almost lost the agency."

"He what? He was working constantly all last year. And last summer, hell, I never saw him, he was working so much."

"Yeah, trying to make up for two major deadbeat clients last spring." Franny shook her head in annoyance. "These were expensive cases, too. Berto had to call in Jannie Miller, you know, the cyberspace contractor, and bodyguards. He made sure they got paid, and out of his own money."

"I had no idea. He never said anything."

"He didn't tell Marisol, either, and said he'd fire me if I said anything to either of you." Franny looked slightly abashed. "Which means you can't tell him I told you."

"Why wouldn't he say he was in trouble?"

"Marisol. He didn't want her to worry. That's why he didn't want you to know what was going on. Because he knew you'd tell her, and she'd be even more worried because he hadn't told her in the first place."

I groaned. "That's typical Berto bullshit."

"Excuse me?" Franny glared again.

I got up and started pacing. "Oh, come on, Franny. It was his stupid macho pride and trying to stay out of trouble with Marisol."

The phone rang. Franny picked it up.

"Esparza Investigations... Hello, Mrs. Bachner, how are you today...? I know it doesn't sound like it, but that's actually good news... Oh. I'm afraid Mr. Esparza is with another client today. I'll tell you what..."

I waved at her not to send me.

"Mr. Esparza's new associate is free. Her name is Daria Barnes. I'll send her right out... It's no trouble. She just stepped out of the office for a minute, but as soon as she gets back, I'll send her on her way... You're very welcome, Mrs. Bachner. Good-bye."

"Bitch," I said as she hung up.

"I'll do whatever it takes."

"I only said I'd ask a few questions," I said, pacing. "I'm

not taking over for him."

Franny's stony glare pierced through me to my stomach.

"I ought to send you." I sighed. "All right. Give me the file and bring me up to speed."

"There's my girl."

"Fuck you."

"I do not like that kind of language."

"Fuck you."

Franny shook her head and got the file. She also made a big deal out of validating my parking.

Mrs. Tiffany Bachner was the latest trophy wife of Mr. Gunther Bachner, a filthy-rich television producer who'd started out in the days when TV was still live. He'd made hit after hit and was still making them even in today's youth-obsessed Industry. I wasn't sure if Tiffany Bachner was wife number four or five. Given that Bachner had to be somewhere around 90, at least, the odds were very good that he could have been her great-grandfather.

Some tortured soul had thought it would convince the young and beautiful Mrs. Bachner to leave her husband and marry him if he sent her close-up photos of his erect penis. She'd received three already. The first two, she'd thrown away, which is what most people do. The third she'd saved for Berto, although she'd thrown the envelope away.

The scary part was that the perp had found the couple's home address in Beverly Hills - which is doable, but not easy since Mr. Bachner had had the good sense to have a shell company buy the property, which meant his name was not on the property tax rolls. People used to be able to get stars' addresses from the DMV since drivers' licenses must have actual home addresses on them. That's gotten a lot harder to do since the Theresa Saldana killing.

Berto had concluded that while the perp was weird, he was most likely harmless. The file had the letter and the picture, and there was nothing angry or anguished in the writing. He'd had the handwriting analyzed, and the analyst had also concurred that the writer didn't show any signs of being violent at that time. Unfortunately, there was no guarantee that he wouldn't eventually get violent. Still, it hadn't seemed likely when the case was opened.

I can't say I was thrilled to be driving out to Beverly Hills, especially since it had started raining again, but I wasn't in as foul a mood as maybe I should have been considering how little I wanted to be sleuthing. I cranked up the stereo on my CRV and filled the small cab with Celtic tunes sung by Great Big Sea, a group from Newfoundland. They used to be obscure as hell. They're damn good, so I still listen to them.

Of course, my less than foul mood could have been a result of being in my CRV. Just looking at it fills me with pleasure. It's one of those little compact SUVs with five speeds and the luxury interior in light tan. The exterior paint is boring white. You can't have everything, and I'd gotten one hell of a deal on it.

It had come off lease about two or three months before I bought it and I'd test driven it once, along with several other cars I'd been considering at the time. I knew I wanted it and had the cash but waited until the timing was just right. Finally, that December, the last weekend, when everyone was out celebrating the remnants of Christmas and the coming New Year, it rained. It couldn't have been better. The salesman was so desperate for a sale, he let it go for a song. I only had to threaten to walk out twice. Okay, I also had to get up once, but from then on, that man was mine and so was the CRV, at barely two hundred dollars over Kelly wholesale, including the trade-in.

Mrs. Bachner had said to come in through the gates and park in the driveway. It still took a few minutes for somebody to answer the intercom when I arrived, then a couple more for him to find Mrs. Bachner and find out if I was legit or not.

The house was a white plantation-style colonial. To the left of the semi-circular driveway was a matching guest house that looked like it might be bigger than my house. The door to the main house was answered by a maid who looked like she was originally from India or Pakistan. The dark wood floors were polished to a fare-thee-well, and the décor had that professional kind of perfection that gave no clue about the people who lived there.

I was led into a dark green living room with over-stuffed sofas, a huge fireplace, and antique tables, the odd antique mirror, and paintings of landscapes. Everything was too perfect to feel like a home. A fire burned in the fireplace, which I guess was supposed to make the room feel cozy. Only it was a gas log, so all it did was make the room feel even more sterile.

Mrs. Bachner came in and while I smiled comfortingly, I groaned inside. She had actress written all over her. From her impossibly thin body to the puffy, erect boobs to perfectly fluffed blonde hair and the perfectly vapid face. She also seemed vaguely familiar.

"Hello. You must be Daria. I'm Tiffany Bachner," she said extending a hand that was just tanned enough to look pretty without begging for skin cancer. She was perfectly poised, too. Possibly had done some time as a model or in beauty contests.

I winced. Normally, I prefer to be called by my first name, but not by total strangers. She flipped her hair back over her shoulder. She was wearing a full, hand-knit turtleneck sweater made of a fuzzy pink yarn with little flecks of golden yellow in it. Skin-tight khaki covered what little butt she had.

She invited me to sit down across from her on one of the facing couches, then signaled the maid away. Mrs. Bachner looked at me with the barest hint of a puzzled frown, then waved at the coffee table between us.

"There's the latest," she said. "I can't bear to touch it."

"I don't blame you," I said, nonetheless reaching for the package.

It was a box about twelve inches by four inches by four inches, basic brown cardboard and taped with the clear kind of packing tape available everywhere. Mrs. Bachner hadn't opened it yet.

"It came with today's mail?" I asked, picking it up. The postmark made it obvious that there would be plenty of fingerprints on the package and lifting prints off paper is possible, but not that easy. "Is this the same return address as the letters?"

"I don't know. I don't remember."

"Hm. He did a really neat job. I'm debating getting this x-rayed before we open it."

"You don't think...?" Mrs. Bachner gasped and drew her legs up into her lap in fear.

"A bomb? Nah. At least, it's not likely. The handwriting analysis came back, and your perp does not appear to be the violent type."

"Are you sure?"

I shrugged. "Nothing's ever sure, Mrs. Bachner. Believe it or not, the vast majority of these weirdos are not violent. You only hear about the ones who are and that's maybe one percent of these kinds of cases where you have a stranger involved." I was quoting Berto's standard speech almost verbatim and was amazed at how easily I did it. "Violent stalkers are almost always going after former wives or girlfriends. I'm ninety-nine percent certain this box has nothing dangerous in it, but why take a chance when I can get it x-rayed easily enough?" I looked at her carefully. "Just to be sure, you don't recognize the guy in the photo at all, do you?"

"No." Mrs. Bachner rolled her eyes in disgust. "It's not like I was some sort of angel before I got married. I think I would remember that funny little spot on his... You know."

I nodded. That was one nice feature of this case, the penis was distinctive.

"Are you sure he's not violent?" she asked again.

I sighed. "Well, it's not likely. I wouldn't worry too much about it right now. You've got good security here. You've got your assistant when you go out, so you're not alone. If there's even a hint that he might get violent, we'll get you increased protection, and, if you want the hard truth, him getting violent might be the best thing that happens to you."

"You can't be serious!" Her perfect hand flew to her throat and the huge diamond on her engagement ring sparkled in the dull light.

"Let me explain. Right now, he's just harassing you

from a distance. If the address on this package isn't his correct return address, and I'm willing to bet it isn't, he's going to be hard to find. Secondly, this kind of harassment isn't considered a serious crime. It's icky, but he's not actually threatening you. If we catch him and it's a first offense, we're talking a fine at worst, maybe court-ordered counseling, if you're lucky, and he's still free to send you things. If it's not a first offense, jail time is minimal. Now, say he gets violent, he'll most likely have to come out of hiding to do it, which makes him easier to find. With protection, you'll be very safe, he'll be busted on a much more serious charge and possibly a decent amount of time in lock-up, and with an ongoing restraining order, so that if he harasses you again, it's back to jail. It's not the best option, but it can work for you."

She shuddered. "I don't think so."

"If you're that worried, we can send out a bodyguard team for you. We've got some guys who are fairly reasonable, though it will still cost you something."

"Gunther says to do whatever you think is necessary."

"I don't think bodyguards are necessary yet. If they'll help you sleep at night, they may be worth it to you."

She looked down at her perfectly manicured nails. "Well, if you're sure they're not necessary."

"I can't be absolutely sure, Mrs. Bachner. Nobody can. Let's do this. I'll get this x-rayed and we'll find out what's in it and make a decision about a bodyguard then."

"How long will that take?"

I thought. "I can probably get you an answer by tomorrow morning."

She looked at me again, at first searching for reassurance, and then something else.

"I've met you before," she said suddenly.

I thought about it. "Maybe we have met. I thought you looked familiar because you were an actress."

"Yes, I am. Wait! I know where I met you. When I was doing that play, um, about the painter."

It all flooded back. The Death of an Artist. She played the model. I had produced it for my buddy Larry Peterson, a director who had also written the play, and remembered her as one of the least fun parts of that whole painful process. She was constantly late. She couldn't find her way into the proverbial paper bag, let alone act her way out of it. Her only asset, as far as Larry was concerned, was that she didn't mind being naked in front of an audience. Larry had draped her several times to cover her privates, but she kept dropping the drape the entire run.

So, she'd bagged a rich producer. It figured. Lord knows, she wasn't going to get anywhere on acting ability, and her looks, while stunning, weren't stunning enough to set her apart in Hollywood.

"Well," I said, finally. I got up. "It's nice seeing you again, Mrs. Bachner."

"When did you become a P.I.?" she asked.

"It's a long story. Anyway, I'll have an answer for you about the package tomorrow. Is this the way out?"

"Sure." She got up and followed me to the front of the house. "That is so cool. Wow, you were such a great director. I really found my center as an actor in that play. It was such an emotional release."

"Uh. Yeah. Well." The front door loomed ahead. I lunged for it. "I'll catch you later."

I got off the property as fast as I could, cursing Franny, Berto, and the asshole that had hit him every inch of the way. Still, there was work I needed to do.

I stopped at a stop sign just long enough to get my phone into its dashboard holder. Just before Sunset, I punched the key to dial Berto's office and hit the speaker button. I know. I could have voice dialed, but it takes too long. Franny picked up.

"It's Daria," I told her, then grunted as I leaned forward looking for a break among the cars zooming back and forth along Sunset Boulevard. "Do you have the number for the guy Berto uses to x-ray packages?"

"Yes, he's over at Cedars."

"Like I haven't spent enough time over there today. Hang on." There was something resembling a break in the traffic, and I gunned the engine as I made the left turn.

"Okay, I'm back. I also need a reverse lookup on an address."

I gave it to her. She gave me the phone number for the x-ray tech.

"You need to come back to the office first," Franny said. "Mr. Winston is here."

"Great. What the hell does he want?"

"I don't know, but he really wants to see you."

"You don't need to twist my arm anymore, Franny."

"I'm not." It sounded like she was telling the truth. "He asked to see you, specifically."

"This is not good."

"He's not happy, either."

Chapter Four

As Franny had said, Mr. Luke Winston was not happy when I got there. Fortunately, it didn't have anything to do with me. He was wearing a nice, cotton shirt with dark jeans and an open vest and no tie. I shed my pea coat and he followed me into Berto's office.

"We've got an unfortunate development," he said.

"Will you sit down?" I asked, pointing him at the couch while I grabbed a yellow legal pad and a pen off Berto's desk.

I sat down on the perpendicular couch and waited.

"It's my assistant Jay," Winston said, a little nervously. "He didn't show up to work today. Didn't call. Nothing."

"Have you tried to reach him?" I asked.

"Oh, yeah. After Jean, the receptionist, couldn't get an answer at his place, I went over there myself. It's an apartment over in West Hollywood. There's no way of saying whether or not he's in there. I got no answer when I knocked and didn't hear anything on the inside."

"How reliable is Jay?"

"What do you mean?"

I sighed. "We-ell, he's fresh out of college. It's not unheard of for young people to just take off for the day and forget to tell anyone."

Winston nodded, then looked at me. "Think I'm overreacting?"

"I don't know," I said. "On the surface of it, you might be. Unless you have some reason you haven't told me to believe there's something wrong."

Winston frowned. "No, I don't."

"It looks a little funny that you're this worried with no real reason," I said.

"That's the thing of it. I can't say why, but there's

something wrong. Jay did have a problem with being late and I almost let him go. But for the past couple months, he's been very punctual, and the one time he was late, he called right away. He'd gotten rear-ended, and when I talked to him, he kept apologizing and everything, so I knew he was serious about changing things."

He fidgeted and looked vaguely around the room.

"After all that," he continued, "I just can't see him not showing and not calling."

"Unless he got another job suddenly. Any hints that he might have been looking?"

Winston shook his head. I made a note absently, then sighed.

"Look, there's a reason the police wait for seventy-two hours before declaring someone missing," I said. "Unless there's good evidence that something's wrong. How about his car? Do you know what it looks like?"

"Uh, yeah. He drove a green Kia Soul. Kind of flashy, I thought, but he's young."

"Does he have an assigned parking space?"

"Don't know."

"Do you have his license plate number?"

"Actually, Jean does. For the parking permit on the street round the office." Winston pulled a mobile phone from his vest. "Let me get it for you."

"Good. I'll go ahead and check his place out. I doubt I'll be able to find anything. It's probably just a serious relapse of the old irresponsibility bug. Or it could be he called someone else in the office and they didn't get the message. Or he could have gotten the wrong answering machine. It's not likely to be anything serious."

Winston smiled weakly at me as Jean picked up on the other end. He had me talk to her to get the information I needed and disconnected when I handed the phone back to him.

"I, uh, feel kind of silly," he said, finally.

I smiled. "I wouldn't worry about it, Mr. Winston. I can imagine everyone's a little edgy at your office these days."

"Yeah." He remained seated.

I wasn't sure if he had something else to say or not. He finally took a deep breath and watched his fingers as they fidgeted with the mobile phone.

"Ms. Barnes," he said slowly. "I don't quite know how to say this. I expect I'm just imagining things."

"Mr. Winston, is there something going on that you're not telling me?"

"No." His laugh sounded embarrassed. "That's the problem. I have to confess that I was hoping you and Mr. Esparza would tell me I was imagining things about Larry being murdered. Now that you're taking me seriously, I... I have to say it's a little unsettling."

"Mr. Winston, are you afraid someone is trying to kill you?"

He chuckled nervously. "Well, when you put it like that, it does sound kind of paranoid, don't it?"

"It sounds pretty normal to me."

He suddenly looked at me, blue flecks emerging through the brown in his eyes.

"It does?" He looked away again. "I thought I was being just a complete coward."

"Well, not to scare you or anything. You know as well as I do that someone as famous as you are is a target. Then, all of a sudden, someone close to you gets killed and it's kind of suspicious. I'd be scared, too. We haven't proven that Mr. Ochoa's death was murder. It could still have been an accident."

He kept his face down and I could barely hear a sniff. I reached out and put my hand on his shoulder.

"Mr. Winston, do you have someone you can talk to about this? I mean, your feelings of grief over your friend and stuff?"

"I did." I could see his eyes blinking furiously even though his gaze was fixed on the floor. "But she... And I used to talk to Larry." He got a grip on himself again and looked at me with a wan grin. "I don't want to talk like people should feel sorry for me. For God's sake, I've got everything anybody could want. I'm famous. I'm rich. If you'll pardon the expression, I got fuck-you money coming out my ears."

He suddenly sighed. "It does get a little lonely sometimes."

"Yeah."

I was going to say I could imagine it would. I knew I couldn't imagine being where he was, not in a million years. There was part of me that resented the hell out of him. He'd had every one of his dreams come true. Mine, well, hell, I didn't even know what mine were at that point. The worst of it was, at the same time, he was so sweet. There was something so completely unaffected about him. Average Joes I knew were more pretentious.

He had a handkerchief out and was wiping his nose.

"I'm, uh, sorry about that," he said.

"Oh, please. Don't worry about it." I ducked my head, nonetheless. "I have little to no respect for men who can't be human. Except maybe Berto, but then he has his moments, too."

"I get more than a few," Winston conceded, finally getting up. "Around the office, they accuse me of crying over TV commercials." He smiled as he sniffed again. "I've done it, too."

I got up as well and again laid my hand on his shoulder. "Well, I'd say right about now, you've got a lot more reason to. You know, I know a good grief counselor. I could get her number for you."

Winston started to protest, then thought better of it. "Why don't you do that. You know, that's the most comforting thing I've heard in a while."

"Well, at Esparza Investigations, we aim to serve."

There was an awkward pause, then I just went with my gut and hugged the guy. You could tell he really needed one. He nodded thanks, got out his handkerchief and headed out of the office pretty quickly.

I rooted around on Berto's desk for a sticky note so I could write down a reminder to get that number for Winston without having to put it in the official notes.

I found the sticky notes. As I was scribbling down my reminder, I also saw a note scribbled in Berto's hand for Dellis Archer, L.A. County Probation Dept., a phone number, the name Cliff Sims, and a date, actually, a date from the week before.

"Franny!" I called, hurrying to the office door. "Franny, could you look up a case involving a Cliff Sims, please?"

"You got something?" she asked.

"Maybe. I've got to make a phone call. Think it would be okay if I did it in here?"

"Sure. Sims?"

"Yeah, S-I-M-S, Cliff."

"He the victim?"

I stopped. "I'm not sure. I think perp."

Back at the desk, I called Archer and left a message on his voice mail. As I did, I found three other cryptic notes, six credit reports and pages of notes on cases that went back several months. There were also a few bills, several stacks of statements from bills that had been paid and junk mail up the wazoo. Berto wasn't prone to throwing things away.

I wasn't real thrilled, but there only seemed one thing to do. I called the hospital. Marisol answered the phone.

"Hey, Marisol, it's Daria. I've got a tough one to ask."

"What?" Her voice was steady, so I plunged ahead.

"Is Berto up to the news that his accident was no accident?"

She sighed. "He already figured it out. He still doesn't remember what happened, then I let it slip that it happened in the parking garage, and he put two and two together."

"Fine, then will you tell him that the police want us to go through some of his past cases and I, uh, accidentally found a couple things on his desk that have me wondering?"

I waited while Marisol talked to him.

"He wants to know what you found," she said.

"Well, that's just it. I don't know. I want permission to go through all this junk on his desk. I promise not to throw anything away, but I've got to restore some order here if I'm going to make sense of it."

I waited again.

"He says you can, and he wants updates every day."

I rolled my eyes. "I'll do what I can. Tell him if he doesn't stay down and get well, I'll break both his legs again myself." The second line on the phone lit up as another call came in.

"Listen, I've got to run."

"All right. Be careful."

"I will, Marisol. You, too."

I hung up as Franny's voice popped through on the intercom. "Daria, it's Leo McKesson."

I sighed and picked up the phone again. "What can I do for you, Mr. McKesson?"

"I was just checking in. Your girl says Mr. Esparza is not in the office today?"

"No, he's out. I think Mr. Esparza said it would take some time. Mr. Winston was here earlier, and he seemed satisfied with the progress."

"I see. And what did he come for?"

"He was a little concerned that Mr. Swanson did not show up for work today. Do you know anything about that?"

"Well, hell, he's a kid. We've had problems with him before."

"So I understand. Has anyone heard from him yet?"

"Not as far as I know."

"Well, if anyone does, would you let us know right away?"

"Sure thing."

I hung up feeling a little funny about the call and not sure what to make of it. Then I looked at the papers littering Berto's desk and felt it all just overwhelm me. Naturally, that's when Franny came in.

"I've got that reverse lookup you wanted," she said, putting a piece of paper and a file in front of me. "Here's the file on that Sims fellow. He's a nasty one."

"I'm not surprised. It looks like he was released from prison last week if this note makes any sense." I waved it at her. "Looks like we have a suspect."

She nodded and left. I looked again at the papers. When I'm feeling that overwhelmed, I know it's time to start making to-do lists. I sifted through the papers, then pulled the legal pad toward me and started writing.

I had just finished when my stomach gurgled. It was close to two-thirty, and I hadn't eaten lunch yet. I grabbed my list and the file and headed to the front office.

"Hey, Franny," I started.

She waved at me that she was on the phone.

"We'll look for the check then this week," she told someone at the other end of the headset. "Thank you."

Exasperated, she slapped at the button on the box next to the phone that hung it up.

"You've been busy, haven't you?" I fidgeted with the papers.

"Oh, yes."

"I'm sorry. I didn't mean to dump my stuff on you."

Franny looked at me. "What do you mean?"

"That reverse look-up and the file. I could have gotten that stuff myself. I mean, it's not like I'm the boss. Maybe we ought to clarify the boundaries."

"Don't start that psycho-babble nonsense with me." Franny frowned at the computer screen, then glared at me. "Look, Daria, you don't know where everything is around here. You don't know how to do the notes so they're consistent. I've got all the website codes for the SSN searches and stuff like that."

"I just don't think it's fair to add to your workload."

"It's my job. Besides, I'll tell you when you're dumping too much on me."

I grinned. "I bet you will. Okay. Why don't I spring for lunch?"

"I already ate." Franny paused and grinned also. "I'll let you buy tomorrow. By the way, your parking card came up a while ago. Here are your keys." Franny held up a split ring key holder. It held four identical bronze keys with square heads and small square tags taped to them, plus a smaller silver key with a round head. She pointed first to the bronze keys. "This one is the front office, file room, Berto's office, the bathroom and the after-hours key for the elevator. Payday is every other Friday, which means you get your first check this Friday. I need you to sign your W-2 and see your driver's license and your Social Security Card."

"Oh, shit." I sighed. She had me. I suppose it was inevitable, but five minutes later I was officially an employee of Esparza Investigations, Inc.

It was almost three before I put my new parking card into the thingie in the garage and watched as the gate swung up. I pulled the card, got in gear, and got out of there.

My first errand, after swinging through the Mickey D's at Sunset and Laurel Canyon, was to Cedars, although not to see Berto. Instead, I went to the radiology department. Dr. David Stein was waiting for me.

He's a medium-sized man with dark, curly hair in his late 30s. He's kind of cute, and although he doesn't wear a wedding band, I've always had the feeling that he's married.

"So Berto finally got you to sign on," he said with an evil grin.

I rolled my eyes for the five-hundredth time that day. "More or less. I don't know how long it's going to last."

"He'll need you for a while. Those are pretty nasty breaks he's got."

I sighed. "You know he's here. Damn. We're trying to keep that quiet."

"I'm doing the imaging for his surgery."

"What?"

Stein's bushy eyebrows rose. "You didn't know? They'll have to pin his legs back together. They're only waiting for the swelling to go down first. I think he goes in tomorrow."

"Great. Marisol didn't say anything about that."

"He only went on the schedule about an hour ago. What do you have for me?"

I handed him the box. He sniffed it.

"Latex?" he muttered. "I don't smell anything else, so I'm willing to bet it's nothing dangerous."

If he had the least suspicion there really was a bomb in the box, he'd have called the cops immediately. Instead, he put the box on the x-ray table, and fiddled with the camera and did all the things x-ray people do. As a radiologist, Stein didn't usually work the x-ray equipment, but he liked to every now and then and usually x-rayed Berto's stuff himself.

While we waited for the film to pop up on the computer, we stood around and chatted, mostly about the Lakers. About three minutes later, he pulled the file up on the computer's big screen.

"Looks like some sort of phallus," he said., "and there's some kind of motor in it."

"Safe to open?" I asked.

"I don't see any signs of containers. Here." He tossed a pair of rubber gloves and a mask at me. I got them on while he got on gloves and a mask himself.

He slit open the tape with a scalpel then let me lift the lid. Inside was a latex phallus - a huge one - with a switch at the bottom. Slightly disgusted, I flipped the switch, and the thing began to whir and vibrate. Wouldn't you know, batteries were included.

Stein laughed. "What's that all about?"

"Somebody obviously thinks that a fair damsel with a superannuated husband is apparently not getting enough," I said, finally chuckling myself.

"Too bad that's evidence in a case. When was the last time you were out on a date?"

"Cute. Real cute."

"Well?" he insisted, his grin ever more evil.

It had been a while, but I wasn't going to let him know that.

"Are you asking me out?" I challenged.

His eyes almost popped out of his skull. "Oo. Sorry. I didn't mean to mislead you. Honest. It would really piss off my girlfriend if I did. Besides, you're not Jewish, are you?"

"Nope." I picked up the box. "Well, thanks for your help."

I was glad the box didn't have anything dangerous in it, I left the radiology department feeling mildly miffed, although not directly at Stein. It had been too darned long since I'd been out with a man. Of course, working at a domestic violence shelter didn't provide a lot of opportunity for social interaction with available, suitable men. While I love working in the theatre, I have to admit that a lot of the guys there are either gay or flakes. The last time I'd been this desperate, I had given in and let Berto set me up, which I will never, ever, ever do again.

As I got in my CRV, I debated calling on Mrs. Bachner

to let her know what was in the box. I decided I just couldn't stomach another meeting with her quite so soon. I wriggled around out of the garage and eventually onto Beverly Boulevard still feeling at loose ends, my list notwithstanding. Above me, the Beverly Center loomed, dark and monolithic. The sky above was grey and threatening again. Even more threatening was La Cienega Boulevard. With the time getting on for four-thirty, the traffic was piling up. I looked at the list, then at the last second pulled into the monolith.

The Beverly Center is a good-sized mall built during the heyday of malls back in the 1980s. I hadn't been in there in years - most of the stores in there are more than a little beyond my income. Nor did I pay attention to the way the place had changed beyond figuring out that the food court was still on the top floor where it had always been. I bought an over-priced muffin and got my parking validated, then found a reasonably clean table and whipped out the old mobile phone.

I checked in with Franny, and Dellis Archer had gotten back to me but would be gone by five. I dialed him first.

"Archer," he growled into his phone.

"Mr. Archer, my name is Daria Barnes. I'm Berto Esparza's new associate," I told him.

"Yeah, he told me he was working on getting one." Archer's voice was deep, with a strong African American flavor.

"Oh. Well, maybe you've already talked to him recently."

"Actually, I've been trying to get a hold of him since last Thursday. I've left messages."

"About Cliff Sims?"

"Yeah. Did you work that case?"

I paused. I wasn't sure how much I wanted to tell him. "No, I didn't. I've only just started."

"Berto got him busted about eight years ago."

I swallowed, then plunged in. "Here's the thing. Someone tried to run Berto over yesterday and hurt him pretty badly. We're looking at some of his past cases, to try and find who's out to get him."

Archer chuckled grimly. "That'll be a long list."

"That's what I'm afraid of. Anyway, I found a note on Berto's desk about your call and the timing looks mighty interesting."

"Ah-h-h-h." I could almost hear the frown on his face. "That's the thing. How much do you know about this case?"

"I'm afraid I've just barely had time to glance over the file. He was married to what's-her-name. Miriam Watts, the actress." I opened the file and sifted through the notes. "She booted him because he hit her, and he stalked her."

"He hit her pretty hard and pretty often, at least that's what Berto told me. Basically thought he owned her. After she walked, he started showing up whenever she left her new place. He'd get into her building and leave threatening letters and vandalized her door and mailbox a few times."

"Sounds like a real charmer." I winced because he also sounded far too familiar.

"Yeah, well, he was brought up on aggravated assault charges. The D.A. let him plead down and the judge only gave him fifteen years with no counseling."

"Great, and he's out on the streets, free to terrorize again."

"And I'm his parole officer and he's already broken parole."

"Shit."

"That's about sums it up," Archer said. "I was hoping Berto would have a current address for his ex and could warn her that Cliff is out."

I made a note on my list. "I'll check it out. On the off chance you do run into him, would you be so good as to find out what he was doing yesterday evening?"

"Yeah, like I'm going to see him." Archer chuckled again. "Good luck to you. By the way, where is Berto? I'd like to come by and say hi."

"Security is pretty tight. I'll check with his wife and see if it's okay."

We said good-bye and I pushed the end button. Thumbing through the file again, I found an updated address and phone number for Miriam Watts, a young actress currently starring in her second sitcom on Netflix.

She'd been in the first when she'd gotten married to Sims and that blew up.

I also finally looked at the slip of paper that had the reverse lookup on the address that had come from Mrs. Bachner's box. It was a company that made sex toys and had a rather high-end catalog. It seemed to me they were located somewhere on the East Coast. I checked the time on my smartphone. It was just after five, which meant it was just after eight back east. No point in calling them, then.

The muffin was gone and so was any reason I had for hanging around.

Chapter Five

By the time I had left the Beverly Center and was heading north on La Cienega, it was raining and already dark. I wasn't that far from Jay Swanson's address in West Hollywood, so I went there.

It was one of those huge buildings on a side street off Santa Monica, kind of apricot-colored, obviously built within the past couple decades, as opposed to some of its neighbors. There was a gated garage underneath. That didn't mean there was any street parking.

Or there wasn't much. I'm always inherently suspicious when I find a space just outside whatever building I'm parking for, but sure enough, there was a space open just outside of Swanson's building.

Better yet, a car pulled up and opened the garage gate, and I was able to walk into the garage right behind it. I found Swanson's Kia Soul easily enough, and in a space that matched his apartment number. There was an elevator into the rest of the building, and I got on with a young woman, presumably the one who had just driven into the garage.

Swanson's apartment was in the middle of a long hallway with dark industrial carpeting and dim lighting. I knocked on Swanson's door and got no answer. Nor was there any sound of life inside. Of course, that wasn't conclusive. For all we're tied to our cars out here in L.A., there really is public transportation and it was within walking distance of Swanson's place, as was a mini mall with several food stores and a dry cleaner.

I went down to the manager's office. Judging from the newspapers in the office, I guessed he was an immigrant from one of the Middle Eastern countries - most likely Iran. He certainly looked at me with plenty of suspicion, but that was his job.

"Your tenant in two-twenty-four, have you seen him at all today?" I asked the man.

"Why you want to know?"

I got out one of the agency business cards. "I'm with Esparza Investigations. We're investigating a case for Mr. Swanson's boss and Mr. Swanson didn't show up for work today. We just want to be sure that he's okay."

The man looked down at the card and shrugged.

"I no see him," he said, finally.

"Just today or in general?"

"I no see him. He move in. Rent paid. I no see."

I thought that over. "Okay. Um. If you do see him, could you call me at that number, please?"

"Sure. I no see."

I left the building through the front. As I opened the door to my CRV, I got the creepy feeling that I was being watched. I did a full turn and didn't see anything. No surprise, it was raining pretty hard.

I got in my car and wrinkled my nose at the smell of wet wool. I'd gotten my pea coat from a cousin who'd been in the Navy. The damned thing weighed a ton, especially when it got wet, but it was amazing how it repelled water. My hair was dribbling rainwater onto my forehead. Under my coat, I was as dry as toast.

Before starting the CRV, I went ahead and called the latest number I had for Miriam Watts.

"I'm Daria Barnes, from Esparza Investigations," I told her when she answered. "I'm trying to follow up on something regarding your former husband's release from jail."

"Mr. Esparza called me about that on Thursday," she said.

"Yes, well, I'm Mr. Esparza's new associate," I told her, wondering just how much I should tell her. "We were wondering if your ex has approached you at all or if you've heard from him."

"No, I've been fine." She chuckled, but it was a frightened sound. "I don't think he'll be able to find me that easily. I had a shell company buy the house so that my address isn't on any of the public records, and I haven't given the address to anyone, not even my mother."

"That's as safe as you can make it," I said, knowing full well that determined batterers sometimes found a way. "Um, there's another case that I'm working for Mr. Esparza that might involve Mr. Sims. Is there a time I can come by, maybe tomorrow, to get some background on him?"

"I'll be home, for a change." She sighed deeply. "We're not shooting this week. Come by any time."

"I'll give you a call in the morning, once I know how my day is shaping up."

"Okay. Thanks."

I hung up feeling frustrated.

I tried to think of somebody worth bothering after hours and couldn't think of anybody. There was only one thing to do. Eat dinner and head home.

The swing through MacDonald's earlier that afternoon had been an emergency measure. I usually make it a practice not to eat at any restaurant that's within five miles of my home unless I'm within five miles of my home. I was feeling only moderately adventurous and tried a little Argentinian restaurant. The tables were crammed together but the thin steak and sauce were darned good. I left feeling I'd definitely put in a full day's work.

When I got home, I shouldn't have looked at my answering machine. I went ahead and played my messages, anyway. My buddy Lisa had called to say hi. Not a bad thing, however, the return call would probably take an hour or longer and I wasn't up to it. Berto had called, wanting to get an update. Then Tim Wing had called, insisting that I call him immediately, he had absolutely huge news and he desperately needed me.

Tim's an exceptionally talented director and a nice guy. Aside from working with him off and on for many, many years, we've also dated off and on. Although it had been a year since we'd last gone out, both the work and the sex were an awful lot of fun. Still, I wasn't sure if I wanted to talk to him at that moment in my life.

I called Berto first at the hospital. He was, indeed, going in for surgery the next day. He was pleased that I'd picked up on the Sims thing and had talked to Watts, not that she would likely know where Sims was. But she would know who his family was and have some idea of who his friends were. Berto also recommended a couple of bodyguards, just in case, and gave me permission to tell her why we wanted to know where Sims was. He agreed with my assessment of the Swanson thing and suggested I check out a few things at his office just to be on the safe side. I hung up quickly because he sounded really weak, and I didn't want to tire him out.

Then I called Tim, holding my breath as the phone rang on the other end.

"Yes!" I hissed as the voice mail picked up. I waited for the beep.

Instead, Tim picked up the phone.

"Hi, it's Daria," I answered.

"Daria! It's so good to hear your voice. I can't tell you how much I've missed you."

"I've missed you, too, Tim. What's the big news?" I tried not to sound as lacking in enthusiasm as I felt. I took the phone, working the cord around from the phone table and flopped onto the couch. I'm probably the last person on the planet to use a hard-wired phone. The cordless ones I've tried have never worked, so I refuse to use them.

"You won't believe this, but I have just gotten a major grant, really major. I mean, I've got the space for a song. Neri Mikelson has an absolutely amazing script ready. I just need a really good producer."

"Oh, shit."

There it was. Exactly what I wanted, and yet I balked

"Daria, we're talking our own company, and there's money," Tim went on, not noticing. "We've got sixty thou and we don't have to pay it back."

"Tim, honey, that's really terrific." It was, too. I bit my lip. "I don't know if I can, though. I just got so burnt out. I'm still crispy around the edges."

"Please, Daria, think about it. Will you? I heard you

quit the shelter and I was just hoping and praying you were coming back to us."

I sighed. "Not for the time being. I'm up to my hips working for Berto at the moment. There's no telling when that will clear up."

"Fuck. I really need you, too." Tim stopped. "No. I'm not going to do the manipulation thing."

"It never worked with me anyway," I said, smiling in spite of myself. "A show does sound tempting, though."

"Can I send you the script? It's really wonderful. Neri's outdone herself with this one. She could take it to Broadway, I swear."

"She should have been on Broadway years ago. Yeah, send it. Just don't get too excited. I'm serious, Tim, I'm really not sure I want to get back into that grind. I've kind of gotten used to eating regularly, you know?"

He groaned. "Too well. What's going on with Berto?"

I gave him a rough run-down about Berto's accident and that there was a new case and got an extended discourse on the hell bound state of the world in general, which left me feeling better than I had all day. After finally hanging up, I plopped onto my couch, let MacCavity and Little Dora (my other cat) plop themselves on me, and clicked through a bunch of cable channels until it was time for the news, which I watched, then went to bed.

I got into the office by ten the next morning. Franny had been there since nine but didn't say anything about the time. She did give me the once-over and nodded as if she approved of my ensemble. Well, I had decided to try and dress more professionally, although it was more casual professional than hardcore suit and skirt professional. I used to have a couple of suits, back when I was acting more often. However, I've always preferred comfort to looking good, which is probably why I never got more into acting. That day, I wore one of my nicer shirts – a dark green polished cotton broadcloth, with a paisley-patterned vest and light gray dress slacks over dark-colored running shoes.

I spent most of the next hour trying to get through to the head of the sex toys company that had sent Mrs. Bachner the latex penis. When I finally got him, I explained why I really needed to find out who had ordered the dildo. He was sympathetic but couldn't just give me that information. I agreed to send him a letter on Berto's letterhead explaining the situation and requesting the information that way. The CEO was pretty decent about the whole thing. He just needed a paper trail in case he got sued for disclosing private information.

Then I spent the next half-hour working on the letter, itself. Then I wasted a bit more time trying to find Berto's letterhead. Then I finally did what I should have done in the first case, which was ask Franny.

She sighed. "What you need is the voice recorder, that little one that looks like a microcassette machine? You dictate the letter into the recorder, then give it to me. I download the letter and I type it up for you. You sign it and I send it. Are you clear on that?"

"Uh, okay. What do I do about the letter I have?"

She sighed. "Save it to the L drive, in the Franny folder, and I'll take care of the rest."

"Okay. By the way, have you ever bought anything from that company?"

"I beg your pardon?" It was a pro forma protest, and yet...

"For gifts, and you're married." I felt my face growing hot. "I mean, why not? Hell, I've ordered stuff from the catalog. For some newlyweds. Shower gifts. I'm not asking what you've bought."

"Then why are you asking?"

"The writing on the box. It was all hand-printed. The company is pretty discreet, only the box that I got still had the logo on the outside. And there was no packing slip with the..., uh, you know."

Franny's eyebrows raised. "Hm. That's interesting. You think the perp had the thing sent to him first and then sent it to Mrs. Bachner?"

"Probably." I checked the clock on Franny's desk. "Oh no. I've got to get over to Luke Winston's office. I'll bring lunch back with me."

"I brought mine today."

I pulled my pea coat off the coat rack. "Hey, I thought I was buying."

"I forgot."

I rolled my eyes yet again. "Listen, I may swing by the hospital after Winston's. Berto should be out of surgery by then. You going, and can I tell him anything for you?"

"I'll be heading over myself. Your letter will be on the conference table when it's ready."

"Thanks." I left with the distinct feeling that Franny was training me and not enjoying it much.

Winston was out auditioning drummers when I got to his office, and most of the staff was with him. Jean, the receptionist, was expecting me, however, and had apparently been told to give me free rein. She looked to be in her late 20s, with naturally dark blonde hair, and just enough smarts to do her job well, and not enough to aspire to more. She sat at a curved desk placed in the dead center of the entry area of the house and busied herself making me a master key card for the offices within. The doors on either side of her were closed and one had a punch-key lock on it.

"Have you heard from Mr. Swanson yet?" I asked her. She hadn't asked me to sit down, and there really wasn't any place to sit, anyway. I hovered over her as she sat behind the curved desk.

She grimaced. "Nope. He's going to be in trouble, which is kind of too bad. He's a real sweet guy."

"I noticed." I debated taking off my pea coat. It was getting warm, but there wasn't anywhere to put it. "What time does the staff come in in the mornings?"

"About nine. I come in at eight and sometimes people are here earlier." Something on the computer was taking too long so she played with a pencil, absently stroking her thumb along the side.

"I take it Mr. Swanson did not call in sick."

"I don't think so." Her face scrunched up as she tried to remember. "He could have. Sometimes people will call in early, and we have the office voice mail, you know. I usually pick it up first thing, and whoever comes in first usually checks it, 'cause, like, there could be a message for them."

"Doesn't each staffer have individual voice mail?"

She smiled. "Oh, yeah. But you know how people freak when they get sent to voice mail. Somebody calls and they don't know the right extension, or, like, they freak when they don't want to press the button for the directory? So, they leave messages in the general mailbox all the time. We've got a couple people who don't clear their messages, so their mailboxes are always full, so the general mailbox is the only one with room, and so people leave messages there. The first person in the mornings checks the messages."

"Who picked up the messages yesterday morning?"

"Oh, I did. There weren't any."

I nodded. "Is that unusual?"

"Oh, no. Happens all the time."

"If anybody in the office can pick up the messages from the general mailbox, is it possible that someone got a message from Jay saying that he wasn't coming in and that person forgot to tell anyone?"

She nodded sagely. "That's what I'm thinking." She suddenly blushed. "I was, like, really late yesterday and practically everybody was here already, so I don't know who got here first. I wouldn't know, anyway, 'cause, like, a lot of people here come in through the back."

I glanced at the door with the cipher lock on it. Coming in through the back would make sense. Having been in the back already, I knew that with the offices all being closed off, no one else would know when other people had arrived, either. I glanced at the ceiling around where it met the walls. Sure enough, in each of the corners at the back of the entryway were two very discreet video cameras. I'd have to double check in the body of the offices. I had a bad feeling these were the only two cameras.

After Jean finally got around to handing me the key card and letting me in the back, I found out I was right. I saw the key card locks on all the outside doors, yet when I called the security company and convinced Winston's security supervisor that I was legit, I was told that the locks didn't track which cards and when they were used. There were cameras on the doors, however, they only activated if someone tried to break in. The supervisor wasn't too thrilled about the possibility of someone stealing a key card and using it to wreak havoc, but Winston had been adamant that he did not want to spy on his staff and refused to give them any reason to think that he might.

Swanson's office was right next door to Winston's, which made sense. I didn't really find much except for the usual ephemera. Swanson's office seemed a tad neater than one might expect, although it also looked like his job didn't involve a lot of paperwork in the first place. There were several files in the lower left-hand drawer: blank petty cash vouchers, menus from a wide range of local restaurants, price lists from catering companies, travel vouchers, expense sheets, things like that. Behind the files was an orange plastic bowl and a fork, both of which reeked of stale ramen soup. The usual office supplies were scattered among the sections of the drawer tray in the top center drawer, along with a few Hershey miniature candy bars still sporting their Christmas season wrappers, and a couple of the same wrappers missing their candy bars.

The desk had a collection of miniature sports balls strewn about the surface, as well as several Matchbox cars. The only framed photo on the desktop showed Swanson and some sweet young thing grinning at the camera on a local beach. The frame was pink and decorated with hand-painted flowers and hearts. Swanson had a girlfriend.

What few papers littered the surface were printouts of Winston's schedule and a couple catering price lists. The Rolodex had been left open to a local company that I knew by its ultra-trendy and pricey reputation. I flipped through the Rolodex, and it seemed that most of the cards, including the caterer's, pre-dated Swanson. However, I did hit gold in another way. All of Swanson's various passwords, written carefully on a card which he had, logically enough, filed under S, between a card for Eric Scrogway (a soundman, apparently) and Laura Seeton (a make-up artist), as in the card was filed as "secret."

I pulled the card and booted up Swanson's desktop.

While waiting for the computer to do its thing, I studied the phone. It was a pretty standard office phone with twelve lines, each of them neatly labeled, by someone who pre-dated Swanson. Winston's line clearly had priority. There were also twelve speed-dial buttons, all of them labeled by the same predecessor, except one labeled "Katelyn." I debated pressing it, and instead hit the button labeled "Voice Mail."

Checking the card, I punched in his password (which was ridiculously simple – I wondered that he'd felt it necessary to write it down). There was a message from the previous day, around nine a.m. from the caterer, returning Swanson's call. Another from Winston, a few minutes later, saying that he'd be late. Then, after the mechanical voice announced that the call had come in at 2:13 p.m., a worried young female voice came on.

"Jay, honey, I'm getting a little worried. You sounded so upset last night, and you didn't pick up at your place just now. I know I'm not supposed to call you at work, but you told me you were going to call me at lunch time, and I haven't heard from you." She paused. "I guess I'm just being paranoid. Listen, will you call me? Please?"

The young woman had called again just before five o'clock, and again that morning. That last message was practically hysterical. She could have been a relative. I was betting on the girlfriend. I saved the messages, rang off, then pressed the button labeled "Katelyn."

Of all the annoyances possible, she wasn't picking up. She was probably at work. I went ahead and left a message, leaving Berto's office number. Since the computer was already booted up, I went ahead, signed in, and did a text search for the name "Katelyn," and didn't turn anything up there, either. I went through the Outlook files and found Luke's schedule, and didn't find anything that looked out of place.

I browsed through the call record feature of Outlook and noted several calls to McKesson. The funny thing is, at least some of them, probably most, should have gone to his extension, but these calls were made to an outside line. I wrote the number down.

I thumbed through the Rolodex. Sure enough, there was only the outside line listed for Leo McKesson.

I played around on the computer for a few minutes more and didn't really see anything strange. I paused for a moment, debating. I would have preferred to slip out discreetly. The I realized I did need something from Winston, after all, and it was something I should have looked at earlier.

Fortunately, Winston was back from his auditions and on the phone in his office, nervously drumming his fingers on his desk. I stopped in his doorway.

"You know I'd rather not do it," he told somebody on the other end then sighed. "I suppose that's true. So, what the hell am I supposed to talk to him about? I can't tell that same old lame tour story... No, we did that one last time... Well, I suppose, if you think I should. Now, what are we going to do about that choreographer...? I don't mind the ballet thing, but she just doesn't get the music... Good. You take care of it, then, and can you talk to Doreen, while you're at it...? I'm pretty sure we can swing it. If you want, you can talk to Felicity first. Don't forget she knows I need Doreen, too, and she'll be right about it... Can you talk to her manager then? I don't think Felicity would mind that... Thanks, Leo. I'll talk to you later."

He smiled at me as he hung up. "What can I do for you, Daria?"

"I should probably search Mr. Ochoa's place if it hasn't been packed up yet."

Winston nodded and drummed again. "No, it hasn't. His folks came out from Texas for the funeral last week, but his mother just couldn't face it. So, they just got his bank account settled as much as they could and left."

"His folks?"

"Mom, dad, and a couple of sisters."

"Huh. Did Mr. Ochoa leave a will?"

"Well, now." Winston sucked on the ends of his mustache for a moment. "I don't know. We didn't find one here, and this is where he kept most of his financial stuff, since Leo helps everyone with the business side of things.

I figured his family would know. They didn't even want to go into his house. I think the one sister did. If she found anything, she hasn't told me."

"Really."

"It's like I said the other day. They weren't close. Larry's old drug habit, you know. He'd burnt a few bridges. I think he'd gotten his mom to talk to him right before he died, but that's about it."

"That's nice. You wouldn't happen to have a key, would you?"

"As it happens, I do." Winston pushed himself back from his desk slightly and opened up the center drawer. "He made sure I had a spare for emergencies, me being just about the only family he had. I mean, with him and his folks being estranged and all."

"You were friends," I said.

"Yeah." He got up and handed me the key.

"Right-o. Thanks. Oh. I'd like to try to talk to Mr. Ochoa's family and I've also got to set up some times to talk with your band members. They knew Mr. Ochoa, also, and may have seen something you didn't."

"Set it up with Jean, then. I've already told her to get you anything you need."

"I'll do that. Thanks again." I paused. "I'll be in touch."

"Thank you."

I left and stopped at the reception desk and asked Jean to set me up with Winston's band members, to which she agreed, and the Ochoa family's numbers, which she wrote out for me.

"Jean, I've got kind of an odd question," I asked her, after giving her the office number so she could get back to me.

The phone rang.

"The Winston Company." She smiled up at me and raised a finger. "I'll put you through to Mr. McKesson's secretary now, sir," she said and punched a series of buttons. "Now, what's your question, Ms. Barnes?"

"Can't you transfer a call directly to Mr. McKesson?"

"No." She shook her head genially. "He doesn't have a

phone in his office."

"He doesn't?"

"He does. It's just not a regular phone phone. He uses his mobile phone all the time and doesn't bother with the regular ones, so we took it out, like, years ago. I can't transfer calls to the mobile. I think Agnes can. No, wait. She just makes it a three-way call, then hangs up. I could do the same, I suppose. I usually just transfer the calls to Agnes and let her sort them out."

The phone rang again and as Jean answered it, I waved at her, mouthed a "thank you," and took off.

However, I paused outside the garage that was McKesson's office. Winston had said that Agnes had vouched for McKesson's presence in the office. On the other hand, Berto was of the opinion that it never hurt to ask again.

Agnes was a trim woman in her early thirties who looked like something out of an old Fred and Ginger movie. Her short blonde hair was combed into a perky flip and her blue dress easily dated back to the Depression era. Except that her attention, when I walked in, was focused on the computer monitor on her side desk. The keys rattled quietly as she typed. I cleared my throat.

"Hello. How might I help you?" Her voice was soft and her accent solidly British.

"I'm Daria Barnes," I started.

"Oh, yes. The private detective. Mr. McKesson said you might be by."

"Yeah." I looked around. "Is he in?"

"Yes, but he's not to be disturbed."

"How do you know he's in there?"

She chuckled lightly. "I saw him go in just a little while ago and he hasn't come out." She nodded at a door to my left and behind her. "That's the only door in and out of there and I've been here the whole time."

"No kidding. There's no way he could have snuck out?"

"No." She smiled brightly. "Mr. Winston asked me the same thing the day after the… accident. He even asked about the windows. They've been stuck shut for years, and they're actually quite a bit higher over the ground than you might think because of the slope in the back yard."

"Mr. Winston asked you?"

"Oh, yes. He said he was worried about anyone getting the wrong idea."

"Can't have that, now, can we?" I smiled, although I couldn't help wondering why Winston would have started investigating, himself, unless there was something else going on. "By the way, I've heard Mr. McKesson can be a bit difficult to work for."

Agnes winced. "I must say, he's always been kind to me. He does get into a bit of a lather, at times, but he always apologizes."

"I see." I gravely feared that she didn't. Maybe I was reading too much into it. Her description of McKesson's losing it then apologizing sure fit the pattern of an abuser.

I thanked her and left. I got into my CRV and didn't start the engine right away. Instead, I pulled out my smartphone and called Berto's office.

"Franny, you got a second?" I asked when she picked up.

"I do. What do you need?"

"I had to leave messages for some people just now, only I didn't want to leave my cell phone number, so I left the office number."

Franny chuckled. "Well, at least you got that right. Who is the somebody, and do you want me to patch you in when this person calls?"

"Wow, you mean make it a three-way call, then hang up?"

"Yes."

"Isn't that expensive?"

"Daria, where have you been this last decade? Three-way calling is a standard part of any phone services package, along with caller ID, call waiting and all that other nonsense."

"Okay. Well, yeah. Any messages?"

"Yes. Miriam Watts asked you to call her right away."

I looked over at the notepad on the passenger seat. "Shit. I was supposed to call her this morning. Did she leave a number?"

Franny gave it to me, and I rang off with her, then dialed Watts' number. She picked up and what she told me made my heart stop.

Chapter Six

I hustled my CRV to Miriam Watts' place in the Hollywood Hills as fast as I could drive. The phone call had been short and sweet, and I got the icky feeling that I was about to get my background on Clifford Sims in an up close and personal way. I called Franny back as I pulled out from Winston's office and had her call the bodyguards. In the meantime, Watts needed somebody there and I would have to do, scared spitless or not.

Watts' sprawling 1920s hacienda-style home was east of the 101 freeway, close to, although not technically in, the Los Feliz district. It had been built on a street that had a forty-five-degree tilt. Okay, maybe it wasn't that bad, but it seemed like it as I parallel parked out front of her home and cut my wheels so that my CRV wouldn't roll down the steep hill.

I had been debating with myself all the way over and as I cut the ignition and set the parking brake, I was no closer to an answer. You see, there was a gun under my seat. I have the permit for it and the concealed weapon license. I know how to use it, too. It was the result of some serious arm-twisting on Berto's part because I am seriously anti-gun. Thanks to some of the skanky joints I'd been working in and that one time I got attacked, Berto not only bought the gun for me, he'd personally shown me how to use it and dragged me out to the shooting range on a regular basis to practice. He also made me take self-defense classes pretty regularly, too.

I had no reason to believe that Sims was at Watts' house. The police had been by earlier and had, presumably, scared him off. The problem was for how long?

Sims was not a nice person. And he was angry, having

been recently released from jail. Not only that, he had violated his parole in record time. None of that automatically meant that he was carrying a firearm on him, and while it's not unheard of, abusers don't usually carry heat because most people, in general, don't. Abuse is usually a spontaneous thing, although planned attacks have happened.

Which is why I finally pulled the .357 magnum automatic from under my seat and dropped it into the pocket of my pea coat as I got out of the car.

The exterior of the house had been done in a nice pink stucco, complementing the red clay tiles of the roof. The windows and trim were all in white, and the yard was filled with neatly trimmed bushes and a rich green lawn. The beds were still dormant, but I was betting that once we got sun, they'd be filled with color. All in all, it was a peaceful, pretty place, which made the spray paint all over the porch really scary.

Somebody... Okay, Sims, in all likelihood, had sprayed the words *You + me 4ever* and *your mine* all over the door and front stoop in blood red paint.

I rang the bell and hollered, "Ms. Watts? It's Daria Barnes from Esparza Investigations. I'm alone."

There was a peephole in the door and a long pause. I was about to ring again when the door cracked open.

"Hi," said the soft voice on the other side. "Can you come in quickly, please? Just in case."

I slid in through the crack into a long hallway with a stairway and wrought iron banister on one side. On the other side was a spacious living room, lovingly decorated with Mission-style furniture on top of well-polished dark hardwood floors. Watts was wraith-thin, like almost every actress in Hollywood. Still, the round-faced brunette carried herself with a sense of substance – something you don't see in Hollywood very often.

"Can I get you some water or some tea?" she asked, leading me into the living room.

"Water's fine. Thank you." I said, looking around.

There was a window that faced onto the street, but it was fairly small for the room, which was much longer than it was wide. At the far end of the room, there was an open door that led into the dining room. Watts had gone through the dining room to the kitchen, which I couldn't see, and returned quickly with a glass filled with ice water on a small wooden tray.

"Thanks," I said, taking the glass. "How long ago did the cops leave?"

"Only a few minutes ago," she said. "Please, have a seat."

"Sure. Just a second." I walked the perimeter of the room, looking out the windows, just like I'd seen Berto do. If only I'd remembered to check the whole floor.

"Can I take your coat?" she asked as I set the glass down on an end table.

"Thanks." I slipped out of it and was about to hand it over when I realized there was something in it I needed. I hesitated, then got the gun out of the pocket.

Watts gasped.

"I don't really think we'll need this," I explained, laying it on the coffee table, where I could get it quickly. "It's just that if we don't have it…"

Watts nodded and smiled wanly. "You know, I was just getting used to not being afraid all the time."

"You'll get there again," I said, laying my pea coat across the back of the sofa. "Sims has already violated parole. He'll be going back to jail pretty quickly. Besides, there's why I wanted to come by today, even before…" I waved at the front door, and she shuddered.

"Cliff's idea of showing eternal devotion," she said, pacing the room.

I winced. "Yeah. That happens. Anyway, the reason I need background on him is good news for you. If he's done what we think he might have, we'll have him on attempted murder charges."

Watts looked at me with a curious frown. "What's he done?"

"We don't know. It's possible he pulled a hit and run on someone. That's why I need to know about any friends he has, family. We'll need to talk to them, see if we can find out where he was Monday afternoon, evening."

Watts suddenly swallowed. "Why isn't Mr. Esparza here?"

I took a deep breath. "Because he was the one who got hit. With Sims breaking parole last week, the timing looks interesting."

"Is Mr. Esparza all right?"

"He got hurt pretty badly," I said, with tears suddenly threatening. I sniffed them back. "But it looks like he'll be okay. Why did you think of Berto?"

"Because he's not here, and there really isn't anybody else that Cliff would be mad at," Watts said. "I mean, I have friends, but Cliff didn't really know them." She sniffed. "If only I hadn't…"

"You can't blame yourself," I told her.

"Oh, I know. I just can't help wondering, though."

"Well, let's see if there's any evidence to get on him. What friends did he have?"

Watts snorted. "Almost none. He didn't like people getting too close to him. There was his church group, but they don't seem to want anything to do with him, at least, that's what his pastor said when I called him Friday. I had to warn them, you know." She pressed her eyes shut. "He's why we're not shooting this week. My producer didn't want him following me home from the studio and finding out where I live. Only I guess he already had."

She was trying so hard not to break down in tears that I felt guilty pressing her, but I needed the information if we were going to stop this asshole.

"What about family?" I asked as gently as I could.

"There's only his mother." She took a deep breath and got a better grip on herself. "His dad was killed in some sort of bar fight, I'm not sure. It was years ago, long before Cliff and I met. Cliff's mom is not exactly mellow. Cliff said he couldn't wait to get away from her, and I've gotten the impression, she couldn't wait for him to get away. She's in Pacoima. I think I've still got the address." Watts grabbed her phone and went scrolling through her contacts. "Yeah. Here it is. Let me text it to you."

A minute later, my phone buzzed with the incoming

text.

"Got it," I said, looking at it to be sure. "Thanks." I checked the time while I was at it. "The bodyguards should be here any time now."

"Great." Watts sank into a chair and closed her eyes. "The sad thing is my family thinks Cliff is great. He can be a real charmer, you know. Figures. They're just as fucked up as Cliff's family, in their own way." She shook her head, then looked at me. "Tell me about your family. It's got to be less fucked than mine."

"I don't know about that," I said, with a chuckle. "My mom and I get on really well, but her family is a complete mess."

"What about your dad's family?"

I grinned, in spite of myself. "I don't have a dad."

Watts looked at me. "I don't get it."

"There was some sperm involved," I conceded, coming over and sitting down on the couch. "But, well... When I was little and it was just my mom and me, and people would ask where my dad was, Mom would make up all these crazy stories, and I started making up a few. Just between us, Mom said I didn't have a father. Only when I was eight and found out about the facts of life, Mom finally 'fessed up that she didn't actually give birth to me. Her sister had, only it was such a disgrace to the family because my aunt had refused to give me up for adoption, that Mom, who was leaving to live in Los Angeles and be an artist anyway, agreed to take me."

"Why didn't your..."

"I call her my aunt."

"Your aunt, why didn't she get an abortion?"

"She had issues with it."

Watts was looking carefully at me, which felt a little weird, but at least, she seemed to have calmed down.

"How old are you?" she asked suddenly.

"I'm forty."

Watts' jaw dropped. "You're kidding."

"I'm kind of in shock about that, myself. I sure don't feel like I am." I noticed Watts eyeing my neck. "I haven't had any work done, either."

She laughed. "I'm sorry. I was going to say, you've got one hell of a surgeon."

"Nope. I can't get into that. I don't even color my hair. On good days, you can see the grays poking through."

We both smiled. Then the glass shattered. The sound came from the back of the house. Slowly, I reached and got a grip on my gun. Watts swallowed.

"He's here," she whispered, her face growing whiter by the second.

I nodded, trying not to let on that I had no clue what to do next. Well, I did grab my phone and hit 911. But beyond that, no idea what I was going to do.

The operator picked up right away and I softly told her to get cops to this address with a break-in in progress. Isabel once told me that if you even think somebody might be in the house, tell the cops it's a break-in in progress and that will get them out the fastest. They'd rather find no one there than have you wait and get hurt because someone really was.

The operator asked me to stay on the line, only Sims loomed up in the archway and let me know with an ugly glare and a drawn fist that he wanted me off the phone. He was a big man, linebacker big, with soft brown hair and the kind of gorgeous, rough-hewn face that explained in part why Watts had fallen for him.

Since I had the gun, I just smiled.

"He's here now," I told the operator.

Sims lunged at Watts and just barely missed her. Watts scrambled behind me and the couch.

"You can't do this," Sims snarled. "That is my wife. What God has brought together, let no man tear asunder."

"Good thing I'm a woman, then," I said.

That did it for Sims. He suddenly lunged at me, and he was fast. I instinctively drew back, which was a mistake. The coffee table saved my ass, however, tripping up Sims so that he fell on top of me, knocking both of us down on the couch.

Sims got an iron grip on my left wrist and pinned it. I managed to bang him in the side of his ribs with the butt of the gun. He didn't let go of my wrist and flailed as he tried to get my right hand and the gun. As he shifted, he fell off the couch onto his backside.

I rolled over, got my feet steady and put the gun in his nose.

"That wasn't smart, Sims," I growled. "I wasn't going to shoot you before. Now you've pissed me off. I've got every right to blow your head straight to kingdom come. It's called self-defense."

"She's my wife."

"She was your wife. You abused her and now she's not your wife."

"The Bible says—"

"You can stuff your Bible up your ass, buddy."

"You're going to hell. Do you know that? You have blasphemed against the Holy Spirit and you are going to hell."

"Shut the fuck up, or I'll make sure you beat me there."

I held him there for about five or so minutes, when the first cops showed. They had been already on the way since Watts' alarm had silently triggered when Sims had broken the window on the back-porch door. The officers came in through that door, guns drawn, ready for action, because, as I later found out, they were the same officers who'd already been there earlier when Watts had called about the vandalism. They didn't seem too happy that I'd already done their work for them. In fact, they were a little snippy as they checked my concealed weapon license.

They were still there when a second set of cops, responding to my 911 call, arrived on the scene about ten minutes later. Then the guys from the bodyguard company showed up. There were two bodyguards. One, a former boxer almost as big as Sims, was there to explain the service to Watts and take care of the paperwork. The other was the first shift. Given that Sims was being arrested, it seemed a tad unnecessary, although there were no guarantees that Sims wouldn't be able to post bail and walk. As a parolee, he should have gone straight back to prison, but things have gotten mixed up before.

Once I was sure that Watts was in safe hands, I went ahead and slipped out of the house. I was shaking and royally pissed at myself. I hadn't handled myself well, and while I was glad that things had worked out okay, it could just as easily have gone the other direction.

Sims had obviously known that I wasn't going to fire that gun, or he wouldn't have charged Watts, or me for that matter. Berto always said that I had to plan on shooting.

"The most dangerous gun is the one the owner won't shoot," he'd told me. "They get chicken about shooting and then they get their guns used against them."

Which means I'd just set myself and Watts up badly. Yeah, I'd gotten out of it, but I shouldn't have been in that position in the first place. It really made me wonder what Berto had been thinking when he'd said I'd be good at this private detective thing.

I debated calling him at the hospital then realized that if he was out of surgery, he was probably too groggy to give me a decent answer. On the other hand, it would probably be worthwhile to swing by Cedars on the way back to the office to at least say hi. I called his room before starting my CRV.

Marisol answered and said that Berto was still in surgery and would likely be under for the rest of the afternoon.

"Well, I'll come by tonight, then," I told her. "Do you have my cell phone number?"

"Uh, no. Let me get my phone and I'll put it in."

While we were pressing buttons, I put her number in my phone, wondering how the hell I'd gotten so techno enslaved.

After ringing off with Marisol, I discovered that Franny had left a couple of messages for me. The manager at Jay Swanson's apartment had called – Swanson's truck had been moved to the wrong spot and someone was peeved about it. Swanson was still not answering at his place, so the manager was hoping I knew something. Katelyn Everett had called, returning my message, and hoping that I knew something about what was going with Swanson.

I called Everett, who sounded exactly like the worried girl who'd left all those messages on Swanson's voice mail, which, of course, she was.

"This just isn't like Jay," she said, her voice under control, although just barely. "He doesn't get freaked easily, and the other night, he was, like, totally messed up."

"Did he tell you about what?" I asked.

"No! That's the worst part. He said that if I knew too much, it would get me in big trouble. He was really scared of something."

"Did he call the cops?"

"Well, I told him to."

"Right. That doesn't mean he did." I sighed. "Listen, do you have a key to his apartment?"

"Yeah."

"What time can you meet me over there?"

"Um. Well, I suppose I can get out of here at six. Hang on. Kristen?" Her voice got softer, but I could still hear her talk Kristen into finishing the prep work in case she couldn't get things done herself. "It's no big deal. You could probably start wrapping the knives and forks now while I finish packing the soft drinks." Everett came back on the line to me. "I should be able to get there at six-thirty. Is that okay with you?"

"Sure. I'll meet you outside the manager's office."

"Okay, six-thirty."

I ended the call and, after mounting the phone in its holder on my dash, started my CRV. Since I didn't have a key to Swanson's truck, I decided against calling the apartment manager back. That left Ochoa's place to search.

I have since decided that there is something inherently just plain wrong about searching someone's crib after they've died. I suppose it'd be different if you were family or something. Searching Ochoa's place left me feeling like… Well, like a peeping Tom, or like somebody who bitches constantly about daytime talk shows and won't miss seeing them.

The thing is, I'm not a squeamish kind of person. Yeah, I've got issues with people shooting me, but who doesn't?

Blood and guts? They don't bother me. I didn't blink an eye during Mel Gibson's The Passion, although my friend Sally said that was probably because I didn't have any emotional investment in the whole Jesus thing. I've been to my share of funerals and was even with Berto the day we came across a stiff instead of the client we were supposed to meet for lunch. It didn't faze me, and that was one messed up stiff.

Still, I had butterflies in my stomach as I drove up to Ochoa's house in Venice. It wasn't right on the beach, although it was within walking distance if you don't mind a decent hike. The neighborhood had probably been built in the 1920s or '30s and was mostly clapboard houses built up instead of out on postage-stamp-sized lots. Even back then, beach property was at a premium. Ochoa had a yellow Cape Cod-ish place, with white trim.

His garage door had been modernized, a roll-up style with windows. I peeked in before walking over to the front door. There was a Jaguar inside – somebody had apparently gotten Ochoa's car home, assuming he didn't have a second one somewhere.

Taking a deep breath, I went up the small walkway to the front door and let myself in.

Ochoa had been a minimalist at heart. There was next to no furniture in the place, although you could tell it had been decorated by a professional – or someone with a real eye. The hardwood floors gleamed without a rug in sight. The kitchen was spare and modern, and the cabinets were filled with professional quality pots and pans and tools and ingredient foods, like canned tomatoes as opposed to ready-made tomato sauce.

While the place had a clean functionality to its décor, the shelves that lined the walls of almost every other room besides the kitchen and the bathrooms were overflowing. There were books – Ochoa had very eclectic tastes. I spotted a copy of a treatise on natural theology by St. Thomas Aquinas next to a trashy murder mystery by Robert Crais next to one of Octavia Butler's more ethereal sci-fi works next to Plato's Republic next to Dickens' Tale of Two Cities.

The bulk of Ochoa's passions appeared to center on

recorded music. He had extensive collections of just about every medium that has existed since Edison first figured out how to get sound onto something tangible that could be replayed. There were cylinders, 78 records, LPs, 45s, reel to reel tapes, cassette tapes, 8-tracks, CDs, and even floppy disks, and I was sure there was a host of mp3s on his computer. He had at least two mp3 players, plus a cylinder player, a real Victrola, something tall that looked like a Victrola that had half-inch thick records in its cabinet. He had a whole collection of turntables, two reel-to-reel units, cassette players up the wazoo, and five (I couldn't believe it), five 8-track players.

It was all neatly organized, and I got the distinct impression that Ochoa was a hardcore collector. There was sound stuff everywhere, including the two bathrooms. His living room, kitchen, and dining area were on the first floor, then you walked up to the bedroom. Another floor up, Ochoa had put in a small recording studio, which held his synthesizer and an impressive collection of rhythm instruments from simple tribal drums from three different cultures all the way to a full drum set, a kettle drum, a brace of cymbals, and small hand instruments.

He had several framed blow-ups of Luke Winston albums on his walls, plus a plaque honoring himself as country drummer of the year. There were a couple of other albums prominently displayed, albums of experimental music of his own. I found one of the CDs back downstairs and briefly debated putting it on. I love obscure music and I'll listen to just about anything that isn't on a major label.

Ochoa apparently liked the obscure stuff, too. I found a cassette tape that I also had of the Dixie Belles, a Dixieland jazz band made up of women over 60, or something like that. I didn't think anybody else had that cassette.

The place had an eerie feel of expectancy as if it were waiting for someone to come home. There was a coffee maker in the kitchen with about a cup's worth of coffee in it waiting to be drunk. I opened the dishwasher, and that was a mistake. It was only about a third full, but over a week's worth of waiting had left a serious stink. A book lay open next to the bed, and some dirty clothes waited on top of a hamper in the bedroom. Ochoa had clearly expected to be back that evening.

I looked in a few of his drawers and didn't find anything of interest. I turned on the computer and found out that, as I had suspected, the hard drive was mostly given over to downloaded music. There were no word processing files and the only spreadsheet files just cataloged his incredible collection. I shut it down.

The one interesting thing that I did find was his answering machine. Aside from the fact that he even had one, as opposed to using the phone company's voice mail, it was an older stand-alone model that still used real tape. There were two messages. The time and date stamp announced that the first one had come in on the day Ochoa had died, in fact, right around the time he had passed. It was from McKesson, asking Ochoa to call him about a meeting.

The second message was dated two days after Ochoa's death.

"Larry, it's Rita," said the voice in strung out tones. "Look, you gotta stop calling. I don't care about this ree-conciling thing. It's not like you haven't already fucked up my life enough. *Papí* says you call again, he coming after you." There was a pause. "I oughta let him. Bye."

I gazed at the machine, wondering what to do next. It and the phone were on a table next to the kitchen. I opened a small drawer under the tabletop and found an address book. There weren't any Ritas listed. Under the address book was a sheet from a legal pad with a list of names and phone numbers. The sheet was labeled Step # 7.

I nodded. Ochoa was a recovering drug addict and was apparently still working his Twelve-Steps. You can't work as long in theatre as I have and not know someone doing the Twelve-Step recovery program made famous by Alcoholics Anonymous. It seems like there's a Twelve-Step program for everything, including picking your nose. I know one of the steps involves asking for forgiveness from the people you've hurt with your addiction. Funny thing is, I've been hurt by plenty of addicts in my time, some of whom have done Narcotics Anonymous, and I've yet to have anyone ask me for forgiveness.

Looking at the sheet made me realize there was something missing in the house – ashtrays. I mean, nobody had said anything about Ochoa being a smoker, although even recovering drug addicts usually find the nicotine habit impossible to break. I had yet to meet a drunk or a druggie that didn't also smoke cigarettes, and even fewer musicians who didn't smoke.

I went back up to the bedroom and sniffed at the dirty clothes in the hamper. There was a definite whiff of cigarette smoke, but nothing strong enough to pin it on Ochoa. It could easily have come from someone else's cigarette, especially since odds were very high there were at least several smokers among Winston's people.

Coming back downstairs, I looked at the list of people on the legal pad and saw that there was a Rita Camacho on the list. I didn't recognize the area code attached to her phone number, which didn't mean much.

I noted the day and time of the calls on a notepad I had in my pea coat, then took Ochoa's list. If Rita wasn't a suspect, it was possible others on the list might be. The question was what to do about it.

I headed back toward Hollywood. It was only four-thirty and the traffic on Olympic was non-existent. It was still pretty sticky getting back up to Sunset on La Cienega. Fortunately, the bulk of the traffic seemed to be south bound, so I got back to Berto's office just before five.

Franny showed me how to fill out the notes forms and took off for home. I wrote up my notes for her, then spent another twenty minutes playing solitaire on her computer.

I wasn't happy. I had the uncomfortable feeling I had missed something regarding the Ochoa case. Then, in addition to almost letting Cliff Sims get at my gun, I had let Watts out of my sight and had forgotten to secure the back of the house. This wasn't the sort of business where you could get away with being sloppy.

Berto was nuts. I wasn't cut out for investigating. If only he weren't in some drugged-up stupor, I would have turned in my parking pass and run. But he needed help, and I was his best shot at it. It wasn't like I hadn't followed him around plenty of times. But the learning curve had suddenly gotten a lot steeper than I suspected even he would have liked. But he didn't have anyone else to pick up the slack. But if I didn't get myself or anyone else killed, it was entirely possible I would kill his business. But if I didn't help out, the business would surely die. But. But. But.

I clicked a red four onto a black five, then realized I'd lost yet another game. It was just after six at that point and I had one more meeting before I could get away with going home. I was, indeed, well and truly stuck.

Chapter Seven

It had started to drizzle by the time I made it out to Jay Swanson's apartment. The parking god had decided that I had used up my allotment of premium spaces for the time being, and I ended up parking down the street and around the corner. My hair was just starting to drip when I walked up to the foyer of Swanson's apartment building.

I could see a young woman pacing in the lighted foyer. She didn't look entirely like the sweet young thing in the photo on Swanson's desk, which didn't mean anything. Oddly enough, I have a rough time recognizing people from photographs. I recognized her outfit, though. She wore the standard waiter's uniform – white shirt and black pants – under her parka. If that wasn't obvious enough, her matchstick frame cemented it. She was an actress working food service until she got her big break.

Everett saw me step into the pool of light outside the locked exterior door and had the door open before I had a chance to knock.

"Are you Daria?" she asked.

"Yes, I am. Are you Katelyn Everett?"

"Yes. I'm so glad you're here. I suppose I could have gone upstairs without you, but…"

She was blonde, though her dark roots suggested she was not naturally so. While her face had that pretty, almost vulnerable thing so popular with casting directors, there was an intelligent spark in her eyes that almost made me wonder what she'd seen in Jay Swanson.

"It's probably just as well," I said, though I don't know why. "Why don't we go on up?"

Everett led the way into the building and to the elevator. She smiled and made an honest, but lame, attempt at small talk while we waited. She got on the elevator first and pushed the button for Swanson's floor. We rode up in silence.

I followed her to Swanson's apartment, even though I'd been there before, and let her open the door. She froze in the open doorway, and it was easy to see why.

The place had been trashed – and not the kind of trashed from Swanson being a lousy housekeeper. Over Everett's shoulder, I could see a couch overturned, stuffing all over the place, a wrought iron frame in the middle of a pool of broken glass and an overturned shelving unit.

I gently pushed Everett aside, and remembering that I still had my gun in my peacoat pocket, I drew it and slowly went inside. There wasn't any foul smell, which boded well. The silence of the place was deafening.

I motioned for Everett to stay put, then walked slowly through the one-bedroom apartment. Fortunately, the living room was the only trashed room. The kitchen, bedroom, and bathroom were all empty of people. I put my gun back in my pocket and came into the living room.

"He's not here," I told Everett. "This mess, however, means we'll have to call the police. With your boyfriend missing, and all this damage, I think we've got a crime scene on our hands."

"I knew something was wrong." Everett blinked back tears, yet somehow remained calm. "Wait. Did you find Muffy?"

I looked at her.

"His cat." Everett blinked back tears again. "Here, Muffy. Kitty, kitty, kitty. If she's not here, then Jay left on his own. He would never have left her behind. He loved her and she's rare. Kitty, kitty, kitty."

If Muffy was there, then she was too danged scared to come just because someone was calling her. That's little enough motive for a cat even if not terrified, but there's one lure that no cat can resist. I took a chance on messing up evidence and found what I needed in the kitchen: a can and can opener.

Sure enough, a large fluffy orange tabby with white

paws and nose emerged from who knows what hiding place and slid into the kitchen. If indeed female, then that was one rare kitty, indeed. Orange tabbies are almost never female. As Muffy stood there, eyeing me suspiciously, Everett came in right behind the cat.

"At least you're safe," she said. "Only what do we do with you?"

"Well, you're closest," I said. "Can you take her?"

"Oh no." Everett sounded like she just might break down at that point. "I wish I could. I can't have pets at my place. We can't even keep them for someone else. I can't afford to lose it. I'm in Santa Monica."

Which meant she had a rent-controlled place, and given the ridiculous cost of housing in the L.A. area, if she'd scored a rent-controlled apartment, she wasn't going to risk losing it even for a beautiful homeless rare cat.

"Well, I guess you can come home with me," I said to Muffy, all the while thinking what a ridiculous name that was, even for something so ridiculously fluffy.

I went ahead and fed her from the can I'd opened and called the police as she ate. Then I slid out of my peacoat and as Muffy licked the last little bit of meat out of her bowl, I dropped the coat on her and got her safely bundled inside.

She didn't take to it. She wasn't heavy – all that hair made her look bigger than she was – but she struggled like a champ. I'm still not sure how I was able to keep her under wraps long enough for the cops to arrive, take statements and dismiss Everett and me. I made sure I had all of Everett's phone numbers, then headed home to spring Muffy on MacCavity and Little Dora.

Believe it or not, I'm actually a dog person. Not that I don't love cats. It's just that after getting nothing but attitude all day and night from actors, stage-hands, fellow producers, directors and all the other egos involved in the theatre, I couldn't see coming home and getting it from my pets. Dogs do not give you attitude.

However, at that time in my life, I was dog-less. I usually had at least two, and have had up to four at one time, which I know is really pushing it. I'd only buried my last dog – a beagle mix named Roxy who'd died of old age – about three months before. Five months before that I'd buried Simba, another geriatric case. For some odd reason, no homeless doggies had found me yet.

It's probably a major sign of just how unsettled I'd been feeling about my life that I hadn't gone to the animal shelter to find Simba's successor, let alone Roxy's. I do believe in a decent grieving period. Still, this was the first time I'd been without a dog for more than a month since before I could remember.

The cops had let me take a pillowcase from Swanson's apartment to transport Muffy. They also let me take her food and litter box, which was more than decent of them. Actually, it was probably sloppy police work – after all, Swanson's place was technically a crime scene. I'd checked the litter box for secret messages before I left and didn't find any, which is why I didn't worry about it. Muffy would feel a lot better in the strange new place with the strange new kitties with her old litter box.

I also called the hospital as I drove back to Eagle Rock. The surgery had gone well, Marisol told me, but Berto was still pretty groggy and out of it. She suggested I come by the next morning so he could get some rest. Which made things a lot easier for me, I had to concede.

As soon as I got home, I got Muffy settled in the bathroom, to the extreme annoyance of both MacCavity and Little Dora.

MacCavity is a smoke-blue cat, about medium size, who has gotten pretty docile since he turned twelve. As a kitten, however, he was always getting into and breaking things, hence his name. His mom had been a feral cat that had been eaten, along with Mac's siblings, by a coyote. My mom had found Mac near his family's nest while hiking up in the foothills and insisted I take him. It was either that or be euthanized at the animal shelter and neither Mom nor I could bear that after Mac had already so narrowly escaped death.

Little Dora, on the other hand, had had a much gentler start, even though she's very small. She's a little black tortoise shell with a super-soft coat. She came through a friend of a friend who's a breeder who couldn't show her because she was so small. In spite of her name, she was a pistol as a kitten, but at three years old, was finally mellowing out.

She and Mac had always gotten along, even though Mac had been nine years old when Dora came to join us. She'd loved Roxy and Simba, even chased old Simba around, which was hysterical to watch because Simba was this huge old hairy hound and Dora was so tiny compared to him.

Even so, animals don't like surprises, and cats can be pretty territorial – another reason I tend to prefer dogs. I left Muffy in the bathroom for a full hour before I let Mac and Dora meet her. The wait did not go over well with either Mac, Dora or Muffy, for that matter. I decided what the heck and let Mac and Dora in to meet their new playmate.

As expected, there was a lot of hissing and yowling. What I didn't expect was to find the three of them sleeping together peacefully on my bed a few hours later, when I came in after the news.

The news, for once, had made me somewhat happy. Swanson's disappearance under extremely suspicious circumstances had somehow slipped past the attention of the newshounds. That was fine with me. I had enough to worry about.

Fortunately, that didn't stop me from getting a decent night's sleep. I had planned to make it into the office at nine. Then I realized I needed to swing by Cedar's and visit Berto, landing there about eight-thirty.

Berto was still pretty out of it. It didn't stop him from asking for an update, which I gave him. I did skip the altercation with Sims, however. No point in upsetting him, I thought, although the only reason he didn't catch the omission was that he was too doped up on pain meds, thanks be.

I ran into Marisol as I was leaving. She was coming off the elevator as I was getting on.

"Were you visiting Berto?" she asked.

"Yeah. The nurses are still insisting on keeping it short

and he's pretty doped up," I replied, deciding not to get on the elevator after all.

Marisol fidgeted nervously.

"How are the kids doing?" I asked.

"Fine, I guess. The boys aren't acting out so much, but everyone's still pretty worried." She fidgeted with her wedding rings. "Daria, do you got a minute?"

"Sure," I said.

We went down to the cafeteria where I bought coffee for both of us, doctoring mine heavily. Marisol, gutsy broad that she is, took hers black.

"I drink church coffee black," she said, smiling weakly as we sat down at a table. "Hospital coffee is almost good compared to that."

I chuckled and waited while she fidgeted some more.

"This is hard, Daria," she said, finally. "We haven't seen you in the longest time, and there was something terribly wrong last summer with Berto. I've been worried that the two of you were mad at each other or something. You're practically family. If you and Berto..."

I shook my head. "It wasn't us. I was just too tired from my job to do much except eat and sleep. And apparently, there was something wrong with Berto and I only just found out about it, myself." I sighed. "We can't blame Franny. Berto swore her to secrecy because - and you're going to love this - he didn't want you to worry."

"About what?"

"Some majorly deadbeat clients and that Berto was close to losing the agency. He was working overtime, Marisol. He didn't tell me because he didn't want me telling you. I hardly saw him until October, and even then, we haven't done lunch that much or anything."

You could see all the feelings ripple their way through Marisol's body. First, the relief, then the anger, then the utter disgust and frustration. She swore in Spanish, then shaking her head, looked at me.

"I've been so angry. I should have known. Can you forgive me?"

I laughed. "Of course, Marisol. It was upsetting, but

I think we can get past this and thump Berto on the head together." I took her hands. "And, really, you're pretty much family to me, too."

Marisol suddenly sniffed and smiled. "You know, he said the same thing about you. I'm glad. The kids have been really bugging me about when *Tía* Daria is coming over."

"Great. Like they don't have enough aunts and uncles?"

"Yeah, only they miss you, too. So…?"

I sighed. "I don't know. I'm pretty busy playing Berto right now, and not doing very well at it, either. Don't tell him I said that. I don't want him freaking."

"He has a lot of confidence in you, Daria."

"That's what worries me. I made a stupid mistake yesterday and almost got a client killed. It's not like I have a lot of room to screw up here."

"No. You'll be fine. If it makes you feel any better, Berto worries about the same things. And that cop, Detective Lancaster, she thinks you've got a good head on your shoulders, too. You're good at this, Daria. You'll see."

I have to admit, I felt a little better. But not much.

Franny started to give me the evil eye as I walked into the office, although I cut that short with the announcement that Berto was doing better, even if he was pretty strung out on the pain meds. Besides, it was only nine-fifteen.

I went into Berto's office and called Winston. He wasn't in yet.

I called the Ochoa family next. The parents were still together, and the daughters were married and out of the house. No one was home. The parents didn't even have an answering machine. I made a couple more calls and left messages with the sisters.

I called Isabel. She was in, but pre-occupied.

"Tonight?" she asked. "Oh. Yeah. Barhopping. Definitely still up for that. You mind Rumors in North Hollywood?"

"You mean that dive on Magnolia?" I grimaced and it must have transmitted over the phone wires.

"I don't know what you have against that place."

"It's noisy, trashy and too many of the dykes have a chip on their shoulder. Can't we go to a more refined lesbian bar?"

"I thought you preferred the butch girls." It was part of our usual banter, even though Isabel did not sound like she was enjoying it.

"I prefer the butch men. A failing of mine, I know. I'm sorry."

"Mm. Cranky."

"You, too, dear."

Isabel finally chuckled. "I guess we both need a night out. Listen, I'm not up to rich bitches."

"Then let's compromise. How about that new place in Silver Lake?"

"Ooh. Artsy-fartsy. Sounds good. Seven early enough?"

"Perfect. Oh, and I may have someone for you to look at on Berto's accident."

"Really? Who?"

"Cliff Sims. Miriam Watts' abusive ex. Freshly paroled last week and already in violation. They picked him up yesterday at Watts' house and are, hopefully, still holding him. I don't know if he has an alibi for Berto. He certainly has motive and a mother in Pacoima."

"He does. How convenient. I'll check him out. Thanks, Daria."

"You're welcome, Iz. I'll text you the address for the mom and see you tonight."

I hung up, then drummed my fingers on Berto's desk, debating what to do next. The pile of papers still needed going through. I thought I'd buzz Franny on the intercom first.

"Franny, did you find any potential former perps for Berto?"

"Yes. Can you hold for a second?" The incoming phone line was lighting up. "Daria, it's Mr. Winston on line one."

"Thanks, and I'd like to get with you on those perps after I'm done."

"Sure thing."

I punched the line one button. "This is Daria."

"Hey, Daria. It's Luke. I'm returning your call."

I scrambled for my notes. "Right. Um. Do you know a

Rita Camacho?”

"Who?”

“Rita Camacho. She left a phone message for Mr. Ochoa about two days after he died. It sounded like they had some sort of relationship.”

“Never heard of her.”

“Hm.” I picked up Ochoa's Seventh Step list. “How about some of these people?”

There were a couple that Winston couldn't I.D., but he'd known most of them, some from as far back as his and Ochoa's days at Julliard.

“You think any of them could have killed Larry?” Winston asked.

“It's possible. Apparently, Mr. Ochoa was trying to make amends with them, so I'd guess they'd be considered suspects.”

“Except that none of them work with me and I thought we'd agreed it was someone from inside the organization.”

“We have to stay open, Mr. Winston.”

“Please, call me Luke.”

“Sure, Luke. Anyway, it's entirely possible someone got past security onto the sound stage. Any word from Mr. Swanson?”

“Jay? No.”

I made a note. “Well, the police are looking for him now. I'll see if I can check out a couple leads in the meantime. You got his family's information?”

Luke transferred me to Jean again, and I made a couple of phone calls. Swanson's mother was worried sick but had no idea where he was and had no reason to believe he'd been mixed up in anything dangerous. Swanson's dad was surly and drunk, and even allowing for being on the East Coast and three hours ahead, it was still pretty early to be drinking that heavily.

As Dellis Archer had said, there was a long list of people who might have it in for Berto. Franny had made phone calls on a good many and eliminated several based on their being in jail, others were living in other countries and not likely to have left. A couple had died. One was in drug rehab, and another was in a theological seminary, having fully confessed all his sins and completely turned his life around.

That left, besides Sims, two solid possibles for me to do the leg work on. I mean, there were more perps, however, the cases were so old, we figured they were less likely to have gone after Berto.

The first on my short list was Lester Margolis. The case had started out as your standard stalker case. About four years before, Margolis had gotten the hots for Melanie Wiedeman, who owned a medium-sized computer company. At least, that's what we thought when he kept sending her messages saying, "You want me." However, what Margolis had really wanted was Wiedeman's company, and thought that if he couldn't woo his way into an ownership stake, he could scare Wiedeman into selling out. Apparently, throwing pots of money at her through a shell company that Margolis owned wasn't working.

Berto saw to it that Margolis got arrested. Margolis sued Berto for slander. Sadly, Margolis' stalking conviction pretty much blew his case out of the water. Margolis got parole, did his community service, and pretty much disappeared from the face of the earth. Or had he?

Then there was Sophie Reisner, as in the local news anchor for one of the owned and operated network affiliates in town. In fact, I suspect Berto had solicited the job the previous summer when he needed the extra work because this was not a stalker case. Rumors had been floating around about her for years that she hadn't just padded her resume, she'd flat out lied. Then right after the affiliate had made a lot of noise about paying her more than any other woman news anchor on TV, the local alternative paper printed a story that called into question her qualifications as a journalist, suggesting instead that her pay hike had more to do with her D-cups and her willingness to let the brass play with them.

The funny thing is, her resume checked out, so she really didn't have a motive. At the time, however, she had gotten really nasty with Berto when she found out he'd been investigating her, and she'd even made some threats about seeing to it that he'd regret it. Berto said she was directing her anger at him since she couldn't direct it at her bosses. It had certainly seemed so, except that all of a sudden, she wanted to interview him and had called asking for the interview the afternoon Berto had had his accident. Berto had said they'd made it up. Franny hadn't noted whether or not Berto had gotten back to her and I'm guessing she didn't know. I could tell Franny had her doubts about Reisner and I was willing to go with Franny's doubts.

I debated making a list then realized that I really couldn't until I'd gone through Berto's papers. I started making piles. Ads and circulars went in one (the largest), bills in another, and paid bills in another, phone message slips in another, case papers in another, stray sticky notes I pasted onto a legal pad, then piled the magazines on the floor.

I didn't think the phone message slips would reveal anything, although I went through them pro forma. Since Franny had written them all, she would have told me if there was anything suspicious there. I set aside a couple, just in case.

The case papers were pretty straightforward, mostly copies of notes that Berto hadn't gotten around to having Franny file. There were the notes on the Kramer case - Nita Kramer, the rich daughter of some biotech magnate living in Pasadena, had been trying to get rid of her drug-addicted boyfriend, Matt Ridley. It had taken some pressure, but Berto was at last able to convince Ridley's parents that if their son got arrested, the stalking charges would be the least of it.

Then, in Berto's cramped handwriting on the last page, was one final note, from Monday, before the accident. It had me swearing like a drunk stagehand.

Chapter Eight

“What in Heaven's name?” Franny demanded as she came into the office.

“Berto does it again,” I snarled and handed her the Kramer case notes. “What does this look like to you?”

“Mm-mm.” Franny looked like she was going to finally break down and cuss. “I remember putting that call through Monday morning.”

The call, according to Berto's note, was from a rehab facility in Santa Barbara, from which Matt Ridley had escaped shortly after arriving there the previous Saturday. Nice of them to wait two days before asking Berto where the kid was.

“Berto obviously wasn't too worried about Ridley,” I grumbled. “You haven't heard anything from the Kramers, have you?”

“I talked to Mr. Kramer yesterday, asking about the check. He said it's in the mail.”

“Don't they all.”

Franny shrugged. “I won't say I haven't heard that before, but I can usually tell when someone's playing me.”

“I take it Kramer isn't.”

“He didn't sound like it.”

I sighed. “I'll go ahead and call the rehab facility and Ridley's family. Maybe if we can pin the kid down, we won't have to call the Kramers.”

“Let's hope.” Franny went back to her office.

It was a wild hope, at best. Granted, it wasn't at all Berto's fault that the rehab people couldn't hold onto the Ridley kid. That didn't stop some clients from thinking so, anyway. I could only hope that the Kramers wouldn't.

I called the rehab people and found out that the Ridley

kid was still missing.

"What are the odds he's at his folks' place?" I asked the facility's director, Dr. Herbert something-or-other. He had that mincing, I-know-everything-and-you-know-shit kind of attitude.

"I can't really say."

"Really, now. What does 'can't' mean?"

"I think it's pretty obvious."

"Can't, as in there's some legal issue here, which given that there is a plausible threat against a young woman, is pretty well moot, or can't, as in you don't know?"

"I can't say."

"Would you be able to say if I had an investigator from the local law enforcement agency asking you? After all, there's been an attempt on Mr. Esparza's life, which means that this is also a criminal investigation, and means you're liable if you do anything to impede it. If anything happens to the Kramer girl or Mr. Esparza because you weren't up front with me, we would all certainly have cause to drag this into a couple really nasty, really public court cases."

"I think I am well aware of my legal responsibilities." The man even sniffed.

"Which means you don't know where the kid is."

"I did not say that."

"Don't give me that shit. If you knew where he was, you'd tell me because you know damn well the kid is a danger to himself and others and your ass would be covered."

"I don't know how to respond to that."

"I do. Fuck you." I hung up.

I hate losing my temper, but assholes like that prick, boy, oh, boy, they get me every time. I took a few deep breaths to try to calm down, then paced into the outer office.

"Sounds like that went really well," Franny observed drily as she pounded away at her keyboard.

"You think they'd mind next door if I snuck into their break room and bought a soda?" I asked, glancing next door at the lawyers' office.

"One of the partners owns the soda machine, so what do you think?"

"I think I'm getting me a soda. Want one?"

"No, thanks."

Okay, a Dr. Pepper isn't exactly the equivalent of an hour of Zen meditation. It was, however, what I needed at that moment. The real stuff, by the way. I mean, Diet Dr. P is as drinkable a diet drink as they come. Yet I so seldom drink soda that I figure it's worth risking the high fructose corn syrup.

I called all the numbers I had for the Ridleys and got no answer. I left messages all round, then tried Ridley's school. They hadn't seen him, nor did they know he was supposed to be in rehab. The school secretary didn't sound surprised and promised to call me if anybody saw Ridley.

I debated calling the Kramers, then put that off in favor of going through the rest of Berto's stuff. There didn't seem to be anything, still I handed off the case papers and phone messages to Franny to make sure.

Then I sat down and finally made my list.

About an hour later, with my stomach grumbling, tasks neatly prioritized and even an appointment made, I told Franny I was going to get lunch and check several things out. I also asked her to do the reverse lookups from Ochoa's Seventh Step list, just in case. Franny smiled. At last, I was getting the idea.

I found a sandwich shop not far from the Winston offices and indulged in a roast beef sub with avocado and mayonnaise, and, naturally, dripped avocado down the front of my best ivory turtleneck. Five minutes in the restroom took care of the stain, but the wet spot was going to be there for a bit. I fanned at my chest and headed for Luke's offices.

Guitarist Tab Michaels was waiting for me in the foyer, and we went into the downstairs conference room and shut the door. He was tall and scrawny, with small eyes and no lips, at least none that could be seen under the bushy reddish blonde mustache he wore. He sprawled in one of the chairs, bored and distracted and obviously wanting to be someplace else.

"I presume Mr. Winston told you why you're here?" I flipped out a notepad and clicked a pen.

"Yeah." He nodded, his fingers drumming on the table.

"I understand you're the bass player in the band?"

"Yep."

"How long have you been playing for Mr. Winston?"

His eyes shifted over to me. "Huh? Oh. About six years." He stopped. "I'm sorry, Miss Barnes. I been up all night working on a bass line for one of Luke's new songs and I just got it down right before you got here and it's all I can think about." He ducked his head. "I sure miss Larry. He and I used to work stuff out all the time. It don't work as well with him gone."

"I hear it's been pretty rough since the accident." I stopped writing to look at him.

"Yeah, it has." Michaels hung his head and tried to cover his sniff. "We all miss him, 'specially Luke. It's kinda like if we'd paid better attention, maybe it wouldn't have happened, you know?"

"Do you know of anybody who was angry at Mr. Ochoa? Maybe one of the other band members?"

"Nah, nobody could stay angry at Larry," Michaels smiled. "He was the best. Always laughing and teasing. He was always at your back. Even Kemper - he got issues with Mexicans, you know. Come to think of it, he got issues with everybody who ain't White. He loved Larry, though, and Larry helped him out of more than one jam, I can tell you that. I remember one time, we were doing three nights in Chicago. We went out to an after-hours place and there was some Black kids there and Kemper started going off on 'em, calling 'em names. Larry had to deck him to shut him up, then bought a round for everybody in the place while me and Tracy pulled Kemper outta there. Larry damn near got his face cut. He saved Kemper's ass and Kemper knew it. Larry loaned folks money, sobered us up when we got a snoot-full, made sure Tracy kept some condoms on him at all times. Man, that Tracy, he can get around."

"Did you see anybody strange on the stage any time before the accident?"

"Nope. Nope. Everybody I saw, I knew. It was a pretty normal day. Luke and Kemper were working on an arrangement. Larry had a bad kink in his back - he'd had it for about a week. He wouldn't even take an aspirin, and you can probably guess we got a bunch of shit stronger than that. But Larry was clean and going to stay that way, come hell or high water. Luke was real worried about him, 'cause he was in a lot of pain. Larry, he just wouldn't take anything for it."

"Do you know how he injured his back?"

Michaels thought about it. "You know, I don't know. I just kinda figured he bent over wrong, and ping, there it went. You know how that happens. He could be real finicky about setting up his drums. They ain't light and I figured he sprung something hoisting them drums around."

"Don't you have roadies to set up instruments?"

"Hell, yes. Only, like I said, Larry could be real finicky about his drums, and he'd as like as not be hauling 'em to and fro."

I made a note on my pad, then thumped my pen against it, thinking. "Do you know if anybody from Mr. Ochoa's past might have had anything against him?"

Michaels frowned. "Larry didn't talk much about his past. He just said he'd been to hell and didn't want to go back there again."

"Any ex-girlfriends? A Rita Camacho, perhaps?"

Michaels looked at the ceiling. "Hm. He did mention a Rita once or twice. He had an ex-wife. I don't know if her name was Rita or not. Could be." He shifted. "I know I'm not helping much, Miss Barnes, and I'm sorry. I mean we all knew Larry, but we didn't really know him, if you know what I mean. He was real close." He paused. "It's been a real bad month for us, here. You know, Mr. McKesson's wife left him about a week or so before we lost Larry. If things come in threes, kinda leaves you wondering what's next."

"I understand." I pulled out one of the agency business cards and handed it to him. "I appreciate you talking to me. If you think of anything else, would you please give me a call?"

Michaels looked at the card. "How come your name's not on here?"

"I haven't been at the agency that long. Is Mr. Kemper or Mr. Tracy available?"

"I can check, but I don't think so."

I checked the time on my mobile phone. I still had to get back out to South Pasadena to talk to the Ridleys about their son, then drive all the way over to Pacoima, up in the San Fernando Valley, so that I could talk to Sims' mother, then catch up with Isabel at seven. And somewhere in there, I wanted to touch base with Berto.

"You know what, never mind for now," I said, getting up. "I have some other leads to follow up on."

Michaels scrambled to his feet. "Thank you, Miss Barnes. Luke was right. You are real nice to talk to."

I felt my face go warm. "Luke said that? Well, we aim to serve. Anyway, thanks again, and please be in touch."

"I will, ma'am."

I left, wondering why Luke's compliment had me so flustered. Of course, it was the best kind, coming from a third party who had no reason to flatter me. I put it out of my head. I had other things to concentrate on.

I went ahead and dialed the office on my mobile. Mr. Kramer had called to ask if we had an update on Ridley – Berto had, apparently, told Kramer about Ridley's escape on the morning of the accident before meeting with me, then Luke Winston. However, of all the people I'd called earlier, no one had gotten back to me. I called Kramer back first. He was concerned although not rattled.

"The school called this afternoon," he told me.

"Yeah," I said. "We've been trying to get a line on Matt before touching base with you, so we didn't scare you unnecessarily. Unfortunately, no luck, so far. Have you or your daughter heard from him at all?"

"Nothing."

"Good. Unfortunately, I haven't been able to reach any of the Ridleys."

"That's odd. She almost always answers her cell phone. Just in case it's one of the kids, you know."

"Hmm." I started my CRV. "I'm on my way out there now. I'll take a look around. I don't have all the case notes on me at the moment. Do you know where either of the parents works?"

"Yeah. They both own a realty company in South Pas. Ridley and Company. Hang on, I'll get you the number."

I scribbled the number down on the notepad next to me and hung up. It only took about thirty-odd minutes to get out to South Pasadena, where the Ridleys lived. While driving there, I tried the number Mr. Kramer had given me. The person who answered said that neither of the Ridleys was in. In fact, they had left town a few days before. That seemed suspicious, and I definitely wanted to check it out.

Sure enough, the white colonial on a quiet back street in South Pasadena was empty of people, at least as far as I could see. I took a chance on nosy neighbors and looked in all the windows on the front and the place looked pretty vacant. I couldn't get to the back or the upstairs. The garage had windows and it was empty of cars. Not conclusive, by any means, and I definitely had another suspect.

There seemed like little else to be accomplished for the time being. I got back into my car and started the long haul back across L.A. to Pacoima. Google had me take the 210 Freeway over the hills north of Glendale. As I crested the slope down into the flats, the sky fanned out above me, a patchwork of gray and white fluffy clouds, with bits of brilliant blue peeking between.

Pacoima is not exactly known as a garden spot in L.A. It's mostly houses that were built shortly after the Second World War, although there is a small airport there. The address I had for Sims' mother, whose name was Connie Ramón, turned out to be a small bar on San Fernando Road, just south of the airport. It was a largely industrial area, with a couple ratty taco stands and Connie's Place tucked between warehouses, a recycling center, and a parts place.

I blinked as I walked into the dark bar. It was what one might expect, with rickety tables, white resin chairs and single-post stools with cracking red-vinyl upholstery. Neon ads for Corona, Tecate, and Budweiser decorated the walls and provided most of the light. The bar filled most of the side wall, and the lighted shelves behind it held relatively few bottles, most of it higher end liquor. Something told me the bottles were pretty dusty, though. There were two doors on the back wall, both closed. Three men crowded around a table in the corner, laughing at something showing on one of their phones.

Never mind that smoking inside anywhere except your own home is illegal in Los Angeles, the woman behind the bar had a lit cigarette dangling from her lips. She was fairly tall and her body, which was encased in skin-tight workout wear, was tight and well-muscled. Her face was pretty, but there was a hardness to her expression that did her no favors. Her full dark hair hung loose around her shoulders, and she flicked it back every minute or so as she washed glasses.

As I walked up to the bar, the woman put her cigarette in an ashtray under the counter and slapped a cocktail napkin in front of me.

"What can I get you?" Her eyes were wary as they looked me over, probably trying to figure out if I was a cop or not.

I was trying to remember what Berto had told me about interviewing a potentially hostile subject. Oh, yeah. Make friends. Which meant ordering something to drink and probably drinking it.

I looked at the bottle behind her, wondering what to order. I like wine and really hate the taste of beer. Berto says I have snooty taste in liquor, and he has a point, because when it comes to spirits, all I really like are the finer brands.

"Uh, Seven and Seven," I said.

Her eyebrows raised a fraction of an inch, but she went about mixing the drink professionally.

The guys in the corner hooted loudly in Spanish about the size of somebody's dick, and one of the men insisted his was larger. Another, a smaller fellow in dirty work clothes, waved the phone at the woman and asked her how hard it had been to get the dick into her. In return, she insulted his manhood to the uproarious laughter of his pals.

"Are you Connie?" I asked, taking a sip of my drink. It wasn't too bad.

"Yeah, she is," hollered the man who'd compared himself to the porn star he'd been watching. "Constanza La Crema!"

The other men laughed while Connie rolled her eyes.

"Former job?" I asked with a shrug.

"You do what you have to do," she said. "It got me this place."

"I'm looking for your son, Cliff Sims," I said slowly.

Connie took a long, frustrated drag on her cigarette. "What's that little shit done now?"

Given Sims' bulk, little was not the term I would have used, but given that Connie had probably changed his diapers, I could see it.

"I haven't said he's done anything," I said.

"Look, the cops were here this morning asking about him."

"They didn't tell you why they were looking for him?"

"They left a message with my clean up guy." Connie blew smoke out of her mouth with a disgusted snort. "Like I'm going to snitch on my own kid. And before you ask, I don't know where he is, and I don't want to."

"So, you haven't seen him lately."

"Nope. He shows his face around here, I'm going to fix it good."

"Did you know he'd gotten out of prison?"

"For good behavior." Connie snorted and returned to washing glasses. "Must have gone to Bible study or something. I can't believe he didn't hit nobody while he was there."

"How'd you know he was released early?" I asked.

"His parole officer came looking for him. Little bastard keeps giving out this address as his own, like it's some joke." She put the glasses down and pursed her lips. "Can't be bothered to actually talk to me. Since he got religion, I'm not good enough for him. I'm a whore. He doesn't care that I did what I had to do to save his sorry ass."

"I don't understand."

Connie coughed, then sniffled. "His dad, Cliff, Senior. He was a real fuck. He was going to kill Cliffie if I stayed much longer. I had to get out of there, but with no money and no way to pay for diapers, I had to get creative. I still had a good bod. I didn't care about fucking strangers. And I had a friend in the business. He got me some good roles, and that's how I fed Cliffie from the time he was five years old."

"Where's Cliff, Senior?"

"Dead. Blew his head off in a motel room, and I had to pay to clean it up."

"I'm so sorry."

"Don't be. He's done and I don't have to deal with him anymore." She stopped and looked at me. "Why are you asking so many questions?"

"Um." I don't know why I didn't want to mention Berto, but my gut said not to. "He attacked his ex-wife yesterday."

"Her." Connie rolled her eyes. "You know, I tried to warn that scrawny bitch about what she was getting into with him. She didn't listen."

"They don't," I said with a sigh. "She's listening now, though."

"If he put her through half the hell his dad put me." Connie shook her head. "Look. My son is a rat bastard. I'm not proud of it. But he's my son, you know? If you find him, will you ask him to call me?"

"Here okay or do you have another number?"

She reeled off the phone number and I repeated it a couple times to be sure I had it right.

The guys in the corner hooted again.

"Hey, Connie, we got Come and Get It on," one of them yelled.

"Hm," Connie said. "That was a pretty good film."

I smiled. "I'll check it out someday. Thanks for the help."

I left a twenty-dollar bill on the bar and headed outside.

It was a little after five, so I decided to head to Cedars and visit Berto before meeting Isabel. He had the back of his bed tilted up part way and his eyes were clear and he grinned when he saw me.

"Hey, *hermano*," I said as I wandered into his room.

"Hey, *hermana*, what's going down?"

"You had to put it that way," I grumbled, remembering

the bar. "How are you feeling? You look a little more alert."

"Yeah. It's the morphine. It's a good thing."

"No shit. I could use some, myself, about now."

Berto frowned. "Did you get hurt?"

"No!" I paused. "Not yet, at any rate. I'm not exactly getting any hits, either."

"Yeah, you look discouraged. Don't worry about it. Every case hits a dry patch or two."

"It's not that, Berto." I sighed and flopped into the visitor's chair. "Remember yesterday when I told you about Miriam Watts and Cliff Sims coming back?"

"Yeah. You made the collar."

"Yeah. After I nearly got both Watts and me killed. I had the gun out, but I wasn't going to shoot, and Sims charged me. It's just dumb luck that he fell over the coffee table first. Plus, I spent today spinning my wheels. Had to go after the Ridley kid - you know the Kramer case and that note from the rehab center that the kid had escaped that you forgot to tell Franny about?"

"Well, you know, I have this short-term memory problem." Berto grinned. He was feeling no pain, indeed.

"Bullshit, *hermano*. Franny remembered putting the call through. You could have told her. Anything else you forgot to mention?" I glared at him.

"I don't remember." He grinned again, although I could see that he really couldn't.

I softened. "I'm sorry. It's just been a lousy day of not reaching anyone, questioning people who either don't want to talk or who have nothing to say."

"Tell me from the beginning."

So, I did. Berto listened without interrupting beyond a grunt here and there. He laughed at the conversation with the drug rehab director. Then got serious when I told him about Connie Ramón.

"She's bad news."

"What do you mean?" I asked, swallowing.

"She's got a mean streak a mile wide."

"How do you know her?"

"I know of her," Berto said. "Andy Minelli, remember

him?"

"Yeah, your old L.A.P.D. partner, right?"

"Him. He's been working vice these past few years and apparently, Connie nearly shot his balls off when he tried to shut her place down."

I thought about it. "I didn't see any sign of prostitution going on. Some guys were watching her old porn flicks on someone's phone is all."

"She had a whole theater set up in the back, according to Andy. They just couldn't prove she was taking money or showing porn."

"What about the assault? I mean, shooting him in the balls?"

Berto cleared his throat. "Andy may not have been following best practices."

"Oh." I wasn't surprised. Andy Minelli had been one of the reasons Berto left the force. "So, how come you remember that story and nothing about getting hit?"

Berto sighed. "Don't know. But I'm willing to bet you got more out of her than anyone else would have."

"What do you mean?"

"Even with Minelli being a racist fuck, she does not like men. I couldn't have gotten that stuff about her son out of her even if I'd bought a couple cases of beer."

"Okay. That may be encouraging. How about any ideas re who else I should be looking at?"

"There's the Ridley kid you mentioned." He frowned, then winced. "Um, what about that Margolis creep?"

"Already on the list. Along with Sophie Reisner."

"Reisner's okay." He paused. "I think. Maybe you should check her out."

"I'll try to fit her in. There's an awfully long list of people who have issues with you, buddy."

"And the Ochoa case?"

"Going slowly but going. I talked to the bass player today."

"Tab Michaels."

"Yep." I shrugged. "Didn't see anything, didn't know anything. They've been pretty well rocked over there by Ochoa's death. Swanson is still missing. I can't reach Ochoa's family. I did turn up a Rita Camacho. Franny got me the reverse look-up on her phone number - it apparently belongs to a Julio and Concepcion Camacho, and Rita's included on the listing. The address is in El Centro. That's down near San Diego, isn't it?"

"Off Interstate 8, in California, right across the Arizona border from Yuma. How strong a lead is she?"

I looked at my notes. "Not very strong. It seems like distant past because nobody at Winston's place knew her. Then again, Ochoa was doing his Twelve Steps, and you know number seven, make good with the people you hurt?"

"Yeah."

"She's on the list and had left a message at Ochoa's place two days after he died. I don't think she did anything, but she might have an idea of who did."

Berto nodded as well as he could with his head all bandaged up. "That sounds promising."

"Why? If she killed him, why would she leave a message on his machine telling him not to call her again two days after he died?"

"You're right that she probably didn't do it. On the other hand, Ochoa hurt her, so, like you said, decent odds she knows who else he hurt. Revenge is a strong motive, and you haven't got anybody in Winston's organization who has that strong a motive."

"That we know of yet."

"I think you need to go down to El Centro and check her out."

"All the way to El Cento? When? This weekend, maybe?"

"Why not leave tonight?"

"For one thing, I'm going barhopping with Isabel. For another," I stopped. "I guess there is no other. I'm sorry, Berto. I just feel like I'm making a massive mess of this whole thing."

"Daria, you can do this. You are doing it. So, you've made a couple mistakes."

"That could have gotten the client killed!" I almost shrieked.

"It didn't, though, did it? You're alive. Watts is alive and free from that Sims bastard for at least a little while. Learn from the mistake and move on. You know that. I hear you tell people that all the time."

"But why me, Berto? Don't you have some other P.I. friends that can help out for a little while?"

"Because you're here and you're doing it. You've always been here. I trust you like I would my own sister. Come off it, Daria. I've wanted you in the business for years. Because you're good, and because I know what you really want."

I snorted. "Presumptuous bastard."

"Bullshit. Just face it. You want to go back to the theatre. Well, trust me and I'll get you there."

"I know that's what you say."

"Come on. You can make a damn good living as a P.I., part-time, and still have time to yell at actors and directors." Berto leaned back on his pillows, looking perfectly smug. "You think your *padrone* is going to steer you wrong? I know what you love, but you gotta admit, snooping can be fun, too. You've got the brains, and the *corazon* and the *cojones* to do both."

"*Pendejo.*" I sighed. "Neri Mikelson has a great new script and Tim Wing got sixty thou in grant money to mount it. He wants me to produce."

"See? I'm right."

"We'll see. There's still getting shot at." I checked my phone. It was just about six thirty. "Shit. I've got to get out to Silver Lake to meet Isabel. Listen, you big old bastard. You get well, just don't rush, okay? I've got your back and will hopefully not make too big a hash of it. *Te amo, mi hermano.*"

"*Te amo, hermanita.*"

Chapter Nine

I was about halfway to Silver Lake when my phone rang. I touched the button on the screen to answer, then the speaker button.

"It's Isabel," she said. "How far away are you?"

"I'm heading down Fountain from Cedars. I just passed La Brea. Why?"

"Hm. About fifteen to twenty minutes out."

"Meaning no accidents between here and there."

"None that I've picked up on the radio."

I grinned. Even though it was close to seven, the main thoroughfares in L.A. were still packed. However, even with Google's eyes above all, knowing the back streets didn't hurt.

"Okay, what's up?" I asked. "You already there?"

"Not quite. I'm on Sunset, just past Elysian Park. I'm really hungry, is all. Do you know if this joint has food?"

"Nope. Don't you?"

Isabel sighed. "Daria, I haven't been out in months. I have no idea."

"You know, we could try a straight joint, for a change. Besides, I really have to lay off the drinking tonight. I have to drive down to El Centro later."

"Thank God. I didn't want to disappoint you, but I am so not up to flirting tonight."

"Ouch. Sounds like a rough day."

"Pretty normal, actually. Oh, I'll tell you all about it later. Where can we get a good, messy hamburger and fries?"

"House of Pie, just south of Los Feliz on Vermont?"

"Perfect. See you there."

I switched off the phone and turned north on Wilcox to get up to Franklin, which was the actual cross street where the restaurant is located. It's mostly the usual no-so-hot coffee shop food, except the chicken fried steak, which is decent, and they do make a good hamburger, even better than the Fatburger that used to be down the street, which is simply over-priced, in my humble opinion.

Isabel and I somehow managed to score a booth near the back and the noise from the rest of the room gave us just enough privacy. The clientele is mostly seniors, although you do get a few families in. There was the usual L.A. ethnic mix, about evenly divided between Asian, Hispanic, and White with one Black couple and their two kids. Oh, and a pair of old gay men who looked like they'd been partners longer than most of the other seniors. Either that or they were just two guys who'd been friends since the Second World War.

"Got a chance to question Sims about Berto's accident," Isabel told me once we'd ordered. "It was hard to tell between him making like Jesus before Pontius Pilate and spouting Bible verses, but I'm not sure he knows anything about it."

"Making like Jesus before who?"

"The Roman governor of Judea. The Pharisees who wanted to get Jesus crucified had to get Pilate to order it. So, Jesus goes on trial before Pilate and doesn't say a word."

"I get it now. Yeah, Sims seems to have a real fixation with that Bible stuff." I paused. "Any chance they can get him committed?"

"With his messianic complex? Oh, you betcha. He goes for his psych evaluation tomorrow." Isabel sighed. "Probably the best thing that happened all day."

"I'm smelling smoke again. What's going on?"

"The usual shit. The lieutenant won't let me do squat on the Ochoa case, so my hands are completely tied there. The whole clearance thing has been making everybody crazy and the DA's office is getting pissy about it because we're not sending them solid cases. Only they won't let up because elections are coming up again." Isabel stopped and suddenly blinked back tears. "I'm sorry. This stuff never used to get to me, but since Corinne died—"

"Corinne *what*?" I yelped. Corinne was Isabel's wife.

Isabel's jaw dropped. "You didn't know. No wonder I never heard from you. Oh, fuck. You're in the work contacts list."

"Huh? Good lord, what happened, Isabel?"

"It was a little over a year ago, maybe fifteen months. Corinne was diagnosed with ovarian cancer. It was over pretty quickly, less than a month after diagnosis. The problem is, I didn't let a lot of people know at work because you know how they are. I mean, they try, but they get so freaked out, and some of those fuckers are out and out abusive. That's why some of my friends who know me through work never found out. Including you, and come to think of it, probably Berto. Only he would freak out."

"I'm so sorry, Isabel. No wonder you're so crispy. You're grieving."

"Yeah. That's what I'm told." She dabbed neatly at her eyes with her napkin. "Let me tell you, grief fucking sucks. At least, Corinne and I had gotten officially married and had all our paperwork together. Her dad tried to take over, only he couldn't get away with it. Her mom has been wonderful, though. I just miss her so much. Anyway, that's why I haven't been out, either. I'm just not up to flirting yet. I'm kind of glad we landed here."

"We'll have to do a sleep-over soon."

Isabel grinned, in spite of herself.

I rolled my eyes. "I mean flannel jammies and girl talk and pints of ice cream."

"How do you think it started for me, darling?"

"Bullshit. You always knew you were gay, at least that's what you keep telling me."

Isabel shrugged. "How are you doing in the P.I. trade?"

"Oh, do I wish I had cheery news for you there. You'll be so pissed off at me. I'm acting like a perfect amateur."

"You're still alive. It can't be that bad."

I told her about what had happened with Sims, and she had the good grace to laugh when I told her about meeting him in hell. She also said pretty much the same thing as Berto about me being up to handling it all.

"Daria, Berto's a good teacher and you've picked up a

lot. You're not bad at this, at all."

"I know. I'm just so scared all the time."

"Be thankful you are. Not being scared is the fastest way to end up on ice that I know. You don't want to let it paralyze you. Just for crying out loud, trust your gut. If it feels dangerous, it probably is. Be careful out there. You'll be fine."

"Thanks. I could use the encouragement after today. Spinning my wheels getting nowhere."

"That's eighty percent of detective work."

We paused long enough for the waitress to place our food in front of us. Isabel had the hamburger and I had the chicken fried steak. She tucked in gracefully. I just ate.

"Oh, I also talked to Sims' mother, Connie Ramón," I said.

"Ramón? Is she a former porn star with a bar over in Pacoima?"

"Yeah, that's her. How do you know her?"

Iz laughed. "All of L.A.P.D. knows Connie Ramón. The guys are terrified of her."

"Why?" I asked. "She didn't seem that scary to me."

"That's because you don't have a dick." Iz grinned. "She hates men, especially men cops."

"Hm." I thought over what had happened. "She also said that she wouldn't snitch on her son. Does Sims have an alibi?"

"Yeah. Sort of." Iz munched thoughtfully on a bite of burger. "We found a receipt for the red paint in his wallet. He bought it at five sixteen p.m. on Monday night at the Pacoima Lowe's."

I mulled that one over. "Why are you certain that he was the one who bought the paint?"

Iz looked at me. "The receipt was in his wallet when he was arrested."

"But that doesn't technically mean he bought the paint himself." I pushed mashed potatoes and gravy over a bit of steak. "I used to have tons of receipts in my wallet at any given time when I was doing my theatre thing. But most of the stuff had been bought by someone else. I had the receipts so that I could reimburse them or give them credit in the program."

"Oh." Iz glared at me for a moment. "You're right. It was a cash purchase, too, so no card to trace. Son of a bitch!"

"The problem will be finding anybody who would have gone and bought him paint," I said. "I don't think it was his mother, though."

"Why not?"

"She asked me to tell him to call her. Why would she do that if she was buying paint for him?"

Isabel shrugged. "Maybe she's a better actress than you'd think. Or crazy like a fox. Still, it's worth checking out. I'll take care of it. Oh, and in other news, I did manage to get something for you - the official autopsy report on Ochoa."

"What about the lieutenant? Won't you get in trouble?"

"Fuck him. Or you can. I'm not interested. We both know that if Mr. Ochoa had been blonde, blue-eyed Larry Smith, Lieutenant James would be up in arms calling for an immediate arrest."

I sighed. "You're probably right, which means I'm not interested in fucking him either. Now what?"

"Hate to say it, but I actually agree with Berto. Rita Camacho is your strongest lead on that one. Talking to her might not get you anything, or you could hit the jackpot. May as well go down there and eliminate her, if nothing else. More likely, you'll pick up a really strong lead."

I debated looking over the autopsy report. I opted for finishing my dinner first. As I chewed my steak, something started to occur to me.

"Iz, they keep saying that Ochoa died from the fall, right?" I asked.

"Yes. That's what the coroner's office found."

"Is it possible that someone set this up to look like an accident? That they partially doped Ochoa up to get him up to the catwalk, so that they could toss him over?"

Isabel picked up a fry and twirled it thoughtfully. "It seems like an awful lot of trouble to go through. There are a lot of easier ways to do something like that, especially ones that don't involve doing it on a busy soundstage with over a hundred people on the other side of that cyc." She chewed on the french fry for a second. "Also, when you read the report, you'll see there were a whole bunch of contusions around his face and on his belly that are not consistent with the fall. He landed on the back of his neck, you see. The face, as far as we can tell, never hit the ground. Not to mention the fact that based on the injury to his neck, he died instantly, so how did he get the contusions on his belly? Had to have been before he fell."

"He'd messed up his back a week or so before," I said.

"The contusions were all pretty fresh. The pathologist suggested we find out who Ochoa had been fighting with right before his accident."

"From what I've heard so far, doesn't sound like Ochoa was."

"The physical evidence seems to suggest that he was. See if anybody heard anything around the cyc about half an hour before Ochoa was found."

"I'll add it to the list."

Isabel laughed. "Oh, no. Are you a list maker, too?"

"How else do you get everything done? I make up lists of lists. If I didn't have everything down on paper, I'd go crazy."

"You don't have an app for that?"

"I've tried dozens of them. You know what? I'm finding it's actually easier just to write it down on paper. I live my life on legal pads."

Isabel pulled out her leather-bound Day Runner. "This is my entire life. I'm even putting my work contacts in here. I am putting it on the computer because that's easier to update and still keep in order. Only I found this really great website that lets you print out all the organizer forms you could ever want or need."

"You have? Please send me the link!"

That's pretty much how the rest of the meal went. We both agreed we needed to stay in closer touch. It turns out that most of the friends Isabel and Corinne had were actually Corinne's friends and they had a hard time relating to Isabel. I have several close friends, but most of them don't relate to the P.I. thing, either. We decided we needed to form our own little support group, which was a good feeling.

I was still feeling pretty good after a quick trip home to get my overnight things and the cats fed. I did a Google Maps search on my computer and printed out the directions to Rita Camacho's place from the address Franny had gotten me just in case I couldn't get a signal when I needed it. I also grabbed my mail and was happy to see a large manilla envelope with Tim Wing's return address on it. I plopped everything in the CRV and was on the road before nine-thirty.

I waited until I was on Interstate 5, south, to call my mom, who lives in San Diego, which I would have to go through to get to El Centro.

"Just wanted to let you know that I'll be down your way tomorrow and thought I might swing by," I told her after she had answered.

"Oh." She did not sound enthused. "I'm sorry, sweetie. I won't be down there. In fact, I was just thinking about calling you to see if I could catch you in the morning."

"Why?"

"I'm driving up to Paso Robles with Melanie tomorrow to set up for a show over the weekend," she said. Melanie was the college kid she was training to do art shows for her since she had decided she was getting too old for that shit.

"I take it Melanie's not good to go on her own yet."

"Honey, it's only her second show."

"I suppose. Oh, well."

"You could stop by and visit your grandmother, you know."

"Hm." I thought about that. I was overdue for a visit. "That probably would be a good idea. How's she doing?"

"Oh, the usual. The good news is that she's not any worse."

Grandma had had a stroke a few months before and hadn't been in good health, or in good temper, before that.

"Okey-dokey. I should be able to swing by the home," I said.

"What's bringing you down to San Diego?"

"I've got to interview a suspect down in El Centro."

"A suspect?"

I went ahead and told her about working for Berto and his accident, which got the appropriate cautions and sympathies.

"Is he still in the hospital?" Mom asked. "And which one?"

"Cedars Sinai. Why?"

"I told you, I'm coming through L.A. tomorrow. I'll stop in for a short visit. I'm making the note now."

I chuckled. That was my mother all over. She's always considered my friends her friends, as well, and the feeling is almost always mutual.

We continued to chat until I had to merge onto the 91 Freeway and then she had to get to bed. I fumbled with the voice recorder Franny had given me and dictated notes on what I'd been doing that day all the way through the merge with Interstate 15, south to San Diego. After that, I put on a Chris Isaak CD and listened to him wail as I drove through the darkness.

It was sometime after eleven that I pulled onto Interstate 8, and shortly after that pulled into a motel in El Cajon. I brought my mail and the coroner's report on Larry Ochoa in with me. After getting my clothes off and myself into bed and punching up the pillows so I could sit up and read, I went to work.

Most of the mail was the usual junk. I think the electric bill came in, too, but that's neither here nor there. Feeling like I should have been looking at the Ochoa report, I instead opened the envelope from Tim. Sure enough, it was Neri's latest play. I couldn't resist and started reading.

I couldn't put it down. It was fabulous and moving and would make some amazing theatre. I knew it was autobiographical, because Neri had been in an abusive relationship some years ago, and the play had the lead character looking at her culpability for her own death because she chose to stay in the relationship. The only reason I didn't call Tim right that second is that it was after one in the morning by that point, and I still wasn't sure I wanted to take it on.

It's just that Berto's idea about working P.I. part-time was getting its way under my skin. It would be a way to do what I loved. While I wasn't exactly having the time of my life doing the P.I. thing at that moment, I had to concede it wasn't all bad.

I was of the same frame of mind even after reading the coroner's report on Ochoa. There wasn't much in it that Isabel hadn't already told me. It was just more detailed. There had been a fair amount of internal bleeding from the belly contusions, or bruises, which mostly had this odd triangular shape to them. Ochoa might have eventually bled out, only he was nowhere near that point when his neck had broken.

Unfortunately, I did not sleep well, and finally, after tossing and turning a good chunk of the night, gave up around eight a.m.

Fortunately, I had seen a branch of the gym I belong to near the freeway, so I changed into my workout clothes and ran for half an hour on the treadmill, then futzed with the weights. I'm not a big gym-goer. In fact, the only reason I have a membership at this particular club is because my aunt gave it to me during one of her self-righteous fits. This time, she wanted everyone in the family to exercise more, especially my mom. I got the lifetime membership because Aunt Carolyn was also feeling guilty about giving me up as an infant to my wayward mother, who believes that physical exercise is on a par with cruel and unusual punishment.

Mom and I usually find Aunt Carolyn's guilt attacks pretty amusing, however problematic they can be. They are problematic in that they almost always involve significant expense for things or services that I usually have little or no use for. Like the time she decided I needed to date more and got me a gift certificate for a computer dating service.

Telling Caro that she doesn't need to feel guilty is a non-starter. She doesn't know that I know she's the one who gave birth to me. She had a conniption when she found out I knew I was adopted. Not that she said anything directly to me, but Aunt Carolyn called Mom so many times to lecture her that Mom got an answering machine to screen out Caro's calls. Mom and I both agreed it was safer to let Caro believe I didn't know from whence I came.

The real irony is that I am so grateful that Caro gave me up. Her kids, for the most part, are the most miserable, negative, angry people on the planet. Her husband, Uncle Aaron, is quite probably the one who got her preggers with me - they did know each other at the time and my chin and nose are pretty much the same as his and no one on my mom's side of the family has the same. So, given that I come from essentially the same set of genes, you have to figure nurture and not nature is behind my cousins being the way they are. Caro basically saved my ass by giving me up and letting my mother raise me.

Thinking about all that did help clear some of the negativity out of my soul and the workout helped unknot most of the kinks I'd woken up with. I hit the road by ten feeling pretty okay, overall.

Which was good, because if you've ever driven through El Centro, then you know it is one of the more depressing places on the planet, at least the part I was in. I pulled off the freeway onto one of the main drags and headed north for about half a mile until I turned into a mobile home park filled with dilapidated mobile homes. The entire place had been bleached into dull whiteness by the desert sun. Black-haired, brown-skinned children dressed in faded clothes, many in diapers, played in the dirt in front of the trailers, most of them heedless of my CRV as it passed.

I found the Camacho unit near the end of the main row. Someone had attempted to make it less dreary by building a covered porch onto the front and hanging plants all over it. The plants had a listless, dusty look to them, making it all seem even drearier.

A woman in her mid-30s, with straight long black hair, was sitting on the porch, smoking a cigarette, and drinking a malt liquor. She was gaunt and had that dazed and haunted look about her that you see on a lot of long-term addicts. Her upper arm was encircled by a crown of thorns tattoo and there was a butterfly on her collarbone. She wore jeans, a tank top, and a dirty blue sleeveless flannel shirt over the tank top.

I got out of my CRV and walked slowly up to the trailer.

"Hi," I said, smiling.

"Hey." She took a long drag on her cigarette and blinked at me.

"I'm looking for Rita Camacho."

"Why?"

"I'd like to ask her some questions about someone she used to know."

She took yet another long drag. "Who are you?"

"My name is Daria Barnes. I work for Esparza Investigations. We're looking into the death of Larry Ochoa."

"Who? Larry?" That got her. "He's dead? What happened?"

"Are you Rita Camacho?"

"Yeah. Larry's my ex. What happened?"

"He fell over a railing and was killed. I'm sorry to have to tell you this way."

She snorted. "That fuck. I'm glad. He's gone and I don't have to think about him no more. He was calling me, you know. Wanted to ree-concile. Man, I was glad to be away from him."

"Really."

"Hey, I didn't do nothing to him."

I smiled. "That's kind of obvious. You didn't even know he was dead. How long were you two together?"

"Shit, I don't know." She scratched her chin. "We were in Texas. I was living with my *Tía* Mercedes, in El Paso. Then he left. Let's see. Teresa was two?"

"Teresa?"

"My baby. She's not Larry's. See, Larry and me had been together. We got married. Then Larry left for a while, then I got Teresa. Only it was okay because I didn't know Larry was coming back. Only he did and we stayed together until Teresa was two, I think, maybe three."

"How old is Teresa now?"

"She's ten."

"When did you and Larry get divorced?"

She thought about it. "I don't know. He just went."

"And your *Tía* Mercedes, what's her last name?"

"Valenzuela. You a cop?"

"Private investigator. You know anyone that Larry might have hurt or made angry?"

She laughed. "All of us. Mostly my papa, though. If *Papí* ever met Larry, he'd've killed him for sure."

"Oh. Is he here now?"

"Rita!" A man came from around behind the trailer. He was a tall, beefy fellow, with a large, bushy black mustache and wearing a light blue Western shirt stretched over his rounded belly. "Who you talking to?"

"I'm Daria Barnes, Esparza Investigations," I said, extending my right hand.

Mr. Camacho glared and folded his arms. "What are you doing here?"

"She just wants to know about Larry," Rita said, enjoying the show.

"We don't speak that name here. He is gone." Mr. Camacho spat and pulled a small shotgun off the porch. "He's done enough to hurt us. He gives Rita the drugs and she's never the same."

"Sounds like he really messed things up for your family," I said, trying not to eye the shotgun.

"Why are you here?"

"I'm just trying to get some information." I smiled encouragingly. "Um, have you been in the Los Angeles area recently, say, the first part of last week?"

Rita suddenly laughed. "You think *Papí* killed Larry?"

"*Callate!*" Camacho snapped at his daughter and pumped the gun. "I no tell you nothing. You get away from here."

I held up my hands. "Fine. I'm leaving."

I walked as slowly as I dared back to my CRV. The gun exploded and gravel sprayed the CRV's bumper as I scrambled into the seat and turned over the motor. I didn't even bother turning the car around but drove around the last trailer in the row to the next drive and headed up it. Another blast pinged my tailgate as I went past the trailer in front of the Camacho trailer. I didn't dare drive any faster because of all the children playing in the road. Fortunately, Mr. Camacho decided not to chase me up the street.

I paused after I left the trailer park. I debated calling 911 on Camacho. I should have. I wasn't sure what good that would do, especially since what I needed was information.

Still being relatively new to the whole smartphone thing, it took me a minute to realize I didn't have to call information or look it up on the Internet. I pulled up my Maps app and got the address and directions to the El Centro P.D.

It was a pretty standard looking civic building. I went in and asked for the desk sergeant. He turned out to be this tall, rangy-looking guy with short, black hair, could have been Native American, could have been Hispanic, could have been Anglo. Probably was all three - and then some. The name on his badge said Olsen. I got out a business card and took a deep breath.

"I'm trying to get some information on a Julio Camacho," I said.

Olsen chuckled. "What's he done now?"

"Well, for starters, he shot at me just now." I got a grip on my voice. "I'm investigating a murder case up in Los Angeles that may be linked to his daughter, Rita. He pops up, gets real defensive, then starts shooting at me right after I asked him if he'd been up to L.A. recently."

"Hm." Olsen thought it over.

"You know, I don't want to be a pain in the ass or anything, but assault with a deadly weapon is a crime, isn't it?" I asked, just barely hanging onto my temper.

"I get it. You're pissed. I'd be, too." Olsen shook his head. "The only problem is that if Julio wanted to assault you, you'd be dead now. He only misses on purpose. He's got better reason than most to want to scare off strangers."

"I feel so comforted."

Olsen nodded. "I agree, it ain't much. Julio's had a rough time. He's a union organizer for the farm workers. There isn't a major owner in the valley that doesn't hate him. The coyotes hate him because he's always busting their asses for mistreating folks. The border patrol hates him because he's always helping folks over the border. He lost one of his sons to gangs and another is in Pelican Bay for the same reason. You don't even want to mention drugs to him, what with Rita and his two boys getting messed up that way."

I sighed. "Okay. There's some perspective."

"What's the murder case?"

"Larry Ochoa."

"Luke Winston's drummer? Wait. I think Rita used to be married to a Larry Ochoa."

"They had some relationship." I felt myself steadying. "Ochoa had apparently tried to contact Rita to make amends. Which means she has motive. Only given that her father basically blamed Ochoa for Rita's drug use, and how he reacted, I'd say he's probably got motive, too."

"Julio's got motives to take out half this county," Olsen snorted. "Besides, Rita was on drugs long before she hooked up with this Ochoa character. That's why they sent her to live with her aunt in Texas. I'm thinking that's where she and Ochoa met and got married. They had already split up when Rita came back. Concepcion, that's Rita's mom, has made herself damned near crazy, trying to straighten Rita out."

"Sounds like one big, happy family." I paused. "If Rita was already on drugs before she met Ochoa, why would her father say that Ochoa messed her up?"

Olsen's brow furrowed. "That was quite a few years back. I've been going to church with the Camachos for a long time. I seem to remember a few months after Rita was sent away, Concepcion coming into prayer group saying that God had healed her little girl off the drugs, that Rita seemed to be getting her act together. Whether or not she was, who knows? Oh, and there's the baby, too."

"Teresa."

"Yeah. She's an okay kid, as far as I know. Julio said something about Ochoa turning tail and running when he heard Rita was pregnant."

"That's funny. Rita told me that Larry had already gone, and she got pregnant by someone else."

"Hm." Olsen shrugged. "Even odds, that's true."

"I wonder if the aunt would know." I sighed again. "Listen, any way you could find out where Camacho was on Monday the eleventh and let me know?"

It was Olsen's turn to sigh. "Yeah, I'd better. I'm fairly sure he's clear, and even if he is, too many folks would love an excuse to pin something on him."

"You gonna tell me if he isn't?"

Olsen smiled. "I'm sworn to uphold the law. I'm also a big believer in the self-defense plea. Julio's not afraid to defend himself or his family, but he doesn't go after people. Even the drug dealers and he really hates them."

I thanked Olsen, left my card, and got his. I didn't even start trembling again until I got to my CRV.

I waited until I was on the freeway and then recorded my notes on the morning's activities for Franny. I think my voice sounded calm. I didn't feel calm though I tried to figure that I was still alive and in one piece and not bleeding from anywhere, so it was all good. Maybe. I was certainly seriously re-thinking the whole P.I. thing. Part-time might cover my bills, but it wouldn't do me much good if I got killed on the job.

I felt somewhat calmer when I pulled into the parking lot at the convalescent home where my grandmother was. We'd been after her for several years to give up her house in San Diego, when out of the blue, it seemed, she suddenly decided that she wanted to move into one of those graduated care retirement facilities. Mom moved back to San Diego from Glendale, at first to take care of getting Grandma's stuff packed away and distributed the way Grandma wanted. Then Mom realized that even if Grandma was in a graduated care facility, Grandma still needed someone to take care of her and since Caro had Uncle Aaron to take care of, and my cousin Jill had moved back in with her two kids... Well, that was Caro's excuse. Of course, that didn't stop Caro from trying to run the entire operation from her place in Orange County.

Mom and Caro have a brother, Bill, who lives in Massachusetts somewhere. Bill and his family refuse to speak to either of them. I used to ask my mom how she was so healthy when her siblings were so messed up and she'd answer, "Total rebellion and lots of therapy."

Anyway, after Grandma's stroke, she had to be moved to the convalescent home and it was not going well. The biggest problem is that Grandma lost her ability to speak. The physical therapy had gotten her mostly mobile, but the speech thing just was not happening. I sympathized for the most part, because Grandma obviously was alert and coherent, and the fact that she couldn't say anything was making her crazy, and Grandma had never been the mild-tempered type, to begin with. Mother, in one of her rare less than kind moments, would say that Grandma's aphasia was the only thing keeping Mom from going crazy.

Grandma was happy to see me. She may make her daughters crazy, but we've always gotten along. It was a pleasant enough visit. I didn't tell her about getting shot at because that would have stressed her out. Which was a good thing because it forced me to calm down and I was able to grab onto a little perspective about it all. I felt rather sad that I couldn't stay longer. I chatted with the nurses right before I left, and all seemed merry and bright.

The freeway north wasn't, however. It was four before I hit Temecula, then things eased up and I made decent time from there. Not to mention that after Riverside, I was going against the rush hour traffic heading out of L.A.

Tim called right after I merged onto the 91. I turned down the radio - I had it on the news station to keep up on the traffic reports - and hit the speaker button on my phone, which was in its dash mount.

"Did you get the play?" he asked.

"Yes, and I read it."

"Is it fabulous or what?"

"It's utterly amazing. Neri needs to do a little work so that it doesn't come off as the lead character blaming herself for her boyfriend's abuse. Other than that, it's wonderful."

"I knew you'd like it. I'm thinking bare stage with levels, soft blue lighting, maybe a set piece."

"Liev Freeman would be good for the set design. Can

you afford him?"

"I don't know. I don't do budgets. Who do you think for Robert?"

"It'll have to be someone uber charming, so we can see why she fell for him. Um, Tony Blaise, maybe? What about getting Neri to play Catherine?"

"Of course!" Tim was bubbling over.

However, as he went on, something on the radio caught my ear.

"Hold on, Tim," I said, turning the sound up.

"Swanson's body was found late this morning by hikers on a lonely stretch of Angeles Crest Highway," said the man's voice from the radio. "He had been missing since Tuesday, said the spokesperson from country singer Luke Winston's office, where Swanson worked. Maria Torres, from the Los Angeles County Sheriff's department, said that the department is opening an investigation."

"We don't know at this time how the victim came to be in the canyon where he was found," said a voice, presumably belonging to Torres. "We are waiting for the coroner's office to determine the cause and time of death. In the meantime, we're asking anyone who saw anything suspicious along Angeles Crest Highway earlier this week to please notify the Sheriff's Department."

"Shit," I growled, in shock.

"I didn't think it was that bad an idea," said Tim from the phone.

"Not you," I groaned. "Tim, I can't deal with this now. Someone connected to that case I'm working on for Berto just turned up dead."

"That's disgusting."

"No kidding. Listen, I've got to make some calls. Can I talk to you later about this?"

"Sure, but I need to get an answer from you soon."

"Shit. That's fair. Listen, why don't we connect over the weekend? I can cook dinner."

Tim sounded cagey all of a sudden. "Actually, why don't I cook for you? We'll talk later."

"Fine. Bye."

I made the merge from the 91 onto I-5, which was moving like lead, as usual, then finally checked the notifications on the phone. Sure enough, there were five messages.

Chapter Ten

After Franny gave me hell for not checking my messages sooner, she told me that Isabel wanted me to call her as soon as possible, only I should call Berto first.

Berto said that Franny was a pain in the ass, but I really should have checked my messages sooner.

"How the hell was I supposed to know that Swanson was going to turn up dead?" I groaned. "You're right, I should have checked them sooner. Only, you know, I got shot at this morning. I was a little distracted, okay?"

Berto laughed. "You'll get used to it."

"Oh, that's really comforting. I'll call Isabel first, then I've got to call Winston and get him calmed down, so I'll talk to you later."

Isabel said there wasn't much, so far. She'd been out to where they'd found Swanson. They'd called her in as a courtesy, only since the stiff was found in an unincorporated part of the county, L.A. Sheriff's had the case officially.

"Any chance they'll re-open Ochoa now that the White kid got nailed?" I asked.

Isabel snorted. "About the same as the Dodgers signing a decent middle reliever." Isabel is an ardent baseball fan, and while she sniffs at most substitute pitchers, her full contempt is saved for her beloved Dodgers' bullpen. "They should. Swanson clearly had been beaten and there were contusions all over his belly, like on Ochoa. I can't say for sure until we get the coroner's report, but I wouldn't be surprised if Swanson was killed someplace else and then dumped."

"What makes you so sure?"

Isabel paused. "Just something about the way the stiff was positioned, maybe. I don't know. I think it's one of those intuitive things I get sometimes."

Which meant that we were going to find out that Swanson was killed someplace else and then dumped.

"That's odd," I said. "Why dump him? I told you how his place was trashed, and he lived alone. Why go to the trouble of dumping him and possibly getting caught?"

"It could be he came up to the highway on his own after he was beaten, except there was no car found in the area. We'll have to see what the coroner says about time of death, although that could be pretty messy, too."

"Why?"

"It's been pretty cold up there past few nights - possibly below freezing. That can really mess up time of death estimates."

"You know, I was out to Swanson's building on Tuesday evening and Swanson's truck was there in its usual spot. Then on Wednesday, Swanson's truck had been moved to the wrong spot."

"That's interesting. Hm. Listen, I'm not on this case, technically, but I know who is. DeVine Nichols. He's an investigator with Sheriff's homicide. He'll want to talk to you, especially since you discovered that Swanson's apartment was trashed."

"Tonight?" I looked out over the sea of red brake lights in front of me.

The lights of the freeway were reflecting off the clouds in the sky, and the forecasters said we had more rain coming through that night.

"Nah, he's home with his wife and kids by now." Isabel chuckled. "Now, if anything happened to them, we'd have a whole host of suspects."

"Why?"

"You haven't seen Nichols. He comes around, you know who the straight girls and gay boys are by all the tongues hanging out."

"Huh?"

"He is gorgeous. Even I, who find no attraction to men, can see that he is a man of rare beauty."

"Ooh." I grinned in spite of myself. "This could be fun.

Except for the wife and kids."

"The good ones are always taken."

"Indeed. Anything else?"

"Nope. Talk to you later."

I hung up, my moment of gaiety gone. The traffic was still stop and go, which meant I had no excuse except to dial the number Franny had left me for Luke Winston.

"Hello?" It wasn't much, but he sounded okay.

"It's Daria Barnes, Mr. Wins- I mean, Luke. I, uh, just heard about Mr. Swanson."

"Yeah." So much for sounding okay. "We're pretty messed up about that one."

"I don't doubt." My stomach clenched as I realized I was just as messed up. I had to stay professional. "Have you talked to the police at all?"

"We've had a couple guys through, mostly asking about Jay not showing up on Tuesday. I had to tell them you went through his office."

"That's fine. We're on the same side." I bit my lip, hoping the sheriff's investigators would see it that way. "Obviously, anybody in your company have any issues with Mr. Swanson?"

"Oh, no. Everybody liked Jay. Have you talked to Leo yet?"

"Any reason I should?"

"Well, I— You know, he knew Jay. I figured you'd want to talk to anybody who worked with him."

"Of course." I was a little puzzled by Luke's response but didn't get much of a chance to think it over.

"Um, Daria, are you anywhere close to Hollywood right now?"

"Not really. Why?"

"Oh. Well. Not to trouble you or anything. It's just been a rough day, what with calling Jay's folks and all. Plus, I had to identify the body."

"I'm sorry, Luke."

"No, no. I don't mind."

Things were slowing down again. I had made it past Santa Fe Springs. I checked my dashboard clock. It was a little after seven.

"Uh, Luke, do you need me to swing by or something? I'm kind of stuck on the freeway right now. I could be there maybe in an hour or so?"

"Would you? Daria, that'd be just wonderful if you could. You hungry? I could get us some dinner."

"Yeah. Sure." I made a point of sounding more enthused than I felt. "I'll meet you at your office."

It was so the last thing I wanted to be doing at that point, but I felt for the guy. As it turned out, it took longer than an hour to wade through the traffic. It was almost eight-thirty by the time I pulled up outside Luke's office. I called him from the car, then dashed into the building through the raindrops. He appeared in the lobby a few minutes later and took me through to the kitchen, where he had ribs and side dishes in unmarked Styrofoam boxes laid out on the small wooden dining table. He had remembered to set out plates and silverware. The napkins were still on the granite counter next to an open white plastic bag.

"That looks good," I said, stripping off my pea-coat.

"I had one of the interns run up to this place in Burbank," Luke said. "It's not quite North Carolina, but it's about as good as you're going to get out here."

"North Carolina. Is that where you're from?"

Luke nodded as he seated me at the table. "Yep. Winston. It was always kind of embarrassing coming from the same city as my name. It sure works for me now."

"I'll bet," I said. "If you don't mind talking about it, what happened with Mr. Swanson?"

Luke, settled in the seat next to me, shrugged. "Can't say for sure. We got the call from the Sheriff's department sometime in the afternoon - they say he was found around ten this morning. His mom is pretty broken up about it. She's the one who told the Sheriffs he worked here."

"Interesting," I grumbled through a mouthful of rib. Luke was right. It was pretty darned good. "LAPD got called in right away. The homicide detective on the Ochoa case was on the scene."

Luke picked at some cole slaw. "They said Jay was

murdered."

"Yeah, I know." I put down the rib bone I'd just stripped of its meat. "You know, Luke, if you're worried about your personal safety, we can get you a bodyguard."

"Oh, no. I'm fine," Luke said, taking a generous bite of coleslaw to prove it.

His left hand lay on the table, practically next to mine. I debated reaching over and taking it in mine, but something held me back.

"Well, you can change your mind at any time." I went back to eating, keeping one eye on him.

He looked so dejected, and yet, there wasn't much to be said. I didn't say anything, partly because something didn't feel right. I mean, there was no doubt that he was grieving and maybe even pretty scared. Still, there was something else going on. I just couldn't put my finger on what.

Or I couldn't until I got back out to my car. It didn't take long. I only ate another rib or so, then yawned and said I had to get back. Luke insisted on packing up the leftovers and giving them to me. He walked me out to my CRV and lingered for a brief moment as if he were hoping I'd do something. Back on the freeway, which was still slow even after 9 p.m., it hit me. Luke was on the make.

It was the weirdest thing in the world, but I couldn't shake the feeling that the sad puppy routine was just that, a routine to get me to feel sorry for him and fall into bed with him. Except that he really was sad, and it's not like he didn't have reason to feel that way. Even so, there was something vaguely icky about it all and I was truly glad I hadn't stayed any longer than I had.

Chapter Eleven

When the phone rang that Saturday morning, I was in no mood to get it. Granted, by the time I'd left Luke the night before, it was after nine. I still got home before ten, and that's a bit early for me to be going to bed.

Between soothing annoyed pussy cats, who were quite peeved that their dinner was late that night, and vegging out in front of the boob tube, and even though I was tired down to my bone marrow, I didn't get to bed until after midnight.

What with Luke's weird behavior, Jay Swanson biting the big one, oh, and getting shot at earlier that day, sleep didn't really happen, either. When the landline rang, I ignored it - which is easy to do because the phone next to my bed has its ringer turned off. By the time my smartphone rang, I knew who was calling. That phone was a lot harder to ignore since it was in my jeans' pocket, and I'd left those next to my bed. I still tried, pulling the covers up around my ears and rolling away from that side of the bed.

A minute later, the landline rang again. I ignored it. After the voice mail kicked in, my smartphone rang again. Berto was going to keep calling me until I picked up. I still didn't get to the mobile in time before it went to voice mail. I sulked through another round of ringing from the landline, then tapped on the mobile when that rang again.

"*Pendejo,*" I grumbled.

"No, you say, *Bueno,*" said Berto, sounding far more cheerful than anybody calling from a hospital bed on a Saturday morning had any right to sound.

"Fuck you. Why are you bothering me? It's Saturday."

"I remembered something."

"Nice. Tell Marisol."

"I'm just going to keep calling you."

I glanced over at my alarm clock. "Berto, it's not even nine and it's Saturday morning. You know, the weekend?"

"I was talking to Swanson right before the accident."

"Huh?"

"In the parking garage. Swanson met me as I was leaving the office that night, and we rode down on the elevator. He said that manager guy, McKesson, had sent him to get information so that Winston could send some swag. We were in the garage, talking. I don't remember about what. I still don't remember the accident, itself."

"Hm. That's interesting, but it still doesn't tell us much about who hit you and why."

"Except now Swanson's dead."

"So I hear."

"No, Daria. He may have seen something and that's why."

"Except that Isabel told me that the stiff looked a lot like Ochoa. It's more likely Swanson's death is related to that case than who hit you."

Berto thought that one over for a second. "Maybe who hit me is part of the Ochoa case."

"Maybe who hit you was pissed off at you for calling when he could have been sleeping," I complained.

"They were thinking Ochoa was offed by someone close to Winston."

"That's only a maybe, and believe me, between Ochoa's past and how open that venue was, it could have been anybody. Which come to think of it, goes for you, too. They're taking numbers to kill you, *mi hermano*."

Berto laughed. "Check into it."

"I'll see if we can get the surveillance tapes from the parking people. Now that there's a nice young White boy involved, maybe the cops will be more interested in getting that warrant. Can I go back to sleep now?"

Berto complained but let me off the hook. The only problem was, by that point, I was wide awake. I crawled out of bed, taking Berto's name in vain every step of the way.

Of course, just because I couldn't sleep and was, in fact, on my feet, that did not mean that I was feeling particularly chipper. Even after pulling up a Pilates workout I'd saved on my DVR and doing it, I still had that muzzy half-awake feeling. It took a solid jolt of hot coffee before I was able to think clearly enough to decide what to do with my day.

Back when I was still producing plays, on Saturday mornings, I'd either be up and supervising a rehearsal or solving some tech problem; or I'd be in bed after a Friday night performance and probable party. Since I'd given that up in favor of the nine to five grind, Saturdays usually meant sleeping in a little bit later than normal, then cleaning house.

I wasn't sure if I actually could take a day or two off from investigating, although I probably should have. At the same time there were some things to check out, and could I really put them off knowing that whoever had nailed Berto was still out there and possibly looking for a second chance at finishing the job? Not to mention the allure of sweeping floors, scrubbing the toilet, and dusting was in the minus numbers, if you know what I mean.

I got the computer booted up and while I was waiting, I called Ochoa's parents. His mother, Consuela, got on.

"I already told the police Larry didn't mention anybody he was worried about," she told me even before I could ask a question.

"Actually, I was more interested in finding out about Larry's wife, Rita Camacho."

"That little whore. She was the one who got Larry hooked, you know."

"Really. How did that happen?"

"Larry came home from that fancy music school of his and that's when they met," Consuela said. "He had a job in Dallas with an orchestra there. He kept coming back to El Paso on weekends. They met in some bar or something. He kept coming back. Only it wasn't long before he was stoned most of the time. They got married, oh, thirteen, fourteen years back. We got him out of there for a year or so and it looked like he was gonna clean himself up. Then he went back to her and found her knocked up with someone else's kid."

"Do you know when they got divorced?"

"Oh, he left her about eight years ago. It was around that time that he finally went into rehab. I guess he made it stick, but no one here was going to believe it. It's not like Larry hadn't done the rehab thing before, you know?"

"Drugs can make families pretty crazy."

"This family was crazy before he started the drugs." She sniffed suddenly. "It's all kinda confusing. All those folks that worked with Larry, that nice Luke Winston, they all said Larry didn't do drugs no more - that he was cleaner than clean, one fellow put it. Then the cops said he was on pills when he died."

"Yeah, that's what they thought, at first," I said. "There was some Vicodin in his system when he died, but not enough to have killed him and we've uncovered a couple of things that make it look like somebody may have given him the drug without him knowing."

There was a long pause as Consuela thought that one over. "You're going to find out who killed my boy?"

"I'm trying to."

There was another pause. "I wish I knew something. The past few years, Larry would call to say hi. Not much more. He told me he didn't want me to worry about him, that he was staying clean. The last time we talked, he told me I could be proud of him. I told his *papí*. His *papí* said he was proud of Larry. I said, you don't talk to him, how is Larry gonna know? Hernando said Larry knows. Only I don't think he did."

"Do you know if there was a will?"

"Ay. I don't think so. Call his sister, Gloria. She was supposed to look for it. She said there was nothing in the house except all this music stuff."

I made a note to check in with Luke, and probably McKesson, to see if Ochoa had a lawyer. I was betting he didn't. I tried reaching Gloria Warner, Ochoa's sister, and had to leave a message.

While I was on the computer, I went ahead and did a Google to find the El Paso City and El Paso County websites, and from there, found the marriage certificate for Ochoa and Rita Camacho. When I tried to look up the divorce case,

I found I was going to have to call the court office, since the website that the County Clerk linked to didn't want to give me the divorce record because I didn't have all the right information. That went on the list for Monday.

Another Google and I found a phone listing for Camacho's aunt, Mercedes Valenzuela. I probably should have just called her. Instead, I went ahead and gave my house a cursory cleaning, which didn't take long, unfortunately.

Stuck, I went ahead and called Valenzuela. She picked up on the second ring.

"My name is Daria Barnes and I'm looking for the aunt of Rita Camacho," I told her.

"I'm her. Rita's not here," Valenzuela said. "She moved to California a few years ago. I can give you her phone number."

"I've got that, thank you. I'm just trying to pin down a few details about her relationship with a Mr. Larry Ochoa."

"Oh, Larry," she sighed. "He was such a nice boy. There were problems with the drugs, I'm telling you, but he was still the nicest young man."

And she went on to tell me, at length, just how nice Larry was and how he'd begged Rita to go into rehab with him that time before he left her and then, how he found out she was pregnant and alone and came back to help her. And, yes, he did get into the drugs again, but he cared for Teresa like she was his own daughter. And Teresa was just the sweetest little girl, which Mercedes knew because she mostly raised Teresa and it was a blessing that Concepcion was raising her now because poor Rita had so many troubles with the drugs.

"Do you know if Rita and Larry ever formally got divorced?" I asked when Valenzuela paused to catch her breath.

"Well, you know, divorce is wrong, and Larry wouldn't do something mean like that. Larry loved Rita and he told me the only reason he had to leave her was because he couldn't do the drugs anymore. He wanted to stay because of Teresa. I told him he did not need to worry about Teresa because I would take care of her. When he started with that

Luke Winston, he would send money to me for Teresa. Just like she was his own daughter. He called me every week, no matter where he was, he called me. Then Rita moved back to be with her family about a year ago. He still called me to say hello, every Sunday."

"Do you remember what you talked about the last time you spoke with him?"

"Oh, the usual. How am I doing? What's going on in El Paso? I told him about my blood pressure medicine and the doctor kept saying it was fine, but I kept getting dizzy and Larry said he would call my doctor to find out and he did, you know."

"Do you know who Teresa's birth father is?"

"Danny Pacheco. He doesn't call. He barely knows he's got a daughter. He's been in prison for, oh, five, six years now and it's the second time since he got Rita pregnant. Larry was so good to Teresa. He never missed a birthday."

"How has Larry been communicating with Teresa since she and her mother moved to California?"

"My brother Julio won't let him talk to Teresa or give them money or nothing. He's so stubborn that one. I told him just the other day, he should have let Larry talk to Teresa. She misses him. I can tell. Julio wants to blame Larry for everything that happened to Rita. He doesn't listen, no matter what I tell him. Now Larry is dead and it's so sad."

And so it went on for several more minutes. I let Valenzuela go, even though I was antsy and wanted off the phone. Berto always says when you get a talker, it's best to let them talk because you never know what they'll give you. Unfortunately, Valenzuela didn't give me anything useful, as far as I could tell, so when I did finally get off the phone and saw that she'd talked for a good forty minutes, I couldn't help but feel annoyed.

Which is why I wasn't in the best of moods when I finally called Tim Wing. He was delighted to hear from me.

"I wish I was in a better mood," I sighed. "In any case, when do you want to get together?"

"The sooner the better for me," he replied. "You doing anything tonight?"

I yawned. "I'm pretty tired."

"I'll cook dinner."

"Dinner." That sounded really nice. Tim's worked in a lot of restaurants over the years and is an amazing cook.

"Tell you what. I'll pick you up from your place and bring you down here, so you don't have to mess with the parking." Tim had a loft in downtown Los Angeles which he'd bought a few years before, just as the all the new development was going in, right before all the prices had skyrocketed. It was a terrific place. However, parking was a bitch.

"I could take the Gold Line down."

"Where are you going to park overnight? Not to presume, my dear, but do we want to have that make our decisions for us?"

I chuckled. "I guess not."

"You can always get an Uber to the Gold Line if we start fighting and from there, home, I suppose. You can sue me for the fare."

"Okay. Okay. What time do you want to pick me up?"

"How about five? That'll give me plenty of time to get my prep work done."

"Fine. I'll see you then."

I looked at the clock and saw that it was after noon already. I debated cleaning out my hall closet, then realized I could swing by the Ridley place just to see if they were at home, after all.

The house in South Pasadena was not only vacant, there was a For Sale sign on the lawn and a second sign promoting the Open House. I didn't expect to find the owners there. Still, I thought I'd try anyway. I also didn't expect to find the house completely empty of everything and smelling of fresh paint, but it was.

"It's priced for a quick sale," said the agent who was overseeing the open house. She was a short woman, although the kind that filled a room. Her tan silk power suit and four-inch spike heels only added to her presence.

"Really. Why?" I asked.

"A family emergency. The owners also own the agency. They decided this week to sell out and move north. I believe

Mr. Ridley's mother had a stroke or something and they need to go take care of her. It was all pretty sudden."

I nodded. I was thinking it seemed a pretty excessive way to cover up their son's errant behavior unless he'd been up to something besides escaping rehab.

"Listen, I'm a private investigator and I'm checking out—"

"It's about time they hired someone to look into those thefts," the agent said. "Three of them, all on this street. You'd think, for all the money in taxes we're paying, that the cops could come by a little more often."

I went with it. "Well, it would help my investigation if we could narrow down various details, like the cars that belong and those that don't. Could you give me a description of the cars that used to belong to the house?" I asked, pulling out my pad and pen.

"Oh, of course. Grace drove a tan Lexus and Matt, Sr., had a black one. Young Matt had one of those real boxy things - a Scion, they called it. I've got the Mercedes, S-Class outside."

"Great. Well, thanks," I said. "That should do it for now."

"Here's my card. Let me know if there's anything I can do—" She stopped abruptly as another couple meandered into the house.

She dismissed me with a quick smile, and I went ahead and looked around the house, just hoping I'd find some clue about why the Ridleys had pulled up stakes so quickly. The house was little more than a bare and lifeless shell, admittedly one that would sell for more money than I'd ever see in my lifetime, even priced for a quick sale.

I headed back home, stopping for tacos at a little taqueria down in Highland Park. I was pulling into my carport when I noticed the dark Crown Victoria parked in front of my house. Amanda Hitchens wasn't in her yard, but I could see the flutter of her blinds. The Crown Vic was technically unmarked, yet it practically screamed that the person inside was an officer of the law, and I somehow knew that he was waiting for me.

Chapter Twelve

As I got out of my CRV, I debated whether to go out to the Crown Vic or wait for the detective to come to my door. If I went out, it could look like I was being confrontational, and I didn't want that. Waiting inside could be interpreted as me trying to hide something and I didn't want that, either.

Fortunately, the detective spared me and got out of the car. I came around the end of the CRV and smiled.

Then smiled some more. Isabel had not exaggerated, because Deputy Investigator DeVine Nichols was indeed divine. Tall and black, with rich chocolatey skin, and even though you knew his gray suit had to be regulation polyester, he made it look like the best Italian silk, filling it out with a slender but powerful build. Now, I have met Denzel Washington, and he is every bit as gorgeous in person as he is on the screen. Let me tell you, Denzel has nothing on Nichols.

He smiled back, bright white teeth flashing in the fading late afternoon sun. His hair was close-cropped, and his eyes had that lively spark that said he knew just what effect he was having on me.

"You must be Investigator Nichols," I said.

"Are you Ms. Daria Barnes?" he asked.

"Yes. Isabel Lancaster said you wanted to talk to me."

"I sure do."

"Well, come on in." I gestured and he followed me through the carport into the house. "I thought you'd be at home with the wife and kids on a Saturday."

"Sunday and Monday are my days off," he said.

I gestured to the sofa. "Please sit down. Can I get you some water or tea?"

"No thanks." He sat down and got out his notebook.

"I understand you were the one who found Mr. Swanson's apartment trashed."

"Yeah. Wednesday evening. I went over there with Mr. Swanson's girlfriend, Katelyn Everett. She had a key, and she was very worried about Mr. Swanson. Said he'd been really upset Monday night, and when she couldn't contact him on Tuesday, she started freaking out. I went over there earlier, but couldn't get in. By Wednesday, Everett was almost a wreck. We met around six, when she got off work, and went in to see what we could find. Oh, and when I went there on Tuesday, Mr. Swanson's truck was in his parking spot. On Wednesday, it had been moved."

Nichols nodded as he made a note. "Did you have any reason to believe that Mr. Swanson had come to any harm?"

"Not initially." I bit the end of my thumb and thought. "Luke Winston, his boss, was pretty worried about Mr. Swanson not showing up for work on Tuesday."

"I understand you're looking into who killed that drummer, Larry Ochoa."

"Trying," I sighed. "I'm also trying to figure who tried to run down Berto Esparza on Monday evening. He's the one Mr. Winston really hired. Berto said just this morning that he was talking to Mr. Swanson right before his accident."

Nichols' eyebrows rose. "Really. I'd heard he couldn't remember the accident."

"It looks like his short-term memory is starting to come back. He still doesn't remember the accident, itself. But he called me this morning to tell me about Mr. Swanson. Apparently, Mr. Winston's manager, Leo McKesson, had sent Jay over to get information so that Mr. Winston could send everybody some nice swag. Which Mr. Winston did, by the way."

"Hm." Nichols looked at me. "Iz Lancaster says you've got your head on straight. Do you think the two murders are connected?"

"Given what Iz said about the state of the two bodies, I'd have to say it looks that way. Berto said the murders may even be connected to his accident, which could be. It's just that there's a long list of people who want to do Berto in.

Even longer than the list of suspects in the Ochoa case. The problem is, I don't have any evidence or any feeling about either case. Lots of suspects and no hard leads. Do you know if anyone at Mr. Swanson's building saw anything?"

Nichols shook his head. "Nothing. Absolutely nothing. There was no sign of breaking and entering at the apartment, either, so it looks like Swanson let the killer in. We checked up on all the people he works with, and they're all accounted for. So's the girlfriend, as a matter of fact."

It was my turn to shake my head. "I don't know what to tell you. Unless the lab techs come up with something from the apartment, there's really no way of knowing what happened there. Swanson had a cat, but she's not saying anything."

"You know where the cat is?"

"She's right here," I said, picking Muffy up from the couch next to Nichols. "It should have been in the police report. I made sure the officer had my information and he let me take her food and her litter box. Those were all in the kitchen and that wasn't touched."

"Somebody had one hell of a fight in that apartment. It was a mess. The only problem is that we can't find any traces of Swanson having been killed there. He evacuated his bowels when he died, only there's no trace of it in the apartment. No blood, neither."

"Could it be that the lab techs missed it?"

Nichols shook his head and got up. "I had my own guys in there - not to knock LAPD, but they didn't know what they were looking for the other night. My guys are going over Swanson's car now."

I got out a card from my wallet. "Well, here's my info. In fact, let me write my cell phone number on here. If you find anything, would you let me know?"

"Sure." Nichols had his card out, as well. "I'd appreciate it if you kept me up to date, too."

"I'll do that."

I escorted him out and allowed myself one serious ogle as he made his way to the Crown Vic. It was scary how good-looking that man was. I was sure that I'd be hearing about it from Amanda. I decided that I'd deal with that when the time came. In the meantime, Tim would be at the door in a short while and I wanted to get ready.

It wasn't any big deal. I put my hair up. Found my green cotton pullover and paired it with a full jeans skirt that hung just below my knees. Swiped a little mascara over my eyelashes, a little gloss on my lips. Put some earrings in. Found my suede Ginger Rogers pumps. And Tim was at the door.

That's one of the weird things about Tim, compared to most theatre people. Tim is almost compulsively on time. Me, I can be on time if I work at it, except first thing in the morning. Tim runs like clockwork. He says it's part of his Asian heritage.

Tim is Taiwanese. He came here when he was ten, as a parachute kid, to go to school in the care of his older sister, who later returned to Taiwan. His other sister, also older, now lives in San Marino and takes care of their grandmother. The Wing family is pretty darned wealthy and though Tim has been pretty much cut off financially from his parents, he does have a fairly generous trust fund that his grandfather left him. Even so, it ain't that generous, Tim says, and like me, he's pretty frugal.

Tim hadn't really dressed up much, either. He wore a tan sweater over dark jeans, but since they weren't torn, I could tell that he had made an effort. He also had his jazz dance shoes on instead of the running shoes he normally wears. He's several inches taller than I am, which makes him pretty tall for most Chinese. His face is a little long, too, and he wears his shiny black hair in a fade with a long ponytail over the sheared back part. We're both just old enough not to get body art, so his smooth skin is unadorned, except for the earring he wears in his left ear.

"Look who's looking good," he said with a broad smile as I opened the door.

"Looking good yourself," I said in admiration. "Come on in."

We gave each other a long, comfortable hug and as we pulled apart, I couldn't resist landing a lazy kiss on his lips.

"It is so good to see you," he sighed.

"Same here. Let me get my backpack together and we can get going."

I had stashed an extra pair of panties, a toothbrush, and my diaphragm in the bag already. I got my mobile phone and wallet out of my jeans' pockets, collected my keys, double checked that the cat bowls had food and water in them, double checked the timers on my lights and we were off. Like Tim, I wasn't assuming we'd end up in bed. Still, I didn't want to have to say no, either.

We mostly gossiped on the drive to downtown. The usual nonsense about who was doing what, seeing whom, sleeping with whomever else. My friend Sally was preggers again. Tim's friend Steve'd had his heart broken again. Yes, the politicians were ruining the world and if they were really smart, here's what they'd do. There was something about the sameness of it all that was both relaxing and invigorating.

Tim's loft was decorated by our set designer friend Liev Freeman. It's minimalist, furniture from Ikea, but you'd think Liev had gotten everything from the Pacific Design Center. The door opens right into Tim's kitchen, which is under the bedroom overhang. To the right, still under the bedroom, is an office area which is generally littered with scripts and renderings and costume bits.

To the left of the kitchen, the loft is open to its ceiling and there's a dining area, and beyond that, the living room. If you crane your head exactly right, you can see City Hall through the front window.

Tim's kitchen is the best part, though, and it's all about the huge stove. It's a professional-grade Viking, with two wok-wells and six burners. His counters are filled with spices and tools, and he has a huge refrigerator with stainless steel doors right next to the office. Somewhere in that mess is a microwave.

He ushered me into the loft and headed right for the stove.

"I've got some dim sum in the oven," he told me as he bent over to get the sheet pan out. "Give me a sec, and we'll get it all steamed and nice again."

His bamboo steamer sat on top of an ordinary Dutch oven, and Tim had a flame under it in a second.

"There's rice waiting in the fridge," he told me. "Can you get that for me so I can get it in the steamer, too?"

I did as I was asked and then set the table. I knew where everything was and how Tim liked things. Tim smiled at me as he laid out the veggies he'd cut and the various jars and bottles he was pulling together for his sauces. Satisfied that all was ready, he got a bottle of Alsatian Riesling from the fridge and opened it. I got a couple of glasses from the black lacquer breakfront and set them down on the counter between the sink and the dining area.

Minutes later, the dim sum was steamed and ready and we ate off the butcher block table and drank the riesling. Then Tim decided it was show time and started whipping veggies and meats around his two woks, depositing a perfectly fried and sliced fish onto a plate of shredded cabbage, and pouring a glistening sauce over it. There was also some pork with broccoli, bok choy and black bean sauce, and some orange chicken, which Tim only does for me because he thinks it's a ridiculous cliché.

Minutes later, we were at the table piling rice into our bowls and putting various bits of pork and fish and chicken onto it.

"Tim, you've done it again," I said, picking up my chopsticks. "This looks and smells fabulous."

"Thank you, but have I taught you nothing?" he sighed and popped up from his seat. "When are you going to hold your chopsticks correctly?"

"I can get my food more easily this way."

Tim was already behind me reaching around me to correct my grip. His soft hands repositioned my fingers.

"See? That's easier, isn't it?"

Before I could answer, his cheek brushed mine. I leaned into the softness and let out a little sigh. His fingers trailed back up my arms and I felt them softly massage the back of my neck. Tim took a deep breath and went back to his chair.

"You know, this isn't just about the play," he said quietly.

"That's usually when we get together," I said.

"I know." He delicately scooped up a piece of pork trailing strips of bok choy and got it all into his mouth. "I've really missed you, Daria."

I thought about how long it had been and felt myself growing horny. "I've missed you, too, Tim. Then when you didn't call last year, I figured it was the usual."

We'd gone out to a Chinese New Year party, which had been fun. After that, we wound up at my place and for whatever reason started talking as we got naked and had a really nice heart-to-heart about what we wanted for our lives. I was still happy at my job at the shelter and really liked that I was doing something important to help people. Tim was tired of all the sweet young things who regularly threw themselves at him because they thought it would get them somewhere. I conceded that I really loved working in the theatre but was so tired of struggling all the time to make a living. Tim had his vision of a really good repertory company doing both classical and modern plays, plays that mattered, that would speak to people, and maybe even have a children's troupe to help kids get educated in the arts.

We'd made love after that, long and slow and delicious, then drifted off to sleep. When I awoke and saw Tim's face next to mine, I whispered, "I really love waking up next to you, Tim."

I had thought Tim either hadn't heard or it hadn't made an impression on him. I was wrong.

"Yeah. That," he said as he took another slice of fish. "I have a confession to make. I was going to call back right away, only I chickened out."

I stopped eating, puzzled. "Why?"

"Well, the talk was pretty intense. Then there's what you said the next morning."

"About waking up next to you."

"Yeah. That pretty much scared the shit out of me."

"Oh. I didn't mean it to."

"I know." He looked at me, his sweet dark eyes smiling. "Or I realized that about six months ago when it dawned on me that I hadn't slept with anybody since then."

"What? You went celibate for six months?" I gaped in spite of myself.

Tim snorted. "I've been celibate since that night. I can't believe it. You know how we were talking and what I said about those sweet young things. I just don't want that kind of easy sex anymore. I must be getting old or something, but it's been simmering in the back of my brain that what I want is what we have. We're... comfortable."

"Comfortable?"

I must have made a face, which was kind of understandable because the last thing you want an actor to be is comfortable. Tim waved his hands quickly.

"I mean in the good way," he said anxiously. He paused. "It's like seeing one of my favorite films. I may know every frame. Yet every time I see it, I find something new, even though its very familiarity is part of what makes it wonderful."

"We're good together," I said softly.

"Yeah. It's not just the sex or the working together. It's what you said when you woke up that morning. It's the waking up that's special, just being together."

I looked at my food to avoid looking at anything else. "Wow."

"The tricky part is..." Tim hesitated. "I don't know that I want to move in together or get married or anything like that."

I let my breath go. "Whew! Not that it wouldn't be nice."

"I feel the same. It's just that I kind of like being on my own, too, and I think I'd make a lousy husband."

I laughed. "You would. Which is fine with me. I like being single." I paused and looked at him fondly. "Still, it would be nice to have someone around to share with."

"Yeah, and more regular sex."

"You would think of that."

My hand lay on the table next to his. I reached over and took his. It felt good. It felt more than good.

After a gentle squeeze, Tim took his hand back so he could finish eating, but his sweet brown eyes kept giving me the come-hither look. Then there was the cleanup, and you wouldn't think clearing dishes could be an erotic exercise. You haven't had Tim teasing you through the entire process, and didn't I mention somewhere that I hadn't had sex, either, since the last time we'd gotten together?

Tim was in good form that night, too. We managed to get out of the kitchen fully clothed, but then the passion took over and things went fast and furious in the living room after that. We basked in the afterglow and put on some DVD or other and cuddled for a while, then went upstairs to bed.

The thing about not having had sex in a while is that when you finally get some - and especially when it's really good - you just can't get enough. We made love again, this time taking it slow and easy. Tim and I were incredibly good together, that perfect balance of knowing each other really well and still being able to surprise and delight each other.

I woke up first the next morning and simply enjoyed watching Tim sleep for a bit. Then I woke him up, trying to get out of bed to go use the restroom. That was okay. We took our time and showered together. Then I went downstairs and got coffee on and made breakfast while Tim shaved and finished dressing.

It was one of those days when you just let things happen. We didn't really talk about the future. We didn't really avoid it, either. It just wasn't part of the discussion.

Tim drove me home after breakfast and we pitsy-putzed around there. I dared Tim to shag me up against the wall and he did - I'll never know how he got that condom on so fast. Just around three, we both looked at each other and knew it was time to talk.

Tim started. "First off, I want you to know I want to be around, even if you decide you can't do the play with me," he said. "Still, I could really use your help."

I sighed. "That's kind of the weird thing. Berto said I can do the PI thing part-time so that I can do plays. In fact, Berto says he planned it that way."

"And yet, you're not going for it."

"I... I don't know."

We were sitting on my couch in the living room and Tim reached over and pulled me close to him.

"What's holding you back?"

I swallowed. "I'm not sure the PI thing is going to stick." I looked up at him. "I got shot at Friday. Scared me like nothing else. Then that person connected to the case got killed. I'm not sure I'm that good at it, either. Berto and Isabel keep saying I'm doing fine, but... You know, Tim, this isn't like messing up the books on a show or blowing a wad on the wrong set pieces. This is life and death here."

"But every time we talk about the theatre thing, your voice gets so wistful. Daria, you want to go back. I've never known anyone who loves putting on plays like you do and it sure seems like that's what you really want to do."

"Because it is." The tears finally began flowing and I couldn't stop them. "Only, Tim, that last year, I nearly lost my house."

"I thought you bought it outright."

"I did. I couldn't pay the taxes on it, that's how little I was making. My mom had to bail me out. Then I got that temp job and it felt so good having a steady income." I wiped my eyes. "It just totally sucks that the one thing I love doing more than anything else I can't afford to do because there just isn't enough money in it to live on."

It was Tim's turn to sigh. "Don't I know it. I guess you're just going to have to make the PI thing stick."

"I guess."

"It's not all that dismal. That grant for sixty thou? It's seed money, Daria. There's more to be had. Yeah, we'll start with Neri's play, but the foundation wants to do more. They want an education program, and they'll support a repertory company. We've just got to build it."

"I guess we're going to have to." I smiled up at him.

Tim's optimism wasn't always that well-founded. On the other hand, he did pull these sorts of things off just often enough to give it a whirl. Somehow, for the first time in at least three years, it just felt right.

I reached up and kissed him. "I've got a couple of cases to solve first, though."

"We've got six months," said Tim.

"Assuming I don't get myself killed first."

"You're such an optimist. Wait. I've got an idea." Tim dug into his jeans' front pocket and pulled out his smartphone. "There's this app. It's kind of creepy, but it will let me track you. Or track your phone."

"What do you mean?"

Tim grabbed my phone and flipped and pressed through the menu. "My sister had installed this tracking app on my nephew and niece's phones so that she can track them down. Granted, with Jimmy, it's not such a bad idea. Suzy, let's be real, this kid is so straight, it's scary. Only you know what a control freak Su Lin is."

"Pot calling the kettle black, my dear. What are you doing to my phone?"

"That tracking app." Tim finished pressing buttons on the screen and kissed the top of my head. "You've got backup now. Keep it on you, and on, and I can find you anywhere. I've got the locator software and everything. It's all on my laptop, thanks be to Suzy. She thought I'd like it 'cause I'm so good at losing phones."

I chuckled. "How do I keep tabs on you?"

Tim paused, then shrugged. "I'll install it on my phone and give you the sign-in for the account. I figure we've only got a couple weeks before I lose this one."

"Which means you'll have to make sure you get it on with as many sweet young things as you can until you get your new one."

Tim grimaced. "Yuck. I'm done with that."

"We'll see." I leaned back, smirking a little, then got thoughtful. "Listen, if you do change your mind about that, you will please tell me, won't you?"

"Sure, but why?"

"Well, it looks like we're settling into something resembling a steady relationship here, so I think I'd like to go on the Pill. As long as you're faithful, then we can dispense with the barriers."

Tim grinned. "As if I didn't have enough incentive. Shall we see to getting the tests done and then..."

Growling, he nibbled on my neck as I laughed.

Unfortunately, he had to leave shortly after to have

dinner with his grandmother and sister and family. He invited me with the caveat that his grandmother would almost prefer he brought home a man than a Caucasian, which made declining really easy for me. I felt for him, though. I'd seen the miserable aftermath of a visit with his family too many times.

And speaking of miserable aftermaths, my own family, in the form of Aunt Caroline, decided to be miserable, too. I checked my email and saw one from her dated Saturday, the day before.

"Daria," the note said. "I saw your grandmother yesterday, and the nurses told me that you had been there earlier, and that Grandma seemed very agitated after your visit. As you know, Grandma's health is not good and this agitation is not good for her, so I think for the time being, you'd better not visit."

"What?" I howled at the computer. I forwarded the message to my mom, then called her.

"Hello, darling," Mom said, cheerfully. "What's up?"

"I just forwarded you an e-mail from Aunt Caroline. I'd love to know what's going on."

"Oh, dear. Here. Let me get my laptop booted up."

Mom may be an artist, but she's got a geek streak a mile long. In fact, she's my computer guru. That being said, she doesn't like to read email on her phone because it's too hard for her to see.

"How was the show?" I asked her while we waited for her computer to boot.

"We did very well. Melanie is really getting the hang of things. I'm going to let her do the farmer's market on Tuesday by herself." Mom yawned. "I can't tell you how nice it is to be able to just kick back and relax at one of these shows. Melanie did all the packing and drove most of the way home last night. I was able to get out and visit your grandma this afternoon."

"Perfect," I growled.

"Why? Wait. Here's one from you. Subject line visiting. Is that it?

"Yep."

"Hmm." Mom hemmed for a second, then laughed. "She's got to be kidding. The nurses told me that Caro had been there Friday. Which is good because I'd asked Caro to come down since I'd be out of town. Caro only came by the one day and Mother was not happy."

"What about this agitation thing?"

"Mom was fine when I saw her. She's getting better at recognizing letters, so I brought along a letter board, and she said you'd been there and how happy she'd been to see you."

"I was agitated last Friday!" I wailed, suddenly. "I'd just gotten shot at."

"Were you hit?"

"No."

"Well, that's good."

"But I was upset. Maybe I upset Grandma."

"Oh, Daria, darling." My mother's voice was as soothing as Ben and Jerry's chocolate chip cookie dough ice cream on a really bad day. "If Mom was agitated, it was because of Caro, not you."

"Why would Caro want to keep me from seeing Grandma?" I sniffed.

"I expect she's trying to get Mom to change her mind about her will."

Puzzled, I chewed on my thumbnail. "Grandma doesn't have that much to leave."

Mom laughed. "You think that's going to stop Caro? She's convinced that I moved down to San Diego to ingratiate myself with Mom and get Caro cut out. Which is ridiculous since Mom is leaving everything to you and Jeff."

Jeff was my eldest cousin. He had moved away to the East Coast within weeks of graduating from high school and was now finally married to a woman that Caro loathed even more than she loathed the rest of her children's spouses - and that's a lot of loathing. As a kid, he'd been a quiet bookish sort, not really fitting in with his siblings. Truth be told, I hadn't really paid much attention to him, either.

"Why us? I don't want Grandma's money."

"Which is why you and Jeff are getting it. He doesn't

want it, either, and he is decent enough to call Grandma from time to time, and even set up the webcam for her after her stroke so they could see each other."

I sighed. "I don't know why I'm getting so worked up about this."

"Probably because you got shot at," Mom said calmly.

"Why aren't you freaked out? Mom, have you been smoking pot again?"

"No. I'm sober. It is legal now."

"Still..."

"I'm..." Mom sighed. "I had my freak out on Friday, after seeing Berto in the hospital and knowing you were working for him now. Melanie, God bless her fuzzy little heart, put it all in perspective when she pointed out that you stood a much better chance of getting killed in a car accident. Then right after she said it, we almost were. It is ridiculous how fast folks drive in the San Joaquin Valley. So-o-o-o, I'm going to wait to worry until you actually get hurt."

"We'll see how long that lasts."

"Shouldn't be too long," Mom giggled. "I am a work in progress here."

"What do I do about Caro?"

"Ignore her. I mean, if you really want to piss her off, that will do it. It's not like she doesn't deserve it. I swear, Caro could turn Gandhi against her."

"Why does she always have to be so manipulative? I mean, come on. It could be all sorts of things ticking her off besides the will. She'll be a pain in the ass until we finally figure it out."

Mom sighed. "I know, dear, but it's her problem. Not mine. Not yours. Hers. So she's manipulative. Honey, you know people only resort to that kind of behavior because they don't believe they have any real power of their own. Just because you and I recognize Caro as the destructive force of nature that she is doesn't mean that she knows her own power."

"If she did, she'd probably be able to handle it better."

"Exactly. How many supposedly powerful people do we know who actually think very little of themselves? And it always shows."

I bit my lip as my mother veered into the world of politics and her basic take on the hell bound state of things. She was right about Caro. Although by that point, I was realizing that there was someone else I knew who should have known his own power but didn't. Who theoretically had a great deal of power. Suddenly, I started to wonder who was really pulling the strings at the Luke Winston Empire?

Because the funny thing that was starting to bug me about Luke Winston was that he was really good at manipulation. Now, how much that had to do with Jay Swanson talking to Berto right before Berto's accident, I didn't know. That Friday night, when Luke had talked me into going over to his office and had then come on to me, I'd gotten that icky feeling because it wasn't about sex and comfort and stuff like that. He'd had something else up his sleeve. Just what?

Chapter Thirteen

I didn't get long to dwell on Luke Winston. Within minutes of hanging up with my mom, my landline rang again. Sarah Esparza was on the other end.

"*Tía* Daria, my daddy's home from the hospital!" she blurted in a gush so fast I barely made out what she said.

"That's great news, Sarah."

"Mom wants you to come over and see him tonight. Can you? Pretty please?"

Something was up. I wasn't sure what, just that Marisol must have really wanted me over there badly because she knows how hard it is for me to say no to the kids. I looked at the wall clock, it was not even six yet. The sun had just barely gone down and out the window, the western sky still glowed red.

"I—" I started.

"Mom's ordering pizza, isn't that cool, and you can have some, and I really want you to come over."

"Sure, Sarah." I cringed as she shrieked in glee. "Sarah. Sarah?"

"I'm here," she said.

"Tell your mom I'm on my way."

Sarah shrieked again and I hung up, shrugging. Pizza wouldn't be so bad for dinner, and it had been a long time since I'd seen the kids.

Still, something didn't feel right. As I got onto the freeway and headed out to Sherman Oaks, where Berto's house is, I mulled over whether Marisol was still worried that Berto and I were mad at each other. Only that didn't make sense. I was pretty sure Marisol was over that, although we hadn't talked since that day in the hospital. Nope. There was something going on.

The drive was no big deal, most of the traffic was in the other direction, and I got out to Sherman Oaks in record time. Berto and Marisol live south of Ventura Boulevard. It's that southern edge of the San Fernando Valley where the hills are just beginning, and the houses are worth a small fortune. Marisol has worked like a fiend on that place, doing most of the improvements herself. They could hire someone, well, except for that one summer when Berto almost lost the agency. It's just that Marisol likes building things, and she is a full-time parent, so she sort of has the time.

One thing Berto did do was install some top-notch security features, not that you'd really notice them except for the front. The yard is walled, and the driveway is gated, with a combination keypad for the entry. I know the code, but darned few others do. The house is this sprawling split-level ranch and the vegetation out front is pretty low-lying, so Berto can see who's coming before they can see him. He's got cameras trained on all the potential entrances and alarms on everything, too. As Berto says, it's not perfectly safe, but if someone wanted to get at him or the rest of the crew, they'd have to really work at it.

The Esparza place is about a good mile in from Ventura Boulevard, along windy tract-house roads, which may be why I picked up the big black sedan on my tail shortly after I made the turn from Ventura. I mean, I didn't know it was a sedan at first, although I could tell it was following me, which is why I ditched it before turning onto Berto and Marisol's street. I had to double back around to get to Berto and Marisol's. When I pulled up to their driveway and entered in the gate code, there was no one on the street. I parked next to the wall so that no one could see my CRV from the street, just in case.

Marisol met me at the front door, and she was tense – not about me, but in general. The kids were on the ceiling. Daddy was home, *Tía* Daria had come for a visit, and their grandmother (Berto's mom) was in the kitchen making *pan dulces*, aka Mexican sweet bread. Any one of those situations were cause for excitement, especially those *pan dulces*. Mrs. Esparza's *pan dulces* are the best on the planet, bar none.

They're nothing like the rolls with the colored sugar that you see in the markets. These are light and fluffy with just the perfect blend of egginess and sweetness. Mrs. Esparza is wonderfully patient with her grandchildren, too. That day, even she was having a tough time keeping them focused.

I spent several minutes admiring the *pan dulces* and Ruben's hurt finger and trying to make head or tail out of three different stories, all told at the same time, about their father and life at their aunt's and just about anything three kids, age ten and under, can come up with. Marisol finally shushed them and brought me into Berto's and her bedroom and shut the door.

"They're happy to see you," I told Berto, laughing.

"They're happy to see you, too," Berto said. He was sitting up in bed. His head was still bandaged, and the rich green satin comforter covered his legs. His left arm was in a sling and strapped to his chest.

"How are you feeling?" I asked.

He winced. "Could be worse. The doctors are already trying to ease me off the narcotics. They don't want me to get addicted."

"That would not be good." I looked over at Marisol, whose lips were pressed together. "What's wrong?"

"There was someone following us from the hospital," she said. "A big black car. I'm not sure what kind. We lost them near Ventura, but I'm worried."

"Yeah." I gulped. "I think that same car was following me when I came up. I picked it up right around Ventura and lost it before I turned onto your street."

"Which means it's somebody who knows me well enough to recognize your car," said Berto grimly. "The good news is that we should be safe enough here."

"I'm calling the security company," said Marisol. "We pay them enough money. They should come out here and earn it, for a change."

She left the room.

"What do you want me to do?" I asked Berto, trying to mask just how nervous I felt.

Berto chuckled. "Find the *pendejo* who wants me

dead?"

I was about to yell at him when I noticed that he was watching the bedroom door with a worried frown.

"It's getting serious, Daria," he said softly.

"No shit. Are you sure there isn't some other P.I who could help out?" I whined, pacing. "Seriously, Berto. I'm way in over my head here."

"Yes and no." Berto sighed. "You're all I got. There are only about two other guys in town that I'd trust with this job and neither of them is going to offer me a discount. If anything, they'll go right after my business, if they haven't already."

"I don't know why you think I'm up to this."

"Because I trained you and I'm right here if you need me." Berto grunted as he shifted. "Where are we on this?"

"Pretty much where we were yesterday morning," I grumbled. "I talked to Ochoa's mom. I talked to his wife's aunt, who knew them in Texas. I went out to check on the Ridleys, and they've blown town. They sold their real estate agency and everything. The woman selling their house has no idea where they went, which looks pretty suspicious. Talked to Deputy Investigator DeVine Nichols, and he told me pretty much the same thing that Isabel told me about Swanson's death. LAPD lab didn't come up with anything on the apartment, so Nichols is having Swanson's car checked. Oh, and I found the marriage certificate for Ochoa and Rita Camacho online. I'll have to call for the divorce certificate. That's on my list for tomorrow, along with the parking tapes and a bunch of other stuff."

"You know who you should also check out," Berto said. "Sophie Reisner."

"Yeah, I told you I was going to."

"Well, I just remembered something a little while ago. She called me that day before the accident, supposedly about interviewing me."

"Okay," I said, trying to think of some mnemonic that would keep her in my brain cells until I could write her name down. "She just moved up on the list."

Berto and I didn't get much further with our

conversation. The kids banged on the door, then burst into the room, loudly proclaiming the arrival of *Tío* Fredo and a whole bunch of pizza.

Fredo is Marisol's youngest brother. We've gotten to be decent buddies over the years. Since I'm a part of Berto's family, I'm a part of Marisol's also. Fredo has Marisol's petite frame and round face, which means he looks like he's fifteen, even with the thick mustache he wears, never mind that he's just over thirty.

We didn't get much of a chance to chat, what with the wired kids and the general tension. It took all of the adults in the house, including Berto, to get the kids bathed and calmed down enough to go to bed. After that, I was so beat, myself, I told Berto I'd talk to him the next day and headed back to Eagle Rock.

Tim called my mobile while I was on my way. His family, for a change, were remarkably well behaved and he agreed that after my evening, I deserved a night alone.

"Not that I won't be thinking about you," he teased languidly.

"Good thing I have my vibrator," I teased back. "I'll call you tomorrow night. It's looking like another miserable long day ahead of me, so don't know when."

"Well, don't worry," he said. "I'm keeping an eye on you. In fact, you're on the 134, heading out of Burbank right now."

Sure enough, I could see the giant Sorcerer's Apprentice hat that's part of the huge Disney Animation building at the Disney studios complex coming up on the left side of the freeway.

"I know that's supposed to reassure me, but there's something really spooky about that," I told him with a chuckle. "Like a bad Sting tune."

"Every breath you take, baby. I'll call you around eight tomorrow night if I don't hear from you sooner."

"Okay. Good night, Tim."

"Good night, Daria."

I wasn't particularly sleepy when I got home, so I got a glass of wine from the fridge and turned on the TV. Channel surfing didn't turn up much that was interesting, except there was a Lakers game on. I'm not much of a sports fan. I know enough about most of them to go to a game and be able to tell what's going on most of the time. I don't follow all the teams, and watching games on TV, especially by myself, is pretty boring as far as I'm concerned. Still, that night, my head wasn't up to much more than a basketball game, and this one was fairly close. I think they were playing Phoenix. The Lakers were hitting most of their free shots, for a change, and eventually pulled off a win.

By the time the game was over, the local CW affiliate had its news broadcast on, so I watched that. Not surprisingly for February, not to mention all the rain we'd gotten the week before, there were mudslides all over the place. I watched them again on the eleven o'clock news, noting that one of the slides was off of Angeles Crest Highway. I wondered if it was anywhere near where Jay Swanson's body had been found. They'd closed the highway again - no surprise there, either. The weather was supposed to dry up over the next few days, and maybe get a little warmer, with the next chance for showers on the coming Friday.

I still wasn't feeling all that sleepy. The sports part of the broadcast was only the highlights of the game I'd already seen. I turned off the TV and went downstairs to go to bed. The cats were all curled up on the bed. MacCavity lifted his fuzzy head just long enough to register my presence and blink at me. Muffy yawned and batted at MacCavity, then both went back to sleep.

I went ahead and got undressed and crawled under the covers, dislodging the cats. Little Dora padded up next to my head and flopped down on the pillow. Muffy scrambled off the bed and MacCavity sat on my legs for a few minutes, then sauntered off elsewhere. I lay back, not turning off the light and watching the ceiling.

I knew I wasn't going to sleep. I wanted to and my body was certainly tired enough. Only my brain wasn't turning off. I was worried about Berto and Marisol and the kids. I couldn't shake the kids' faces and the thought of that car following me on the way to their place.

Berto was right. It was getting serious. Well, even more

serious. All I could think of was someone trying to hurt the kids and I started getting angry. I was still a little scared, but what I really wanted was that perp's ass in a sling. Big time. I wanted whoever that coward was to be hurting like Berto was.

Okay, maybe I wasn't a fully trained professional P.I. like Berto was. Still, he thought I could handle this case, and if he thought so, then damn it, I could. I would because he deserved that from me, and I would be damned before I'd let anyone hurt him or Marisol or the kids. End of sentence.

Chapter Fourteen

The next morning, as I was pulling out of my garage, I suddenly realized that I'd left my list in the house. I stopped my CRV in the driveway, went back in to retrieve it and came out just in time to be greeted by Amanda Hitchens, from next door, who looked unusually cheerful. I braced myself. A cheerful Amanda Hitchens meant nothing good.

"You know that Luke Winston that Berto's working for?" she announced. "He was engaged to Felicity Whiting. She's a country singer, too. Here's the whole story." She waved a magazine at me. "See? They caught her hanging out with Larry Ochoa – that drummer that was killed."

"I know who he is, Amanda," I said, trying not to take the magazine from her.

"Is that the case Berto's working on for Winston?" Amanda clucked, then looked at the magazine. "Then you really have to read this, because if Berto's looking into Ochoa getting himself killed, then maybe it wasn't an accident. If it wasn't an accident, then I'd put Mr. Luke Winston at the top of the suspect list. You better tell Berto. It will look really bad for him if his client turns out to be the killer, you know."

Sighing, I took the magazine. "Thanks, Amanda," I said.

I got into my CRV as fast as I could and got it going while Amanda continued to tell me to tell Berto how to investigate the Ochoa case. Like Amanda so often did, she'd gotten under my skin again because whether I wanted to believe it or not, it was possible that Luke had killed Ochoa and was trying to look innocent by calling in an investigator. Which simply did not make sense. The cops had said it was an accident, and everyone was buying the cops' story. Why would Luke risk everything by stirring things up? Unless he had some sort of weird guilt complex and actually wanted to get caught. Which would also account for his weird behavior.

When I got to the office, I asked Franny to get the file on Sophie Reisner for me, then see if she could find a birth certificate for Teresa Pacheco, Rita Camacho's daughter. Franny smiled again and I wondered if she wanted to pat me on the head and feed me a treat. I beat it into Berto's office and called Isabel and left a message. Then I called the El Paso County Clerk in Texas, waited while numerous people put me on hold (after each one referred me to the very website which I had already tried to get the divorce record from), then finally got a number for the court records office, got put on hold a few more times there only to hear that there was no record of a divorce between Larry Ochoa and Rita Camacho. Surprise, surprise. It didn't mean that they hadn't gotten a divorce somewhere else, but if they hadn't, it did give Rita a good reason for wanting Larry dead.

I went digging through all the papers and notes I'd been collecting since this whole mess had started and found the card for Sergeant Ernesto Olsen of the El Centro Police Department. I called him and he wasn't in either. I left a message.

At that point, Franny came in with Reisner file and the information on Teresa Pacheco. Sure enough, Danny Pacheco was listed as her father. Uncharitably, I wondered what a DNA test would say about it.

Fortunately, Isabel called back.

"Got anything for me?" she asked.

"Not really," I answered. "Any chance I can see the surveillance video from Berto's building? I'm wondering about who came and went right around the time of the accident."

"Like we're not," said Isabel drily. "Actually, I have the file booted up right now. Any particular car you're looking for?"

I shuffled through my notes. "Yeah. A tan Lexus, a black Lexus, or a Scion. Or maybe anything that doesn't look like it belongs."

Isabel tapped on some computer keys. "Tan Lexus

– nope. Black Lexus, I have at least five of them here. No Scions. Two Chevy Suburbans, both white."

"Any of the owners named Ridley or Sims?"

"Nope. I'm guessing you're going through Berto's past cases?"

"Yeah. I've got several. Could be Reisner or Margolis or..." I looked again. "Well, a lot of folks."

"Tell you what. Why don't I email you the list of owner's names and you can see if anybody matches your list? And..." She paused, then lowered her voice. "I probably shouldn't be telling you this, but we do have one hot lead. One of the cars, a black Dodge Charger, is registered to Rottgutt, Incorporated. It's actually a shell company."

"A shell company?"

"It's a company that doesn't really exist except to hide the identity of its owners. A lot of super-rich people have them to avoid taxes, and they're often used to hide assets in divorce cases or launder money or all sorts of things."

"I know what it is. I was just surprised." The penny dropped. "They're also used for trying to buy out another company that otherwise doesn't want to sell to you."

"What?"

"Lester Margolis. One of Berto's old cases." I shuffled through my notes. "He was trying to buy out Weideman Technologies by stalking the owner. He also had a shell company throwing money at her at the same time. It was about four years ago. He got convicted, did his community service then supposedly disappeared. We'd uncovered his shell company. Well, probably just one of them since he was able to disappear so conveniently. I'll have to ask Berto how he figured out that Margolis owned the company that was trying to buy Weideman out."

"How do we find Margolis?"

I sighed. "That's a good question. I'll ask Berto about that, too. Oh, and is the company name spelled like it sounds?"

"Nope. R-O-T-T-G-U-T-T. Double TTs, twice. I've got a buddy in white collar crimes at the FBI who might be able to help. They're always looking at stuff like that." Isabel lowered her voice again. "We have video of Jay Swanson's Kia Soul leaving Berto's office garage just after the 911 call came through on the so-called accident."

"Oh, crap! Berto said he remembered Jay talking to him right before the accident. Or right before he stopped remembering stuff."

"What did Berto say Jay wanted?"

"It was about getting information so Winston could send everyone some cool swag. Which Winston did, by the way." I debated telling her about the wine and CDs.

"Well, we traced the 911 call on the incident to Swanson's cell phone, and now, he's dead."

"Shit. Now what?"

"That's a good question."

"He must have seen something." I bit my lip. "That doesn't mean he's connected to Ochoa's death, does it?"

Isabel paused. "Not necessarily, but it's likely."

"Look, Isabel, I want to stay focused on who tried to off Berto. It's looking ugly on this end, and I want to nab this son of a bitch so badly, I can't see straight. I don't know if it'll help on the Ochoa case, but I'm mostly treading water on that one."

"Fine," Iz said. "As for Berto's case, I did a little digging on Sims. Talked to his pastor and some of the church group. They want nothing to do with him. Sorry, but that's as dead an end as a three-day-old stiff."

"Shit. You think Sims' mom could have bought the paint?"

"If she did, you're the one who's going to have to go after her."

I swallowed as my gut clenched. "I think I'll wait 'til some of the other suspects dry up."

"Well, given that I've got free rein to go after the Swanson killer, do what you want for Berto. Keep me up to date and I'll check in with DeVine, too."

I couldn't help sniggering. "What? Afraid I'll be too blinded by his magnificence?"

Iz chuckled too. "Ah. You've talked to him in person. Nah. I just figure being a cop will get me further than you as a PI."

"Good point. Okay. You know. I just had a thought. Winston was pushing me to talk to his manager, Leo McKesson, about Swanson. Maybe I'll do that next. Can't hurt."

"Sure. Why not? Talk to you later."

"Talk to you later."

I hung up and dialed Leo McKesson's mobile number. What the heck, I had it. He actually picked up, which so startled me I had a hard time getting my first question out – which is probably why I asked about Larry Ochoa first, instead of Jay Swanson.

"I'm headed to the gym right now," he said. "Why don't you meet me there? I can get you a guest pass."

"Um, I'm not set up to work out right now. I don't mind talking to you while you do," I replied. Okay, I was trying to be accommodating. Berto always said that when a subject was willing to talk it was best to go with it in whatever way they wanted to.

I got directions to McKesson's gym – one of those hoity-toity places along Santa Monica Boulevard on the eastern edge of West Hollywood. Okay, so McKesson didn't seem the type to want to work out with all the pretty boys (straight and gay) in WeHo, but I wasn't going to question it. It actually made sense once I got there. When I caught up with him, he was working out bare-chested and it turned out the broad shoulders were on top of some seriously ripped abs. We're talking the full six-pack here.

If the body thing wasn't enough, he was bench pressing some huge amount of weight. Without a spotter, which I know is stupid, only it was pretty obvious that McKesson was all about the showing off. I waited until he was done throwing metal around and had moved on to the treadmill.

"Hey, Daria," he said with barely a gasp as he ran.

"Hey, Leo," I answered. I somehow doubted he'd called me by my first name to be friendly and cozy, which is why I made a point of calling him by his.

"What can I do for you? Something about Larry Ochoa?" There was something strained about his indifference.

"I was wondering if you knew if Larry had a will, or about his ex-wife."

"Why would I know that?" He glared straight ahead.

I grabbed for the first thought I could find. "Luke said that you handled a lot of the business stuff for the band members."

"I handle lots of stuff."

"Do you know where Larry got his divorce?"

"Not really."

"How about the will?"

McKesson continued glaring straight ahead. "Why should that make any difference? His death was an accident, right?"

"Well, we were called in on the possibility that it wasn't. Do you know if he had a will?"

"Nope."

I shifted. He had seemed pretty open about talking to me on the phone.

"What about Jay Swanson?" I finally asked.

"What about him?"

"We think he might have seen something when he went to talk to Berto Esparza about swag from Luke. Did he talk to you about it?"

"Why would Jay talk to me about that?"

"I don't know. That's why I'm asking you."

"Well, you're asking the wrong person. I didn't have much to do with Jay. To tell you the truth, I would've fired that kid's ass the first time he messed up." For the first time, McKesson glanced at me. "I don't know why Luke wanted to keep him around. He was next to useless. Luke's like that. Finds a homeless puppy and keeps trying to fix him. You have any other questions for me?"

I was clearly being dismissed. I debated hanging around a bit longer just to piss him off but couldn't see any benefit to it.

"If I have any more, I'll touch base with you," I said.

I lingered a second longer for no good reason other than busting up his power game, which, by the way, failed miserably. I so know better than to buy into that kind of bullshit, and yet I always do.

As I hit the sidewalk, my phone rang. Luke Winston's phone number flashed on the screen. Not who I wanted to talk to, nor someone I could push off, either.

"Hey, Luke," I said after sliding the phone on.

"Hey, Daria," he said with forced cheerfulness. "What are you doing for lunch today?"

I sighed silently. "Do you want to meet?"

"I'd like that. I'm up in the Valley today. Have to do a taping at the Burbank Studios later."

Figures - the very place next on my list. "Okay. Where do you want to meet?"

He named a coffee shop on Ventura. "I'll buy lunch. That is, if it's not going to take you too far out of your way."

"No. I have to go up to Burbank Studios, myself," I said, then winced at letting that slip.

"Great," he said, and then said good-bye shortly after.

I made it to Ventura and Laurel Canyon in record time. Luke was waiting for me. The place was like any other coffee shop/diner, with vinyl booths, faux wood laminate tables, paper placemats and a menu that features lovely standards such as meat loaf and chicken fried steak. It even offered pot roast, so I ordered that, which raised Luke's eyebrows.

"I'd've figured you for a cobb salad girl," he said with a sly grin.

I smiled back, charmed against my will. "Actually, that was my second choice."

Luke opted for the chicken caesar salad.

We made small talk until the waiter (a simply gorgeous young Hispanic kid who had actor written all over him) brought us our food.

"What did you want to talk to me about?" I asked.

"I guess I wanted to know if you have any updates on Larry's murder," Luke said.

I smiled weakly. "It has been slow going. We did confirm that Larry's wife did put down a Danny Pacheco as her daughter's father on the birth certificate. We haven't been able to find any evidence that she and Larry were ever divorced. It doesn't mean they weren't, but if they never got around to it, and there's no will stipulating otherwise, then she's his first heir, which gives her a motive. It's possible, too, her father was in Los Angeles the day that Larry was murdered. We haven't really gotten much further. We're also trying to get a line on who killed Jay Swanson, although both the Sheriff's and LAPD are working that case."

"That's what I was told."

"Who are you doing your taping for?" I asked, trying to change the subject.

"Randy Witter's show," Luke said. "It's that new late night one."

"Yeah. I heard about that."

"What are you doing up at the studios?"

"Talking to Sophie Reisner," I said, then inwardly slapped my forehead with my hand. That was the second time that day I'd let something slip that I shouldn't have.

"Sophie Reisner. I'll be." Luke chewed, mulling something over. "I remember her."

"You do?" I asked. "Since when?"

Luke chuckled. "It was a number of years back when she was working in Winston-Salem. She was doing a local boy does good story on me or tried to. Not sure why we didn't connect, but she found some footage of an interview I'd done for a syndicating outfit and ran with that."

"Yeah. I've got a friend who does those kinds of interviews," I said. "Small stations buy their footage all the time."

"Yeah, except that the reporters don't cut in shots of themselves asking the questions," Luke said. "Plus, it was an interview we hadn't cleared or something. Leo knows the details of that part better than I do. I just know that I'd remembered doing the interview, just not seeing someone as cute and pert as her asking me the questions. Leo raised a stink about it, only it didn't seem to hurt her career."

It certainly hadn't. Reisner's cheery smile and blonde layered bob decorated the sides of buses all over the Los Angeles area, not to mention billboards, bus stops and just about anything else the local network affiliate could pay money to stick it on. Berto's notes from his investigation that previous summer said that her resume had checked out and that most of her bosses after her problem in Winston-Salem were perfectly fine with her work. Or her D-cups, only that wasn't exactly easy to prove.

Luke talked some more about his upcoming taping. I didn't really listen. How was I going to find out where Reisner had been the Monday night before and how was I going to prove it? I'd done so well with Leo McKesson. Then I thought about Marisol's fearful look through the windows of her home and saw her kids' faces, ecstatic and gleeful that their daddy was home from the hospital, and I began to get really angry again.

I left Luke at the diner soon after and headed toward the TV station studios off Riverside Drive, fueling my resolve with freshly stoked anger.

If Sophie Reisner had been behind hurting Berto, she was going to seriously regret it and I was the one who was going to make that happen. Well, that's what I told myself as I introduced myself to the guard at the studio parking lot. Not that the guard cared. He called Reisner's office to see if it was okay to let me in and I braced myself for the refusal. It didn't happen. That was odd, but I decided to go with it. Bored, the guard got my driver's license information down, wrote something on a clipboard, then slid a permit on my dashboard over my steering wheel and directed me to the visitor's parking area.

If it weren't for the gigantic satellite dishes, you'd never know that a there was a television studio here. It looked like just about any other industrial complex I'd ever seen. The buildings were utterly boxy with horizontal black stripes of windows. The parking lot was overflowing, even including a few of the station's news vans parked along the perimeter of the parking lot.

I drove around back, where a huge loading dock door gaped open. Inside, you could see huge wood-backed set backdrops stacked next to the wall and hefty men in sloppy t-shirts and jeans hanging around, looking bored. They probably weren't. The reality of the entertainment biz is that there is a fair amount of hanging around waiting for others to do their jobs.

Reisner's office was a bit further on, up through the office portion of the studio. It was a testament to how much the station was paying her that she had her own office with a real door and a secretary, too. I did not envy the sweet young thing at the desk in front of Reisner's office. She had mounds of fluffy brown hair and a worried frown on her face. As soon as I told her who I was, she grabbed her phone and made a call.

"The person from Esparza Investigations is here," she told the person on the other end. She paused, then nodded and said, "I will."

She hung up and smiled pathetically at me.

"Ms. Reisner says she'll meet you in Studio B," she said, getting up. "I'll take you right there."

The assistant scurried off and I had to move quickly to keep up with her. We found Reisner in the studio, as stated. The anchorwoman was shorter than you'd think, especially considering the super high heels on the platform pumps that she was wearing. The famed D-cups poufed out her off-white silk blouse and her dark blue skirt was straight. She was talking to someone wearing a headset as we came into the studio. She glanced at me, dismissed me, then went on talking to the man wearing the headset for a few minutes until she realized that her assistant was there, also.

"I thought you said Esparza was here," Reisner snapped.

The assistant pointed to me, and Reisner looked me over with a glare.

"Why isn't Berto here?" she demanded.

"He's recovering from a serious accident," I said. "I'm filling in for the time being."

She glared. "You could have come over a little more camera-ready."

"Excuse me?" I looked down at my pink and white striped oxford shirt and tan slacks, which I was wearing under my peacoat, as usual. The shirt wasn't camera-friendly by a long shot, but why would she want me on camera?

"The interview," Reisner growled. "You're here about the interview, aren't you? I need it for the story I'm doing on celebrity stalking. Berto said he'd come over as soon as he could. We don't have that long before sweeps are over."

It took me a second to decipher what she was saying. She was referring to the advertising sweeps period, which happens every May, November, and February. This is the time that ratings really count in the TV biz because that's when advertising rates are set. Needless to say, Reisner wanted something with some real zing to punch up the station's numbers and celebrity stalking was one of those stories that had zing.

"Um, I'm not here to be interviewed," I told her. "I do want to ask you a few questions, though."

"No, damn it!" Reisner's voice rose although it stayed just shy of a shriek. "I need an expert and I need one now. Take off that shirt. We'll find something in wardrobe, and I'll have to send you to make-up right away."

"I'm not going anywhere," I said, firmly. "I'm here investigating Berto's accident, and I need to ask you a few questions. Is there someplace where we can talk privately?"

"I don't have time for this," Reisner complained.

"Well, I can ask you about Berto investigating you last summer in front of all these people," I said.

Reisner gasped. Nonetheless, I could see her weighing out having a tantrum or giving in and talking to me. She shut her mouth, then smiled.

"Tell you what, you give me my expert quotes and I'll answer any question you have."

There was nothing I wanted to do less. Then I also thought about the business Berto could lose by not doing the interview.

"Can we do a stand up outside?" I asked. I really did not want to go through make-up and wardrobe.

Reisner quickly thought it over. "All right. Let's go to my office." She nodded at the guy wearing the headset. "Reilly, set up a handheld and mike for me."

She led me back to her office. It was one of those modern spaces that was all about her. A credenza behind the glass-topped desk held several tape boxes. The steel blue walls were filled with pictures of Reisner with various celebrities and a few politicians. There was one award plaque among all the photos and a Ficus tree in the corner.

"All right. Ask," she demanded, folding her arms as she stood in front of her desk.

"Where were you a week ago, Monday night around 6 p.m.?" I asked.

"I was on the air," she said.

Well, duh. I should have thought of that.

"I guess I'll have to confirm that," I said. "Why did you call Berto recently, when you were so pissed off about him investigating your background last summer?"

Reisner rolled her eyes. "He's an expert on celebrity stalking and I need the story."

An earnest young man burst into the office. He was wearing a blue chambray work shirt and jeans, still it was clear from Reisner's reaction that he was the boss.

"Sophie, what is this?" he demanded. "You want next Monday night off also? You were off Monday a week ago."

Reisner glanced at me with a scared look on her face. "I've got vacation time. Why can't I take it a day at a time?"

"Yeah. Once a month."

"Uh, Bob, can we talk about this later? I'm prepping an interview for that celebrity stalking story you wanted."

Bob looked at me, glared at Reisner, then stormed out.

I grinned. It was simply pure luck that I caught that break, but these things do happen.

"Uh, Ms. Reisner, didn't you just tell me a minute ago that you were on the air a week ago Monday night?" I asked.

"Oh, that Monday." She stopped and flopped into her desk chair. "I wasn't really thinking straight. I am usually on the air at six every weeknight."

"Uh huh." I waited.

"Well, I am."

"True. You also want me to believe that you got your days mixed up and I'm willing to bet you didn't. You simply lied to me."

"I wasn't hurting Berto," Reisner said, defensively. "Although he damned near hurt me with that investigation."

"Your resume checked out, and the article that started

it got pulled," I said.

Reisner sighed. "Look, I can't tell you where I was that Monday night. I'll lose my job."

"Oh, come on," I growled.

"I'm serious." Reisner glared at the office wall behind me. She suddenly sniffed. "I want you to understand, I'm damned good at what I do. I do most of my own reporting. I write my scripts. I'm here because I'm the best there is in this town." She paused. "But I can't tell you who I was with that Monday night. Let's just say that any stories I do about sexual harassment hit more than a little close to home."

"You do realize that sexual harassment is illegal, don't you? At the very least, if you're that good, you can go to another station."

Reisner snorted. "As if that would make any difference. It doesn't matter where I go. Network executives decide that because I'm cute, pert, and blonde, I must be easy. My former bosses have leaked just enough to their cronies to make sure my rep follows me everywhere. I've earned this job the hard way, and I don't mean on my back. That doesn't mean network executives won't take advantage of me."

I nodded. I mostly believed her, even though I knew actresses who could have sounded just as sincere and hurt. Which is why I didn't scratch her off the suspect list. I also did the interview outside. I had to give Reisner points. She asked the right questions, such as why people stalk celebrities (several reasons, but the scary one is erotomania), and how celebrities can stop it (not easily when they're required to put themselves out there to get jobs).

I was heading back to my car when Jean, the receptionist from Luke Winston's office, saw me from the back of the studio and waved me over. Her dark blonde hair had been scooped back into a ponytail and she was wearing a gray skirt suit.

"Hi, Ms. Barnes," she said with a shy smile as I walked up.

"Everything okay?" I asked.

"Oh, sure," she said. "Mr. Winston just asked me to find you. He said you were on the lot today. Anyway, they're going to start the taping soon, and he said he'd asked you to come see it and you'd said you would."

"He did?" I cast my mind back to our lunch earlier that afternoon. I vaguely recalled mumbling that I wouldn't mind seeing the taping. "Yeah. I'm sorry. It slipped my mind."

"We've got seats," Jean said, gesturing toward the studio. "Really primo ones." She giggled. "I love Randy Witter. This is going to be so much fun. He's hysterical"

"So I've heard," I said. "How did you get away from the front office?"

"I'm subbing until they find Jay's replacement," Jean said, leading me into the cool, slightly darkened audience seating. "It's not a job I want, but it is kind of cool to get away for a change. Here we are."

The metal bleachers in the studio were already filled with audience members who had probably been waiting all day for the taping. A warm-up guy was yukking it up and getting the audience to practice cheering for Witter. I'd seen the show and had not been impressed. Still, it was a network gig and that's where Luke needed to be to sell music.

He was the last guest on - they always have the musicians last. I can't tell if it's because it's tough to interview a whole band at once or if it's that a lot of musicians are not the most articulate folks out there. That being said, they did save time to talk to Luke Winston after his first number. I have to hand it to Luke, that first number was a good, lively, feel-good tune that had the audience clapping and even dancing along.

They stopped the tape for a commercial insert as Luke made his way over to the guest couch. A stagehand handed Luke an acoustic guitar and Luke strummed it to check for tuning, then slid the guitar behind the couch. Oooh. We were getting a surprise second number. I hadn't realized the show was running that far ahead, but then the earlier segment, with the latest pretty boy shilling for a new film I was not going to see, can't have run that long because said pretty boy was an inarticulate moron.

Luke, once they got back to the taping part, was darned articulate, regaling the audience with a silly story about how he and his band got stuck out in the middle of bumfuck Egypt (my term) one night and Luke had to learn how to drive an over-sized bus to get them back on schedule or some such thing. It was inane as hell. Luke told it well, and the audience ate it up. Then Randy Witter segued into a push for Luke's latest album and "talked" Luke into singing something special.

The tune was a sweet love ballad, and while Luke managed to pass his gaze toward several women in the audience, after a minute, I got the icky feeling he was focusing on me. It wasn't just my imagination. I saw one woman down the row glaring at me as if I'd swiped the attention she thought she should have been getting. Witter glanced up to be sure the camera wasn't on him, then squinted to see if he could see who Luke was singing to.

I sat up straight and tried to ignore it, although I was sure there were a few folks in the audience ready to alert the paparazzi. I kept my face blank in the perhaps vain hope that my next role wasn't going to be Luke Winston's new love interest. As soon as the final credits ran out on the studio monitors, I hauled my backside out of there and headed straight for my car.

I was crawling along home on the freeway when my mobile rang. Sure enough, it was Luke. I fumbled to get the phone on speaker.

"I hope you liked the taping," he said.

"Oh, yeah," I said. "It was fun."

"Did you like the song I did?"

"It was a lot of fun. Really lively. I was clapping along with everybody else," I said, even though I knew damned well that was not the song he was talking about. "I also had fun with that story you told about the tour bus."

"That." Luke almost gagged. "I tell that story every talk show I'm on. Leo keeps setting it up that way. I must have told it a hundred times. You'd think the fans would catch on, only they keep eating it up, so I guess Leo's right about telling it."

"Huh." I mentally scrambled for a way to get him off the phone and finally settled on the old losing signal gambit.

"Uh, Luke, you're breaking up. Why don't you call me tomorrow?"

It's a cheesy way out, but, hey, it worked.

"I'll do that," Luke yelled as I tapped the connection off.

I called Berto shortly after I got home and found some leftovers to heat up for dinner. There wasn't much to report, and while I probably shouldn't have said anything about Luke doing his creepy song thing, I did anyway. Berto laughed.

"Sounds like the client is getting sweet on you," he said.

"Ick. Isn't that unprofessional?" I said, toying with the old enchilada on my plate.

"Not from the client," Berto said. "It's only unprofessional if you take him up on it."

"Not likely."

"Good. Relax, Daria. It happens all the time. The client sees you as her savior and thinks she's falling in love."

"As I said before, ick."

"Keep that thought, *hermanita*."

"I will. Any chance you can connect me to the person you used to track down the shell company from the Wiedeman case? Maybe we can find out if it's Margolis who's trying to off you."

"I don't think so. He's got too many other ways to hurt me and hasn't used them. Trust me, he's not the hands-on type."

"Only one of the cars leaving the garage is owned by a Rottgutt, Inc. What if Margolis paid someone to hit you?"

"Huh. I'll email Jannie Miller," Berto said. "She's the best tracker there is. What's the company name again?"

"Rottgutt, Incorporated. I'll text you the spelling."

"Okay. Just don't expect much. Something tells me you need to focus on Jay Swanson."

"We know he saw something," I said swallowing some refried beans. I should have put more cheese on them before re-heating the plate, only there wasn't any cheese in the fridge. "He made the 911 call, you know."

"Exactly," Berto said. "Now you've got your next task in front of you."

"Okay."

We chit-chatted a bit longer until Tim called my landline. Tim and I didn't have much to say, either, but it was nice talking to him. I called him back when Randy Witter's show came on, and the two of us had a grand old time bashing the pretty boy. Then it was time for bed, and that's where I went.

Chapter Fifteen

Going to bed did me no good at all. I spent most of that night tossing and turning, or worse, dreaming vaguely malevolent dreams in which Berto or I or both of us got killed by a faceless killer. Nor was I in better shape when I finally got up and dressed. There was literally nothing to eat in the fridge or in my pantry. I felt like Old Mother Hubbard, except that the cats had food, both dry and canned. I sniffed the can of kitty tuna I'd opened. Turned out that I wasn't that desperate.

Fortunately, there's a Trader Joe's market on the way to the freeway, so I stopped there and picked up yogurt and granola for my breakfast and a wrap for lunch. Or dinner. Given my list for the day, it certainly looked like I was going to be eating more than one meal while behind the wheel of my CRV.

I at least got to eat breakfast at the office. I was slurping down my yogurt when Isabel called.

"Got news," she told me. "Jay Swanson's autopsy report is in, and Larry Ochoa's death is now officially a murder."

"What?" I asked.

"We had to re-open the Ochoa killing. The autopsy on Swanson showed up the exact same triangular contusions as on Ochoa's body, and Swanson was definitely murdered. He'd had the living daylights kicked out of him."

I thought about that. "There's no way they could make it out to be an accident?"

Isabel chuckled. "Well, the actual cause of death was Swanson aspirating on his vomit, and they found his shit all over the back section of his car. We're guessing that's where he died, and his bowels evacuated."

I looked at my granola and my stomach turned. "Uh, Iz.

I'm eating right now."

"So?"

"So how do I remind you that I'm not the hardened homicide detective you are?"

Isabel laughed out loud. "Oh, come on. I've told you worse stories over dinner."

"Maybe, but not as real as this one. I'd met Swanson. He was a nice kid."

"Sure seems like it." Isabel's tone softened. "Still, it's good news about Ochoa getting re-opened, isn't it?"

"Yeah." I yawned. "Are you calling me to tell me to stay out of it?"

"Not really. Do you have any thoughts on it?"

"Besides it being a really stupid way to murder someone?"

"Most murders are stupid ways to kill someone. How do you mean?"

"Okay. You already made this point. They were on one side of the cyclorama, you know those really big backdrops. A whole army of people standing around are on the other. That catwalk was probably visible from where everybody was. If just one person looked up at the wrong moment, game over. Why risk it?"

"Act of desperation. Or maybe it was an accident. The killer and Ochoa go up to the catwalk to have a conversation, it gets heated, blows struck, and Ochoa goes over." Isabel paused. "Besides, you don't know that the catwalk was visible. You weren't on the scene."

"You were. Was it?"

"Fuck. I don't know."

I looked at my list. "I've got to talk to the guitarist today. Maybe he can tell me. Or maybe the set is still up, but I've gotten the impression it isn't."

"Impressions aren't going to help build a case." Isabel sighed. "I'll check on it, too. Maybe we'll catch someone changing his story."

We hung up shortly afterward. I wasn't going to be able to talk to guitarist Rick Kemper until later that afternoon, so I booted up my email on Berto's computer. Berto had emailed Jannie Miller, the digital tracking expert, and she'd already responded to the both of us, inviting me to call her at any time. Which is what I did, we connected, and I agreed to meet her as soon as I could get there at a coffee house on Sunset, just past Alvarado, an area that was just beginning to gentrify.

The coffee house had that comfortable, lived-in look. Various abstract masterpieces by local artists lined the brick walls. The upholstery on the sofas and easy chairs was faded, but clean and intact. Mis-matched wooden chairs surrounded several small round tables in various configurations. Spike bars lined the walls just above the furniture, though only a quarter of the outlets actually had something plugged into them. The tables all had some sort of cord trailing off them, with long rubber humps covering all the cords on the cement floor. Folk music softly played, interrupted by the loud hissing of the huge brass espresso machine as the balding old man, his arms covered in tattoos, steamed milk for each customer's order.

Miller was on the young side of thirty. Her wispy brown hair was mostly caught in a ponytail on the back of her head. She was seated at a table, slightly hunched over a laptop, so it was hard to say how tall she was. A tablet was on one side of the laptop and her smartphone was on the other. Her watch seemed a bit heavy for her slender wrist, and I saw her glance at it, then swipe something on the face. She returned to studying her laptop's screen and didn't look up until I was standing right next to her.

"Daria Barnes, huh?" Her smile was pleasant, and a little guarded. "Theatre impresario extraordinaire, sometime actor and columnist for Left Coast Stage News."

I groaned as I sat down. "You looked up my IMDB profile."

"That and Google. The only thing I hacked was your SAG profile." She leaned back in her chair. "None of the above, however, tells me why you're working as an investigator with Berto Esparza."

I sighed. "Because Equity - that's the stage actors union - says you can hire their actors without paying them union scale wages if the play goes on in theatres with ninety-nine seats or less."

Miller frowned. "Yeah?"

"Ninety-nine seats and under is considered a not economically viable venue. Great for showcasing talent. Not for making money. Even if you're the producer, you're only going to get a small share of whatever grant is funding the production. Which means I need to do other things to stay alive, including help Berto out now and again."

"Plus, your acting residuals are not currently enough to support a feral cat." Miller nodded and glanced at her laptop, then hunched over and scrolled for a moment. She shook her head. "Not him." She blinked and looked up at me. "Sorry. It's a potential target I'm keeping an eye on. Okay, you're moonlighting with Berto for economic reasons. That I get." She looked me up and down again.

"Do I need to show you my I.D.?" I asked.

"No." She didn't grin, but I still got the feeling she'd already seen a lot more than my Screen Actors Guild profile.

"Can you help me trace a shell corporation?"

Miller nodded. "Berto gave me the name. I went ahead and did a basic search. It's owned by a company in Belize, which is probably another anonymous shell. What are you looking for?"

"The person who tried to kill Berto by backing over him in a parking garage."

Miller gasped. "Is he okay?"

"He's pretty banged up. Broken legs, et cetera. Fortunately, he'll recover."

"I was wondering why he was using his home laptop." A guilty smile crossed her face. "I have to be careful. Folks sometimes try to get me to find people for the wrong reasons. I know Berto's IP addresses and his home address, so I was reasonably sure it was him emailing me. That's why I wanted to meet you face to face, though."

"That makes sense."

"All right. It'll probably take a couple of days to get through all the code. Decent odds the Belizean company was set up by a group that does nothing but set up shell companies. It's all perfectly legal unless you're using the shell for tax evasion."

"Among other things," I said. "Berto sometimes has his stalking victims set them up to make it harder for the stalkers to find them."

"A lot of celebrities do the same thing."

Something else from left field suddenly crossed my mind. "I wonder if the Bachners have one."

"Gunther Bachner, the TV producer?" Miller picked up her tablet and started tapping on it.

"Yeah. We're working a case for his wife," I said.

"You know his address or something?"

I gave it to her. Miller typed it in then grunted.

"I've gotta switch VPNs," she grumbled. "This one is so slow. Okay, here it is. Yep. The house is owned by Leland Associates, Inc., which is owned by..." She growled at the tablet again. "...a Belizean company. Huh. Got some of the same people on board as Rottgutt."

"You're kidding. That means—"

"Not much. Like I said, both companies were probably set up by the same outfit in Belize."

"Harrumph. We're also trying to find Lester Margolis."

Miller snorted merrily. "You and the rest of the hacking world. He's the new Carmen San Diego. He's up to something. I catch his code signature all the time. It's almost never from the same physical location twice."

"Odds he's behind what happened to Berto?"

"Limited. He's probably got more money than some small countries, at least he did before he disappeared. When I catch his signature, he's not stealing anything. Just making mischief. The only reason anybody wants to find him is for the challenge of it."

"That's what Berto figured. Only I need to eliminate him just to be certain. It's always possible he paid somebody to try and kill Berto."

Miller scrunched up her nose. "Possibly. Lester may be a spoiled brat, but he's not into petty revenge. He's a gamer, and the whole prison thing actually upped his profile in the hacking world. In some ways, Berto did him a favor when he put Lester away. Melanie hasn't heard a peep from him since."

"Melanie? That woman he got busted for stalking. What was her name? Wiedeman?"

"Yeah. We got to be good friends over the case. We have a lot in common and she's a riot."

"I remember hearing about the case. I wasn't involved," I said.

"It wasn't much." Miller sat up and glared at her laptop screen, then shook her head. She turned back to me. "I was the one who found out that Lester owned the shell company." She waved at the laptop. "Anyway, as soon as I'm done with my lookout shift here, I'll see what I can do to find out who owns that shell you're asking about."

"Thanks. Even if it isn't tied to Margolis, the company owns a car that was caught on tape leaving the scene. Along with about six others, sadly. I'm hoping it might lead us somewhere."

"Sure. Talk to you soon."

I left and went back to my CRV. As I started it up, I suddenly realized I hadn't left my phone number or anything with Miller. I debated going back, then realized she could find it without breaking a sweat.

I also decided to call on Melanie Wiedeman, just to verify what Miller had told me. The drive over to Pasadena took longer than the meeting did, and Wiedeman confirmed that she hadn't heard from anybody she didn't know in an awfully long time. As I left, I checked the time on my phone. My appointment with Kemper was about an hour and a half away. If I drove over to Hollywood at that moment, I'd probably be hanging around for at least a half hour, but if I didn't, I'd be sure to get stuck in traffic.

I ended up hanging around, writing up notes as I waited at the IHOP on Sunset, across from Hollywood High School. Kemper had asked to meet there and was about fifteen minutes late. He had long, light brown hair, a lean frame, and wire-rimmed glasses. His shirt was faded and plaid and his Levi's 501s were almost new and not only fit snugly across his backside, they were solidly pulled up to his waist and belted. The only hint that he had negative feelings about people different from himself was a slightly sullen droop to his mouth and the wary way his eyes darted everywhere, as if he expected someone to jump him at any second. I put my notes away as he entered the restaurant, then came my way without checking in with the host.

He demanded a cup of coffee from the waitress the second she appeared at the table. I requested a cup, myself, then asked Kemper if he wanted anything to eat.

"Nope," he said. As soon as the waitress had left, he leaned over and spoke softly. "You gotta be careful with the folks here. They'll spit on your food as likely as not."

"I'll keep that in mind," I said, trying to smile. "Anyway, as you know, I'm investigating Larry Ochoa's death."

"That was not good." Kemper sighed. "Larry was really good to me, and I wasn't always good to him. I feel really bad about his passing."

"As I understand it, you and Mr. Winston were working on an arrangement together that morning."

"Yeah. Turned out pretty nicely, too. Mr. Winston is a really good musician. We're both classically trained, too, so it makes it easier to work together."

"Did you speak to Mr. Ochoa at all that morning?"

"Early on. He was complaining about his coffee. Well, we were both joking about it. Funny thing is, now that I think about it, the coffee wasn't that bad that morning."

"I've been told he wasn't feeling that well."

"He was in a world of pain. His back had gone out on him the week before and he could barely move. We were all trying to get him to at least take some aspirin, but he was done with all of that. Would not touch any drug at all. Luke and I even joked that we should spike his coffee just to get something down him so he'd feel better."

Okay. I admit it. It went right past me. I did have another question I was really burning to ask. "Were you able to see the catwalk behind the backdrop from where you were?"

"Catwalk?" Kemper asked. "Oh, right. I guess there is one up there. I never really noticed it. Wait. That's where Larry fell from, isn't it?"

"Yes. You didn't happen to see him up there, did you?"

"Even if I was looking, I wouldn't have. Well, not normally. Larry was afraid of heights. That's why I was so sure he had started using again, even though it didn't make sense. It was the only way he'd get up on something that high, if you know what I mean."

Which didn't really bring me any closer to who had killed Larry Ochoa. We already knew he'd been murdered. It was interesting to know that he probably hadn't gotten up on the catwalk of his own free will. It didn't help much, yet it was interesting. I really wanted to see that space.

"Is the sound stage still set up?" I asked.

"Nah. We vacated right after Larry died. It was just too hard to work there." Kemper shifted. It looked like he, too, was feeling the loss. "We're still looking for a new sound stage."

He finished his coffee in a gulp, then looked around.

I took another sip of mine. "Well, I think I've got everything I need for the moment. Is there a number where I can reach you if I have additional questions?"

"Call Leo." He got up, stretched, and stalked off, his head swiveling here and there to make sure he was safe in this so dangerous spot.

I debated getting something to eat at the restaurant, but it's not my favorite place to eat. I'd only agreed to meet Kemper there because that was where he wanted to go. I headed back toward the office and the wrap I'd left there. Except Franny called. Since I was at a red light, I picked it up and put it on speaker.

"How close are you to Hollywood?" Franny asked.

"I'm on Sunset, trying to get past La Brea," I said.

"Turn around and go back to Highland," she said.

"All right," I said. If Franny said go, I would. I was getting it. "Do you mind if I ask why?"

"Don't sass me," she said. "Jay Swanson's mother is in town. She wants to talk to you."

"What? Why?"

"According to her, Mr. Winston said she should."

"That asshole."

"He is the client, and you know how I feel about that kind of language."

"Sorry," I grumbled.

"Here's the address."

It turned out the hotel was behind the big Hollywood and Highland complex, not the big Renaissance (or whoever they are these days). This was a tiny little inn tucked behind that behemoth. The decor was early 1960s and pale teal and sunshine yellow. The desk looked worn but was clean and neat.

The clerk sent me up to Mrs. Swanson's room. The woman who opened the door was of average height and fairly well-rounded. She still looked shrunken and bowed down.

"I'm Daria Barnes," I told her.

"Oh. Mr. Winston said you were looking into Jay's— Jay's—"

"Yes, I am," I said, even though I really wasn't. "How can I help you?"

She led me into the room. It was your basic motel room, with the bonus of a veranda, and the sun was shining. She pushed the gauzy curtains away from the sliding glass door and led me outside.

"We don't get sun like this in Wilmington," she said, sagging into a deck chair.

"Wilmington?" I sat on the chair next to her.

"Delaware. My family has been there since colonial times. When I finally left Jay's father, I took the kids home with me."

"How many brothers and sisters did Jay have?"

She smiled softly. "Two sisters, both younger. I think that's what finally gave me the strength to leave Earl. Jay wouldn't let anyone pick on them, even Earl. Here was this scrawny 12-year-old, standing up to this huge beast of a man." Her eyes filled and she closed her eyelids tight, trying to hold back the tears.

"Did Jay have any contact with his father after you left?'

"Off and on," Mrs. Swanson said, recovering herself. "The girls have done better with Earl, reconciliation-wise, though that's not saying much. Earl has sort of figured out he wasn't the best of fathers, but he's still very, very angry. I'm always amazed that Jay didn't pick up the same anger. He's been surprisingly healthy that way. That may have been the counseling."

"Counseling?"

Mrs. Swanson nodded and took a deep breath. "Yeah. Um. I may as well start at the beginning. Then maybe why I called you here will make more sense." She pressed her eyes closed again, sniffed, then got a hold of herself. "Earl was violent almost from the beginning. I keep thinking I should have seen the signs - the jealousy, the anger, blaming everyone else but himself for his problems. Toward me, he was very gentle, very attentive. He never really hit me until after the kids were born, just shoved me around and put me down. A lot. He never touched the kids when they were infants. Then when Jay turned four, Earl would start slapping him for the least little thing. He constantly yelled at me, putting me down, telling me I was worthless. He moved us to Virginia, early on, which had the effect of separating me from my family. Jay was five when Earl hit me the first time. Earl was so apologetic and swore he'd never do it again, which he didn't for a couple years. When he did it again, I took the kids and moved out. Earl started stalking me, although when we were face to face, he was so sweet. I don't know why, but I gave in and went back to him. It was fine for a month or two and then things got really bad. Work was going badly for Earl, which didn't help. I wanted to leave, only Earl made it clear that if I did, he'd find me and hurt the kids. Finally, when Jay was 12, and standing up to his father to protect his sisters, I found a shelter for abused women and their families. We had to stay in hiding for almost a year, and then we were able to get back to Wilmington to my family. Earl would try to harass us even then. He finally caught on and eventually it stopped. He's tried to make up to the kids a few times. As I said, the girls are a little more open to listening to him. Jay, not so much. Jay told me a week or so ago that Earl had called him. Earl's job took him out here and he wanted to meet with Jay, but

Jay said no. Apparently, Earl was pretty angry about it and made some threats."

"Ah," I said. "Is it possible that your ex-husband could have attacked Jay?"

She looked straight at me. "I wouldn't be a bit surprised. The problem is, I have no reason to believe he did, let alone any proof. I don't want to be the hysterical mom, pointing fingers and all that. That's the fastest way I know to get blown off. Besides, if it wasn't Earl, then turning him into the cops with no good reason isn't going to make him any easier to deal with. May even set him off."

"Do you know how to contact him?"

She nodded.

"Have you heard from him recently?"

"No. He won't talk to me, which, frankly, is fine." She winced. "I don't want to hate him. I don't want the kids to hate him. The counselors, both in Virginia and in Wilmington, were wonderful about helping the kids see their dad as a very hurt person. Me, I'm slowly slouching toward forgiveness, too. It's not an easy thing to forgive. Mostly because of what he did to the kids. If he— he—" She pressed her eyes shut and let out a sob. Her hand covered her mouth and she trembled.

I reached over and rubbed her shoulder. She eventually took a deep breath and nodded.

"This is good information," I told her. "I can't say for certain, but right now it doesn't look like your ex was involved in Jay's death. I will pass this on to the police and they will have to look at your ex."

She nodded. "I understand. It's going to hurt like hell, but it'll be better to know."

I left shortly after, Earl Swanson's contact information in hand and my stomach grumbling loudly. I still had my wrap sandwich back at the office, only traffic was starting to pile up. That meant it would be even longer before I could get something to eat. I found a rather ratty pizza parlor that produced some amazingly good pizza, sighed over my waistline's coming expansion, and ate like a pig.

It was getting on for five o'clock by that point and I

debated even going into the office. It's not that I was trying to avoid overtime. It's just that folks aren't around as much after the working day is through. Plus, I really needed to get some groceries.

There was one more thing on my list. I called Sgt. Olsen, of the El Centro P.D. He was as vague as ever.

"There's kind of a problem," Olsen said. "Julio can't account for his whereabouts on February 11. He was supposed to be at a rally and never showed."

"That's not good," I said. "Any idea where he was on Monday, February 18?"

"He says he was home. Decent odds. Concepcion also told me he was."

"Huh." I tapped my notepad with my pen. "Okay. Well, thanks for the information. Might be worth getting a fix on his whereabouts. The police officially opened up Ochoa's death as a murder case. Turns out some of the autopsy findings matched another victim's. Also, the victim was connected to Ochoa."

"Really?"

"Kid named Jay Swanson. Worked as Luke Winston's personal assistant. They found him the same day as I was down there. In fact, it might be worth checking on Camacho's whereabouts the Tuesday and Wednesday before."

"That's not good. Do you know who's working the case?"

"Detective Isabel Lancaster, with the L.A.P.D., and Detective DeVine Williams, with the L.A. County Sheriff. Swanson was found in an unincorporated part of the county." I gave him their numbers, got his permission to have them call him and ended the call.

I looked at my notes and let out an annoyed grumble. Camacho wasn't alibied for Larry Ochoa's death, sort of alibied for the attack on Berto (which I wasn't certain was connected to Ochoa, anyway), and I had no idea if he was alibied for Jay Swanson. Given what the autopsy had turned up on both Swanson and Ochoa, it was almost a dead cert those two deaths were connected. Which also let Earl Swanson out, mostly, because there was no good reason for him to kill Ochoa. Unless Ochoa had caught him trying to hurt Jay.

I was about to call Tim Wing when my phone rang, and Luke Winston's number flashed on the screen. I seriously considered letting it go to voice mail, but at the last second, I caved.

"Hey, Luke," I said.

"Daria. Any developments?" he asked, sounding mostly cheerful.

"Yeah." I told him about Ochoa's case being re-opened and that there was some similar evidence connected to Swanson's death.

"Oooph." It sounded as though all the air in Luke's lungs escaped at once.

"The good news is that the cops have not asked me to back off yet," I told him. "I'm still looking into things. I appreciate you asking me to speak to Mrs. Swanson, too."

"I thought she might have some good information," Luke said. He sighed deeply again. "Actually, what I called for was to ask if you wanted to come to my place for dinner tonight. Maybe relax a little, that sort of thing."

I bit my lip. It was definitely time to set some boundaries.

"Uh, Luke, I appreciate the offer, only I, uh, have a date with my boyfriend tonight." I hated lying and thought the old "I already have a boyfriend" routine would be the easiest way to let him down.

"Oh. You never said you had a boyfriend," Luke answered.

Damn, he was persistent.

"Well, you know how it is. Trying to keep personal life and professional life separate."

"Yeah. I guess that would make sense."

"Besides, you are a client and I have to keep things ethical, if you know what I mean."

"Oh. Yeah. I suppose you do. Do you mind coming over for lunch tomorrow then? We can go over the case and I promise to keep it professional."

I did not want to put any money on that bet. Still, I

agreed and arranged to meet him at his place at one the next day. I debated calling Berto after that then decided I'd rather have some privacy before talking to him.

That meant my next problem was going to the grocery store. I knew I needed everything but wasn't sure what that meant in terms of which actual items were missing from the pantry. That's when I decided to call Tim. What was the point of having a boyfriend if you couldn't call him when your cupboard was bare?

Chapter Sixteen

Tim not only met me at the grocery store, he brought a list, came home with me, made dinner, and spent the night. I guess I hadn't lied to Luke after all. I wasn't able to discuss much of the case, so I decided to update Berto and Isabel the next morning after I got into the office. Isabel was grateful for the information and said that Sergeant Olsen had already called her. Camacho wasn't entirely alibied for Swanson, but he didn't really have a reason to kill Swanson. Given what we'd found at Swanson's apartment, it didn't make sense that Camacho would go over there first, then drop the body on Wednesday, especially if Camacho had to go back and forth from El Centro.

I was just finishing my update with Berto when Franny brought in the mail.

"Ah. Looks like that response from the sex products company came in," I told Berto, switching the phone to the speaker and opening the envelope. "The Bachner case. I had to send in the written request and all that."

"Oh, her," Berto grumbled. "What a piece of work she is."

"What the fuck?" I groaned. "Piece of work, indeed. She's the one who bought the dildo."

Berto burst into laughter. "Are you serious?"

"Yes." I thought. "The return address on the box was for the company she bought it from. That's how I knew to check with them. Only why would she buy something like this and pretend she had a stalker? The handwriting on the box matched the note."

"Somebody wants attention, I guess. Or maybe a handsome bodyguard to play around with."

"Who do you have that's butt ugly and mean?" I asked,

drumming my fingers on the desk.

"Given that it's her husband that's paying me, why don't we put this one on the back burner? Or better yet, you go scare her."

"What?"

"Set up a meeting, let her know you know she's stalking herself, then threaten to tell her husband. I'll put up good money, she'll cave. Then I'll write up the report from home and give Gunther a call. It'll give me something to do."

"Not excited about talking to her again. On the other hand, threatening her sounds like fun. I'll call you as soon as I've put the fear of God into her."

Berto laughed. "You are good at this, *hermana*. If you can, do it soon. I'm going out of my mind here."

"Bored, huh?" I couldn't help grinning. "Well, why don't we do something about it, like, let you do your own job for a change?"

"I'm paying you good money."

"If it doesn't get me killed, it's okay." I scrabbled through my notes. "All right. Why don't you see what you can dig up on the Ridley family? That was the Kramer case with the perp that escaped from rehab. Apparently, the Ridley family suddenly sold out and went up north to take care of her mother who had a stroke."

"Oh, yeah. That would be fun." Berto perked up. "Anyone else I can look up?"

"Sophie Reisner? Maybe we should check her financials to see if she has a connection to Rottgutt, Incorporated."

"Reisner," Berto mumbled slowly - he was apparently writing this down. "Ridley. How about Camacho and what's his name, the geek from hell?"

"Lester Margolis. He's probably in the wind," I said with a chuckle. "Jannie Miller called him the new Carmen San Diego."

"Well, if Jannie can't find him, I'm not going to try."

"And is there some way you can find out who paid cash for some paint at a Lowe's in Pacoima?"

"Who the fuck do you think I am? Albus Dumbledore?" Berto had clearly been reading to the kids again.

"Couldn't hurt to ask. I told you about the receipt, didn't I?"

"I think so. But tracing a cash transaction. Not happening, Daria. You'll have to check with Sims' mama on your own."

Something I so did not want to do.

I glanced at the time on the desk clock. "It's getting on for 10. If I'm going to scare Tiffany Bachner into a confession, then I'd better get cracking. I have to be at Luke Winston's place by one. He wants me to have lunch with him."

"That doesn't sound good."

"I gave him the ethics speech. He promised to keep it professional. I'm not betting he will, still, it's only fair to give him a chance."

"Daria, if anybody knows how to set boundaries, you do. Have fun."

"You, too."

Berto grumbled and cursed out his physical therapist. He was sounding a lot better and at least the therapy was getting him out of the house every day. While I strongly suspected that Marisol was going to give me utter hell for giving Berto some work to do, I had the feeling it was the best thing for him. For both of them, actually. Berto's not exactly your model patient.

Fortunately, Tiffany Bachner agreed to meet me at a Starbucks in West Hollywood. We found a table outside on the patio. The sun was shining, although there was rain on the way. The air was pleasantly cool, and there was that nice gentle warmth of sunlight across my back.

Bachner, however, was dressed for a frigid winter in Alaska, in a white puffy jacket, designer jeans artistically ripped and high platform shoes. She also wore a pink fluffy snow cap and matching scarf. I remembered her sweater from our last meeting and found my opening.

"Pretty hat," I said as we settled into our seats. "Where did you get it?"

"I made it," She smiled, blushing becomingly. "I started knitting right after I married Gunther."

"Must be getting pretty bored with it by now," I said.

"Oh, no," she said. "It's been what I've really needed, what with this horrible stalker and all."

I grinned. "You've gotten better at acting."

"Thank you." She paused. "Why do you say that? I haven't really done anything recently."

"You put on a great performance last week when you gave me that box."

"I did not!" She got flustered. "I mean, I was really in shock. I mean, who wouldn't be, getting a dildo through the mail?"

"Funny you should mention that." I really had to struggle to keep from laughing hysterically. "We didn't know what was in the box when you gave it to me. Now, all of a sudden, you know. See, while the company you bought it from promises complete discretion, in the cases of stalkers, they can divulge who a customer is. Which is why I have a paper trail showing that there was a significant concern, and how I know that you bought the dildo, yourself."

"Somebody must have used my name." She sat back defensively.

"Forget it, Tiffany. You already blew it when you let me know you knew what was in the box. We've got you cold, girl."

Tiffany blinked. Decent odds the tears were for real.

"You don't get it," she said, finally. "Gunther doesn't care about me. He just likes having someone pretty around. He can't, well, you know. What's a girl to do? If I leave him, I'm out on my ass with nothing."

"I'm pretty sure cheating on him will land you on your ass, too," I said. "If he can't have sex with you, then you've got a case for support that might override the prenup. Check with a lawyer. If you've got enough discretionary cash that you can fake a stalking, then you've probably got enough for a consultation. Just don't jerk me and Berto around because you want your husband to pay attention to you. Or a hunky bodyguard plaything. Now, you've got two choices. Either you back off and we tell Gunther that we've got the perp taken care of, or you keep playing games and we tell Gunther everything. What's it going to be?"

She sighed heavily. "I'll back off."

"Good." I pulled one of Berto's cards from my notepad. "Tell you what. You behave, let us get the report in and get our check. If you're still good, call Berto and we'll get you a good lawyer. Just stay straight in the meantime. You fooled me once, but, honestly, Tiffany. You're not that good an actress and we both know it."

I got up and took off.

There was just enough time to get over to Luke's place. It was in a high-end residential hotel off Sunset, not far from Doheny, one of those tall, older buildings that got rehabbed instead of torn down, with turrets at the top corners. Luke had half the top floor for his unit, and the first thing you saw as you walked into the place was a row of windows overlooking Santa Monica Boulevard and points south. It being a clear day in February, that meant quite a vista. From the turret in the far corner, you could even see Century City and the ocean beyond, including the first clouds of the coming storm gathering on the horizon.

The room was decorated in a casual modern style, with warm browns and yellows. The art on the walls was mostly impersonal florals and landscapes. Not cheap, but not terribly interesting, either. The only signs that this was Luke's personal space was a corner of the living room given over to a violin and three guitars, with a music stand and small table, with sheets of staff paper strewn all over.

Luke hung close until I requested the use of his bathroom. He showed me through his bedroom - a very messy place with clothes all over and the bed unmade - to the huge, marbled bathroom. Notepaper and sticky notes littered the counters and mirrors, along with open magazines. As I washed my hands, I noticed a prescription bottle. I shouldn't have. I picked it up and read the label. It was for Vicodin. The same stuff that had been in Larry Ochoa's system when he died.

Was it possible that Luke had actually spiked Ochoa's coffee instead of joking about it as Kemper had said? Even if he did, did that mean he'd killed Ochoa? More importantly, did I want to confront Luke about it alone in his apartment?

I decided not. I'd left my coat in the CRV. There was still my mobile phone. I texted Tim, asking him to call me and play along.

As it turned out, I wasn't alone in the apartment with Luke. When I got back to the living room, there was a short, busty woman with blonde curly hair caught back in a ponytail. She was glaring at Luke.

"Oh. Now I see why you wanted me here," she told him while looking me over.

She was wearing black yoga pants over her slim butt, with flip flops on her feet and a baggy gray long-sleeved t-shirt on top. Her face may have been scrunched up in a glare, but her brownish eyes had a glint of amusement in them, and no makeup.

Her next glance was aimed at the table Luke had set up near the center of the room. While I'd been in the bathroom, he'd added a pair of candles and a bowl of flowers. Soft, romantic music drifted out of a sound system somewhere.

"I thought we were going to keep this professional." I glared at Luke, as well.

He wilted like a puppy caught piddling in the wrong place. I've seen basset hounds that looked less woebegone.

"Uh, Daria, this is my ex-fiancée, Felicity Whiting," he said, finally. "Felicity, Daria Barnes."

Felicity came over and shook my hand.

"Pleasure," she said, smiling warmly. "Nice to meet Luke's new girlfriend, which is why I assume he brought us both here today."

"Except I'm not his girlfriend," I said, flashing Luke yet another glare. "He's my client. My boss was hired to investigate the death of Larry Ochoa. By Luke."

Felicity's eyebrow lifted. "I'm glad he decided to do that much."

There was something odd in her tone, although I couldn't make out what. Fortunately, Tim was right on cue. The ringing phone echoed in the silence.

I pressed it on. "Hey."

"I'm calling, just like you asked," Tim said, sounding somewhat worried.

"Good," I said. "I knew I could count on you."

"Can you tell me what this is about?"

"No. Not yet."

"Are you in immediate danger?"

"Nah. I guess I can do it. I'll see you in a few. Bye." I clicked off. I smiled at Luke and Felicity. "Hate to bag on lunch and the reunion, but I've gotta go. Mr. Winston, I'll call you later."

I was still shaking when I got back to my CRV. I called Tim back right away, stopping only to slide the phone onto its mount, then put it on speaker, so I could drive away as far and as fast as I could.

"Are you okay?" Tim asked breathlessly after picking up on the first ring.

"I'm fine. Thanks for calling, though. It was even worse than I thought."

"What happened?" Tim almost shrieked.

"I found some evidence in someone's place. I didn't think he was a suspect, only now I have to think he is, and I can't say more because of client confidentiality. It doesn't make any sense. I think I was set up to get between him and his girlfriend. I'm just so glad you called when you did. It got me out of there."

"Daria, are you sure you're safe?"

"Pretty sure. Thanks for being there, Tim. I really appreciate it."

"I love you, Daria. Don't get killed on me, okay?"

"I'll do my best. Listen, I've got to call Berto."

"You do that."

"I love you, Tim. Thanks."

I called Berto next. The bastard laughed when I told my tale.

"Luke did not kill Larry Ochoa. He hired us, remember? People who want to get caught leave clues. They do not hire private investigators."

I had found my way to the Hollywood branch of the L.A. Public Library and was sitting in the parking lot.

"What about the Vicodin?" I asked.

"How reliable is Kemper?"

"How am I supposed to know? I'm new at this."

"Get together with Isabel and confront Winston over the drug. Like you said, it's possible he did spike Ochoa's coffee with it, but that doesn't mean he killed Ochoa. Besides, people saw him on stage the entire time Ochoa was missing. If Winston spiked the coffee, he's probably feeling very guilty right now."

"That makes sense." I swallowed. "Wait. Luke has a motive. He recently broke up with Whiting, and it was supposedly over Ochoa and her having an affair."

"Something else to ask him when you and Isabel confront him. If he did kill Ochoa, this would be the first time I've even heard of someone calling in an investigator on himself."

"Maybe he had someone else do it and wants us to find that person, and not him."

"He's being pretty sloppy about it then. Are you okay?"

"Getting there."

"Good move having Tim call you, only next time, have me do it, please?"

"That would have been a good idea. I guess I got rattled."

"It happens, but you'll learn. Did you talk to Tiffany Bachner yet?"

"Oh, yeah." I blew my breath out and found myself chuckling as I relayed to Berto my conversation with the former actress.

Berto laughed, too, told me I'd done a good job and said he'd send Gunther the report and the invoice.

"Um," I said. "I just thought. Shouldn't that go through Franny?"

"Ye-es," Berto said. "Thank you for reminding me." He paused. "Any ideas on how to tell her I'm getting some work done?"

"Uh, no. Have you told Marisol yet?"

Berto sounded guilty. "She caught me looking up Reisner's financials."

"How badly does she hate me now?"

"Well, she was mad at first, but I haven't bugged her for

two hours now, so she should be cooling off."

"Franny's going to be harder," I said. "You're not bugging her every five minutes."

"Maybe if I send the report through you and you give it to her."

"She'll know it was you. I don't know how to do a final report yet. You are her boss, you know."

"Tell her that." He sighed. "All right. I'll call her."

"*Mas tarde, hermano.* And thanks"

"You're welcome, *hermanita.*"

No sooner had I hung up than my phone rang again. I didn't recognize the area code, let alone the number, and almost let it go to voice mail. Instead, I slid it on and sort of grunted something resembling a greeting.

"I'm looking for Daria Barnes," said a slightly familiar voice. "This is Felicity Whiting."

"Oh, Ms. Whiting. This is Daria."

"Felicity, please." She paused. "Can I buy you lunch? I feel really bad about what happened today."

"It wasn't your fault."

She laughed. "Not by a long country mile, it wasn't. I still think it's only fair to let you know what was really going on."

"Besides Luke setting me up to make you jealous?"

"Yeah, something like that."

She had me meet her in the restaurant at a fancy hotel in Beverly Hills, just north of Wilshire.

"This place is so pretentious," Felicity grumbled at me as we looked over our menus. "Still, the food is really good. They've got a terrific wine list, and if I get recognized, nobody cares."

The room was more than a little snooty with its over-sized sculptures, white tablecloths, fancy crystal, and dim lighting. I noticed a couple of TV execs hunched over a tablet and another name actress and her boyfriend clearly wanting to be seen.

"Yeah, it's a little away from your usual image," I said, cautiously.

I skipped the wine because I was working, although

Felicity had a glass of something white. We both ordered a variety of tapas and once the plates arrived, Felicity sat back in the booth.

"I know I don't have to apologize for Luke's behavior," she said, nibbling on a fried potato wedge. "I still feel bad that you got caught in it."

I shrugged and slurped down some divine Serrano ham. "I appreciate that. It wasn't just you. I'd just found something that…" I sighed. "I can't tell you what I found, but it doesn't make Luke look too good."

"Anything to do with those rumors about me and Larry?" Felicity ate daintily, and clearly enjoyed what she was eating without fear of calories.

"It does give Luke a motive for Mr. Ochoa's murder."

Felicity smiled. "Well, well. The cops finally figured out it was murder. Luke told them he didn't think it was an accident and wouldn't say why."

"I have good reason to believe Luke is holding something back. He never mentioned that he had a good motive for the murder."

"Because he knows he doesn't." Felicity gently slipped an olive pit into her hand and onto her plate. "Those rumors about me and Larry were just that. I know who started them, too. Leo McKesson."

"Why would McKesson do that?"

"Possibly for the publicity. Mostly he just wanted to make trouble. He's had it in for me for a while." She stopped and thought. "Let me explain it this way. Luke is a completely sweet, honorable man. He just doesn't have much of a spine. That doesn't explain it right either. He's very, very focused on his music. He'll fight for that and win. Other than that, he doesn't like conflict of any kind. Which means if someone like Leo McKesson gets a hold of him, Luke is pretty much at his mercy. Until he gets fed up. Now, he won't directly confront anybody, unless it's about the music. Only Luke is a master manipulator. Problem is, Leo has Luke pretty firmly planted under his thumb. I tried to get Luke to stand up for himself, and that's what eventually made me break up with him. I couldn't stand to see him being taken advantage of by Leo."

"Okay. If Luke is manipulating me, what does he really want from me?"

"Has he tried to point your investigation in a specific direction?"

I thought. "Well, he has mentioned Mr. McKesson a couple times, and Mr. Kemper. Problem is, they're both solidly alibied. Mr. Kemper was with Luke the entire time when Mr. Ochoa was probably killed. Besides, McKesson was in his office. Unless his secretary lied to us."

"She didn't. Only don't be so sure Leo was in his office." She looked at her glass then at me. "You sure you don't want a taste of this with these prawns? They're amazing."

"Some other time, thanks." I was deep in thought. I had to have been to have waved off a taste of that wine and those prawns, "This makes no sense. I talked with Agnes - the secretary - and she said there's only one way in and out of that office."

"I know. That's the mystery of it." Felicity took a solid sip of her wine and put the glass down firmly. "I think you need to talk to Leo's wife."

"Candy?"

"Mm-hm."

"I can't. She's in a shelter."

"I shouldn't say this, but Candy and I have found a way to talk since she left that bastard. We have to be careful because we can't let Leo find out where she is."

"I know. I used to work at a domestic violence shelter. The most dangerous time for abuse victims is after they leave. I forget what percentage it is that get killed."

"I think it's still fifty percent of abuse victims who get killed are killed after they leave their abuser." Felicity slipped some ham onto a round of bread and drizzled the chopped tomato sauce on it.

"That was the second time Luke pointed out that McKesson might have had something to do with Ochoa's killing. Problem is, as I told him then, McKesson got the wrong victim. It was Luke that kept McKesson busy so Candy and the kids could get out."

Felicity snorted. "Do you honestly think Leo is going to kill the goose that lays the golden eggs? He needs Luke even more than Luke needs him."

"How would he have known it was Ochoa that helped get Candy and the kids out?"

"That I can't say. That's why you need to talk to Candy. You say you used to work for a shelter?"

"Up until a few weeks ago."

"That could be our in." Felicity got her phone out of her black fringed leather purse. "I'll make a call or two and see if we can get in to visit Candy."

I tapped my phone. "Would it help if I could get the cop investigating this to come with us?"

"I bet it would," Felicity said.

I called Isabel while Felicity called the shelter. The upshot is that the three of us showed up at an over-sized home near the Gold Line tracks and the Southwest Museum. We were admitted and shown to a darkened living room, which grew progressively darker as the clouds began moving in. Candy came in before we could get seated on the two couches. She was a medium-sized woman with dark black hair, cut short and layered. She wore a baggy white t-shirt and jeans, and her feet were bare.

She held Felicity in a tight hug, which was returned. Then she turned to us. I'd seen the look so many times before. There was a letting go in her posture, her eyes, her entire body. She'd been hurt deeply, yet the worst was over, and she'd survived.

"I'm Daria Barnes, Esparza Investigations," I said. "And this is Detective Isabel Lancaster of the L.A.P. D. I don't know how much they told you."

"You're investigating Larry Ochoa's murder," Candy sniffed, started to hold back her tears, then let them run freely. "He saved our lives, you know."

"I understand," said Isabel gently. "Do you think your husband knew he'd helped you?"

"I don't know." Candy pulled tissues from a box on an end table. "It wouldn't surprise me. You get as controlling as Leo, you have to know everything about everyone. That was one of the things that made it so hard to get away. He'd spy on me, you know. I still don't know how he did it. He'd swear he was in his office. Agnes, his secretary, would swear he was there, and then I'd see him behind me. Or he'd tell me about who I had lunch with. Or what I bought at the grocery store. It was pretty creepy."

"I can imagine," Isabel said. "Do you think he had a hold on his secretary? Some reason she'd lie for him?"

"He could. I never got that feeling from her. A couple of the times I called her to ask where Leo was, she was just as astonished as me that he didn't seem to be in his office. One time, he even came out as we were talking. Since he always used his mobile phone, there was no way to tell when you called him if he was really in his office or not."

Isabel coughed softly. "Mrs. McKesson, you said that Mr. Ochoa saved your lives. Do you believe your husband could have killed Mr. Ochoa?"

"That's the odd thing." Candy swallowed and pulled herself together. "I don't think he would have. Leo's problem is rage. He keeps it together at work. He has to. That's why it was such a problem at home. Between Larry's relationship with Luke and the fact that Leo usually keeps a good grip on himself, I don't see it happening. Unless somehow Larry made him angry, and he lost it. Once Leo gets mad, he's perfectly capable of killing somebody. I just can't see Leo getting that mad away from home. He has too much to lose."

Isabel nodded, then looked at me. I shrugged. We left shortly afterward, although Felicity stayed behind. Out on the sidewalk, Isabel started toward her car, then stopped.

"You know," she said slowly. "It's interesting that Candy said that McKesson wouldn't kill anybody unless he was enraged. Kind of fits the point you made about Ochoa's killing being an act of desperation."

"Except how did he get Ochoa up on the catwalk?" I asked. "Ochoa was afraid of heights."

"Except that Ochoa was doped up."

I frowned. "You mean, he carried Ochoa up there?" I thought about it. "It seems far-fetched. McKesson's pretty ripped, and he was tossing around two-hundred-pound weights when I met him at the gym. Still, to carry a full-grown man? Even doped up, I'm pretty sure Ochoa would have struggled."

Isabel shrugged. "We'll get to it. I'd like to have a look at McKesson's office, though."

"I think I can arrange that," I said, pulling out my phone and dialing Luke.

I explained that I needed to inspect McKesson's office, but didn't say why. Luke was all for it. Something told me he knew what I was after.

"Is there something I should be looking for?" I asked him.

"I wish I could say," Luke said. "I have no clue."

I glanced at Isabel. "I see. Do you mind if I bring Detective Lancaster with me? She's investigating Mr. Ochoa's death for the L.A.P.D."

"The more the merrier," Luke said. "I give full permission. In fact, I'll call Agnes and tell her to let you in."

"Thanks, then. I'll touch base with you later," I said, switching off.

Isabel grinned at me. "Good job. Meet you over there?"

"Sure." I gave her the address and we both fought the increasing traffic to get over to Hollywood.

The good news was that it hadn't started to rain yet. It's not like we don't get rain in Southern California - and that year, it was fairly wet. Let a few raindrops hit the road and the entire city falls apart. Go figure.

Isabel got to Luke's office building ahead of me and waited until I found a parking space then walked up the drive. Agnes was working away at the computer though she smiled when she saw us.

"I've just received Mr. Winston's call," she told us. "I'm afraid Mr. McKesson is not in his office at the moment. It's locked."

Isabel and I looked at each other. Someone had figured out how to cover her backside while still following boss's orders, not that it would help her in this instance. I pulled my wallet out and got out the master key card I still had.

"Good thing I still have this, then," I said, brandishing it.

"What? No!" Agnes bounced up, her flip hair-do staying solid. She was wearing a sheath dress in Mondrian block colors.

She scrambled over trying to block the door. I smiled at her gently.

"I have permission, remember?" I told her. "It's not going to be your fault, and if Mr. McKesson tries to make it your fault, then you need to leave. You'll get another job. I'll see to it."

Agnes swallowed. "I overstayed my visa."

"We'll find a way to fix it," I assured her.

Isabel gave her the gentle good cop look. "You can't be deported while you're a witness in a murder case, anyway." She pulled her navy-blue wool suit coat back and showed Agnes her badge. "I am an L.A.P. D. detective investigating Mr. Ochoa's murder. I can't guarantee immunity, but I can sure make it more likely if you tell me the truth about where Mr. McKesson was on the day of the murder."

Agnes started weeping. "I swear, he was here. He went into that office in the morning and did not come out until the call came through about Larry. If he got out, I have no idea how. I've been in there. The windows are painted shut. There is no way to open them."

Isabel nodded at me, and I opened the office door.

"We'll be in touch," Isabel told Agnes, in her really tough cop tone.

I shut the office door behind us and looked at Isabel.

"You think she's telling the truth?" I asked.

"As sure as anyone can be," Isabel said. "People who are lying try to dance around the truth. She answered straight out. Besides, why would she say what she did about McKesson getting out if she was trying to cover his backside?"

"It seems she's heard the rumors, though," I said. "Interesting that she tried to figure it out, too."

"Well, why don't we?" Isabel began looking around.

It was a good-sized room, about half the size of a two-car garage. The back had been retrofitted so that windows ran across the entire back wall, with a matching set on each of the side walls. The wood-paneled walls featured various awards and pictures of Leo, Luke, and assorted celebrities and politicians. A credenza behind the desk displayed more tour photos, along with dozens of shots of McKesson's daughters at various stages in their lives. There were two bookcases along the wall to the front office. Each was loaded with binders and baseballs, and one had three flat screen TVs mounted on the wall over it.

Isabel and I both pried, poked, ran our fingers over each and every window, window frame, and sill. Agnes was right. There was no way to open them. They had screens on them, too, and there was a good-sized drop to the ground. Nothing fatal, just enough to do some damage.

Isabel and I went around back to the alleyway behind the office. There was a door, which we opened. The room beyond was loaded with cardboard boxes and bits and pieces of sets. Obviously, this was the junk storage room, where you put everything you don't really care about but don't want to throw away. We moved boxes and searched the walls. I frowned.

"What?" Isabel asked.

"The floor plan doesn't seem to measure out," I said pointing to a section that jutted out from the side.

It was about six feet deep and had some exposed plumbing leading up to the floor above. Based on the slope the garage was built on, the little section had to have been built against the dirt.

"Let's go upstairs," said Isabel.

We did. Turned out there was a bathroom, which accounted for the plumbing and the space. Agnes was back at work at her computer and ignored us as we went back into McKesson's office. We left the door open and glared at the windows.

"Just because he found a way to sneak out of the office doesn't mean he killed Ochoa," I said softly.

"It significantly increases the odds he did," Isabel grumbled.

We stood for another minute when we heard the outer office door open and Agnes scrambling to her feet.

"Mr. McKesson, Mr. Winston said that the ladies in your office be allowed to look around," Agnes said anxiously.

McKesson stood in the doorway, clad in a dark wool Italian-cut suit. "That's all right, Agnes."

Candy was right about McKesson being able to hold the rage back. I almost saw it in his eyes for a second, then he softened and was all smiles.

"Sorry I couldn't be here to give you the tour, myself," he said.

"We managed," said Isabel, flipping back her equally expensive suit coat to show her badge. "I'm Detective Isabel Lancaster. We've been hearing some rumors that you have a way of getting out of this office without being seen."

McKesson laughed. "Yeah. I've been hearing them, too. Did you find a way out of here?"

"No," said Isabel, standing her ground.

McKesson backed down. It was impressive. That's Iz for you.

"Is there anything else I can do for you ladies? No?" He walked around the desk and sat down in the plush leather chair. "Then if you'll excuse me, I've got plenty of work to get done."

Isabel waited just a fraction of a second. "Good day, Mr. McKesson. I'll contact you if I have further questions."

She stalked out of the office, pausing only long enough to slip one of her business cards to Agnes. I followed with considerably less grace.

"Now what?" I asked as my phone buzzed.

"Not much we can do," Isabel said. "As the man said, there's no way out of the office that we could find, which means his alibi holds unless we can break down Agnes. Even if we break down Agnes, it's always possible she'll tell us what she thinks we want to hear instead of the truth."

"Wait." I showed Isabel my phone. "I just got a text from Jannie Miller. She's a tech expert that Berto put on the case regarding that shell company, what was it? Rottgutt."

"And...?"

I read the text again. "She has the info and will give it to me if I meet her in Silver Lake."

"What?"

"She's real spooky. I'm guessing she wants to be sure she's telling the right person. Come on."

"I'll follow you over," Isabel said dryly.

Miller was back in her hunched over position at the coffee house, only this time, she had two laptops open, in addition to her tablet, and was furiously scribbling in a wire-bound notebook with a fountain pen. I introduced Isabel, and Miller checked out both her badge and her I.D.

"Can't be too careful," Miller said. She pulled a folder out of her bag. "Anyway, fortunately, I didn't have to drill down too many levels. Rottgutt is owned by ZapatoUno, which is owned by Luke Winston Enterprises, Luke Winston, sole owner, managed by Leo McKesson, CEO."

Okay, my jaw dropped.

"Ah. You've figured out who ran Berto down," Jannie said.

I looked at Isabel, who shook her head.

"Not quite," I said. "Somebody's got some 'splaining to do, though."

"Thank you, Ms. Miller," Isabel said, getting up and getting out her business card. "Here's my card. If you get any other information, please let me know. Uh, Daria?"

"Sure. See you," I said.

Out on the sidewalk, Isabel was looking up at the sky.

"We weren't supposed to get rain until Friday," she grumbled.

I shrugged my pea coat around me more tightly. "Last I looked, the storm was coming in faster than expected." I looked at her. "I need to talk to Luke Winston."

"We need back up," Isabel said grimly. "I'll call my partner and have him meet me over there."

Isabel hated her partner, and the feeling was mutual. Still, they were cops and he'd never let her down before.

"I'll see you there," I said, getting increasingly angry.

"Hold on!" Iz grabbed my arm. "Do you want to get yourself killed?"

"He's not the killer," I yelped, tears stinging my eyes. "He's not the person who ran down Berto. He hired us, remember? But, damn it, he knows something and I'm going to wring it out of him one way or another."

I yanked myself away and got in my car. I was shaking by the time I got to Luke's place although not so shaky that I didn't see the huge black Dodge Charger parked near the building. It was discreet enough as sedans go, but now that I knew what it was, it leaped out at me like a laser pointer. Isabel pulled up and parked across the street. I pointed.

"Is that the car from the surveillance tape?" I yelled.

Isabel nodded and waved at me to stay put. I ignored her and ran into the building. The security guard knew me, so he buzzed me in. Isabel had to flash her badge. By that time, I was already on the elevator. I did hold the door for Isabel. She got on, shaking her head.

"We're going to do this by the book," she said as the elevator crawled to Luke's floor.

"He's not the killer. He just knows who the killer is and I'm going to get it out of him."

"And ruin the court case. Come on, Daria. Now, you're acting like an amateur. Get it together."

I was reasonably calm by the time the elevator stopped. The small foyer between the two apartments was deserted. Luke's door was slightly ajar. Isabel had her gun out in an instant. She pushed me to the other side of the door from herself and knocked loudly.

"Mr. Winston. It's the police," she called. "Are you in there?"

The groan started out soft and grew. Isabel waved me back. She pushed the door open slowly and slid in, ready to fire. There was another groan, and she pushed the door open all the way, took a quick look around, then rushed inside, holstering her gun.

I saw why. The room was a shambles as if there had been a fight and I could see Luke Winston's boots sticking out from the other side of the turned-over sofa. I ran in.

Luke's face was a red puffed-up mess, and his nose and mouth were bleeding. He had rolled over onto his side and was clutching his stomach. Isabel was on her radio, calling for help. She patted Luke on the shoulder as he groaned.

"It's all right," she said. "Help is on the way."

"Leo," Luke groaned.

"Do you want him?" Isabel asked.

"No!" Luke coughed. "He— He did this."

Isabel went on instant alert, and I looked around the apartment and pointed toward the bedrooms. Isabel went into search and protect mode. She motioned me back, then went into one bedroom, then the other. Leaving that part of the apartment, she went into the kitchen.

"He's gone," she said, holstering her gun. "How's Winston?"

I found an afghan and put it over him. "I think he's going into shock."

Isabel pushed me out of the way to tend to Luke. Feeling useless, I wandered into the front bedroom, hoping to find some proof or clue. Something. The room looked untouched, as far as I could see. The window looked out over the street. I looked down and saw Leo McKesson pacing back and forth next to the Charger. I got out my phone and dialed. Agnes picked up.

"Agnes, it's Daria Barnes. Is Mr. McKesson in his office?"

"Yes. Well, I haven't seen him leave." She paused. "Has he?"

"Yep. Get the hell out of there now. I'm coming over."

I bolted from the apartment and heard Isabel yelling after me. Okay. It was dumb. I get it. We didn't need to know how Leo McKesson was getting out of his office, just that he was. I had the evidence right before me. I watched from the building's door as McKesson got into the Dodge Charger and barreled out of there. Actually, he headed in the opposite direction from Luke's office, so I thought I might have a couple of minutes on him.

Which is why I made the mistake I did and went over to Winston's office. Damn it, I was going to catch that son of a bitch red-handed. Come hell or high water and whatever other cliché I could think of, I was going to do it.

I didn't see the Charger anywhere on the street when I pulled up to the office. I didn't wait for parking and pulled right into the driveway and entered the code for the gate. I almost left my car blocking the sidewalk, I was so impatient for the gate to open, but it did. I shut down the engine and ran to the garage office.

Agnes had gone, bless her. I ran through to the door, used my key card, and opened it just in time to see Leo McKesson coming in through the wood paneling right above that little section in the storage room where the plumbing was.

"A secret door?" I yelped.

"You bitch!" McKesson screamed.

He started toward me, and I turned and ran for the office door. I would have made it all the way out except something hit me in the back of my head. I fell and lost consciousness.

Chapter Seventeen

When I first came to, McKesson was pacing the office, cussing me out up one side and down the other.

"Fucking cunt bitch!" he yelped and kicked me in the kidneys. "Why did you make me kill you?"

It was an odd question because I wasn't dead. I couldn't answer because I'd passed out again. When I came to the second time, I had been dumped in a tiny, pitch-black closet. I tried to stand and was overcome by spinning and nausea, which was probably just as well because McKesson opened the closet and hauled me roughly out of it, complaining all the while about stupid fucks who made him kill them, first Ochoa, then Swanson. Hell, even Luke had pushed him too far and should have known better.

"Fucking son of a bitch better live," McKesson grumbled, tossing me over his shoulder.

I might have pointed out that I wasn't dead, only I passed out again.

When I, at last, came to for real, I was folded together in a fetal position on top of a rough carpet. It was dark. I could hear an engine running and saw the red glow of a taillight near my head. I was in the trunk of a car. A really, big powerful car.

Slowly, I pieced together where I was and how I'd gotten there. I was still pretty nauseous, but it was better enough that I was able to get into the pocket of my pea coat and pull out my phone. I wondered why McKesson had let me keep it, then realized he thought I was dead. Didn't the idiot know enough to check my pulse? Of course, he'd sounded pretty panicked, I realized, those other two times I'd come to.

I texted Berto first, then Isabel, then Tim. Thank

heavens I'd remembered Tim. I texted him Berto's number because I couldn't remember Isabel's number - the major downside of auto-dialers. I shut the sound off on the phone and fretted because the battery was getting low. Worse yet, there wasn't much of a signal, which would run my battery down even more.

I could hear the car slooshing through water on the road, and when the car finally slowed, I could hear the heavy patter of a downpour. Perfect. I saw the right blinker going and the car turned. Fortunately, McKesson had calmed down enough that he wasn't driving like a maniac. Still, we were on a twisty-turny road. I heard something metallic clank next to my feet as we hit a particularly tight turn. There wasn't a lot of room. I scrunched around and got my hands on what felt like a wrench. There were a couple of them in the trunk, which wasn't all that surprising since lots of guys I know keep toolkits in their trunks. I felt around again and found a ratchet. The wrench was heavier, although only about eight inches long. The ratchet was longer and had a hard knob on the end of its crooked metal body. It was no small trick, but I put the wrench in my coat pocket and grabbed the ratchet.

The car slowed and eventually slid to a stop. The engine ran for a minute, then turned off. In the silence, I could hear McKesson grumbling and complaining about having to dump another body. I couldn't help wondering just how stupid was this guy? I didn't have an answer, given how colossally stupid I'd just been. I gripped the lower end of the ratchet and waited, my heart pounding. At least, I didn't feel like barfing. Much.

The engine started again, and the car turned back onto the road. We only drove a few minutes longer when McKesson stopped the car, put on the brake, and got outside. I heard the door slam and took a deep breath. It felt like forever. McKesson didn't open the trunk. He got back in the car, drove a few feet or something, then stopped the car and got out. I braced myself yet again. McKesson went back to the front of the car, took off the brake and we drove on.

It probably wasn't that long, but it sure felt like it. The car stopped. McKesson killed the engine and turned off the lights. The rain had slowed or perhaps even stopped. In any case, I couldn't hear it pattering on the trunk lid. I heard McKesson get out of the car, then his footsteps crunching on the ground as he got closer and closer to the trunk. It was for real this time.

I played dead just long enough to get clear of the trunk. It hurt like hell when McKesson dropped me onto the wet pavement. At least I didn't lose consciousness.

"Fucking cunt bitch," he grumbled again.

It was almost pitch dark out there, and the rain had stopped. I saw a glow of city lights off the edge of the hill, but there was little other light.

As he reached around me to shut the trunk, I slid to my knees then pushed myself up.

McKesson screamed in terror. I staggered to my feet and pressed my advantage, trying to remember everything I'd learned in every self-defense class I'd ever taken. McKesson backed up and stumbled, then got mad again. Screaming, he lunged at me, I danced back, hit the back of the car, then started swinging the ratchet. McKesson bounced back. It's a good thing that McKesson was more interested in pretty six-pack abs than doing anything with all that muscle he had built, or I would never have survived.

Still swinging, I came at him. He rushed me low and tackled me. We skidded on the asphalt, and I lost my breath as McKesson landed on top of me. Worse yet, I lost the ratchet. McKesson scrambled to his knees over me and hauled back to punch me. I got my knees and feet under his ass, bucked, and sent him tumbling over my head. Scrambling upright, or trying to, I reached for the wrench in my coat pocket. McKesson slammed me down, and I jammed the wrench into his leg. He yelped in pain. Squirming, I got away again. Somehow, my free hand landed on the ratchet. I grabbed it and rolled just as McKesson made another grab for me.

We both scrambled to our feet. I had the road behind me. The moon broke through the clouds, adding a blue cast to the night. I thought I heard a siren in the distance and hoped like hell it was coming this way. McKesson tried another run at me. I dodged him and clipped him with the ratchet. He stumbled but was up again.

We circled each other. I became slowly aware that we were moving off the pavement onto the dirt of the road's shoulder. And even more aware that there wasn't that much shoulder before it fell off into what was presumably a nice deep canyon. I thought the sirens might be getting louder and debated taunting McKesson. Somehow, I didn't think that was going to do much toward keeping myself alive long enough for help to get there.

McKesson came at my other side. I dodged and almost slipped down the hillside. I ran the other way. McKesson was almost on me when I turned and swung. He dodged back. So much for trying to outrun him.

"You aren't going to get me, bitch," McKesson hollered as the soft roar of a helicopter approached.

"I don't have to get you," I called, edging as far away from him as I could. "I just have to stay alive."

McKesson glanced up and apparently saw what I was seeing: the spotlight from a police helicopter. Okay, it was actually a Sheriff's Department chopper, but at the moment all it meant was that, for me, help was coming. For McKesson, it meant that he'd better kill me and shut me up before they got there. He came at me with renewed force. The only advantage I had was that ratchet and the wrench, and the fact that tossing weights around does not make you a good fighter.

I swung the ratchet with all my strength, which knocked him askew for a moment. He bounced back and the next time I swung, he grabbed the ratchet and stopped it cold. I didn't dare let go, but his grip was strong, and he grabbed at me with his free hand. I dodged, then kicked him hard in the knee. He didn't let go, although it stunned him enough that I was able to land a second kick in his belly.

The chopper's thrumming grew loud, and a flash of light blinded me for a second. The good thing was that it blinded McKesson, too. Gasping, he looked up. I swung and the light was back just in time for me to see the edge of the road's shoulder give way under McKesson's feet. McKesson screamed as he slid from view.

I struggled to remain standing for the next few minutes while the Sheriff's cars pulled up, lights blazing and sirens blaring. Behind them, an unmarked Crown Vic that looked suspiciously like the one Isabel had been driving, skid into the circle of light.

A couple of the deputies scurried to the side of the road and looked over. Apparently, the drop was either not that bad or McKesson had gotten insanely lucky. In any case, he was still alive.

A fire truck, paramedics and a couple of ambulances pulled up to join the party. I stood, dazed with ratchet in hand, until Isabel came up and gently took it from my hands.

"I should fucking kill you," she snarled.

"I won't go down easy," I said.

Or rather, I think that's what I said. As Iz pointed out, I was pretty groggy by that point. She rode with me to the hospital in the ambulance, chewing me out the entire way. Most of what happened afterward was a blur. Tim was there. One minute he was gloating about the tracking software that had led to my rescue and the next minute yelling at me for needing it. The nurses took pictures of my bruises and the next morning Isabel came by with a boot and measured it against the marks on my back where McKesson had kicked me. Berto was there, too, in a wheelchair, taking pictures with Iz's mobile phone. Berto and I would have had matching bandages on our heads, except he'd ditched his.

"What are you doing here, *hermano*?" I asked when Isabel finally let me roll over onto my back.

"I got P.T.," he said. "Thought I'd roll by and see how you were doing. Especially since you were such a fucking idiot last night."

"I know!" I groaned. "I get it. I won't do it again."

"Not if I have anything to say about it," Isabel said. She shook the boot. "The only good news is that we've got a match here. Mr. McKesson's pricy lawyers are going to have a hell of a time wriggling out of this one."

"How's Luke doing?" I asked.

"He's pretty banged up," Isabel said. "Fortunately, not life-threatening. In fact, he's down the hall from you. Turns out this wasn't the first time McKesson has hit him."

"You've gotta be kidding," I said.

Isabel went back to work shortly after that. Berto did his physical therapy, then came back and visited. I sorely needed a friendly face. While he was at P.T., Marisol came down and gave me an earful. Then Franny did. Then Tim came back and lectured me some more.

By late afternoon, the doctors determined that I only had a concussion and released me to Tim's not so tender mercies. I did talk the orderly into letting me roll down the hall to see Luke. His face was a puffy mess, but he was otherwise okay and awake. Felicity was with him.

"Hey," Luke said, weakly raising his hand.

"I hear you're going to live," I said.

"Yeah. I'm sorry about what Leo did to you," Luke said.

"What did he do?" Felicity asked.

"He knocked me over the head and thought he'd killed me, so he stuffed me in a car trunk and tried to dispose of me up near Angeles Crest." I shrugged. "That's apparently what happened to Larry Ochoa and to Jay Swanson. He got angry and attacked. Larry was slightly doped up, thanks to his coffee being spiked with Vicodin." I gave Luke a nasty glare and he had the decency to look away. "Jay was an easy-going kid who had an abusive father and couldn't fight back. Both times, McKesson thought he'd killed them then tried to cover it up, first by throwing Larry off the catwalk, and, no, we don't know exactly how he got Larry up there, then by dumping Jay's body."

"That sounds pretty stupid," Felicity said.

"It was, but McKesson panicked each time." I glared at Luke. "Funny thing is, Mr. Winston, I think you knew all along what your manager had done."

"I didn't have any proof. Just a feeling." Luke's eyes darted around the room. "I thought I'd seen Leo on the stage that morning. Except Agnes was sure he'd been in the office the whole time. How crazy would I look if I told the cops that Leo was sneaking out of his office and killing people?"

"You should have at least told Berto and me," I said. "If you had, maybe we could have kept him from running Berto over and protected you."

"I guess that was pretty stupid of me."

"You should have told us about spiking Larry's coffee, too," I added.

He groaned.

"I get it," I said. "You meant well. It's just that you don't do shit like that to addicts."

Felicity cleared her throat and lifted an eyebrow. I figured it out. Luke would be feeling guilty about spiking that coffee for the rest of his life. Good.

"How was McKesson getting out?" Luke asked.

Gee, a real apology would have been nice. I chose to let it go.

"There was a secret door in the garage office to the storage room below," I said. According to the cops, it looks like it may have been there when the place was built in the late 20s. Or some drug dealers could have built it later. We'll probably never know."

"Huh. I remember wanting that office when we moved in," said Luke. "Only Leo said it made more sense for him to be out there."

I sighed, told Luke we'd be billing him and left. Felicity followed me out of the room.

"Hey, Daria," she said softly. "You're right about Luke, but I don't think you understand how strong a hold Leo had on him."

"Actually, I do, Felicity," I said. "I worked in that shelter, remember? It takes an average of seven times for a victim to leave her abuser. Luke had more reason than most to keep McKesson on." I looked back at the room. "You two look like you've made up."

"McKesson was the problem. He's gone." Felicity smiled softly. "Besides, somebody's got to take care of that lunkhead. May as well be me. I do love him." She paused. "I also talked him into going to therapy, so we don't get a repeat episode. That's the thing about Luke. It may take dynamite to get through to him, but once you do, he'll really work on getting better."

"Well, good luck." I tried to keep the skeptical tone out

of my voice. Getting better was always possible, and hope could a powerful thing.

I waved at Tim, who came running to get me. I introduced him to Felicity, the two bantered lightly and then Tim made a great show of taking me home.

He did pamper me with amazing food and some nice sex over the next week or so, as I recovered.

We also got our play staged and it's doing very well, indeed. It may even get to Off-Broadway.

As for all the other loose ends, Sims melted down at his preliminary hearing and earned himself a prescription for some premium drugs and a restraining order. His mother agreed to keep him under psychiatric care, too, but never said whether she or Sims had bought the red paint that he'd sprayed all over Miriam Watt's house. I gave it even odds after the hearing. Berto did some digging and found a divorce decree for Larry Ochoa and Rita Camacho. Ochoa's family inherited although they were kind enough to give Rita's father some money for her care and last I heard, she was in rehab and doing okay. The Feds were even more interested in the Ridley family's whereabouts than we were. Seems the Ridleys had a land-based version of a Ponzi scheme going. In any case, it's not likely Matt is going to be stalking his former girlfriend anymore. Lester Margolis remains in the wind and that's fine.

Sophie Reisner got interesting, though. About a month after I talked to her, she filed suit against the TV station and several other executives, claiming that she was sick and tired of the constant sexual harassment. The guys all claimed that it was consensual, only Reisner had secretly recorded the latest one telling her she'd better play along or get fired. She released the tape, and everyone settled. Now Reisner is working on a woman's news site, and possibly a cable channel. It looks good and it's doing pretty well.

Luke and Felicity got married quietly. Turned out that McKesson had been doing some embezzling, probably thought he had it coming to him. With McKesson plea bargaining for life in prison, it looks like Luke will be able to recover the money. Candy will get the rest of McKesson's assets. She's working for Luke and Felicity, too, and the girls seem to be getting their heads on straight.

The check Luke sent Berto was mighty impressive. Marisol twisted Berto's arm into giving me a goodly chunk of it, with another nice bonus for Franny. Tim turned me on to a good financial advisor. So, while I will have to work some, I'm mostly free to work on producing plays. Because I will be working now and again for Berto (I'm sure as hell not working for anyone else), I'm taking classes in investigation at the local community college. The jury's still out on how much I like it. The whole getting shot at thing, getting beat up thing, and being stupid thing, that stuff still scares me. On the other hand, I did survive all those things that scare me so much. Plus, PI work is not a bad way to pay for my theatre habit, as Berto calls it. The classes are making me feel more confident, too.

I decided to do one other thing. I'm now a volunteer at the shelter where I used to work. It saves them some money on clerical help and gives the regular secretary some breathing space. It's still sad and frustrating at times. Then there are those days when a woman comes in and you can tell that no matter how hurt and beaten down she's been, the worst is over. She has survived and will rebuild her life.

Coming Soon

t's Book Four in the Old Los Angeles series, set in the 1870s.

Death of an Heiress

What do you do when the closest suspect has the least reason to kill?

Timothy Gaines has no reason to kill his sister, Lavina. He's already stolen the bequest from her father. So, he turns to Lavina's friend, physician and winemaker Maddie Wilcox, to help him find the killer and divert suspcion from himself.

But Lavina's murder bears an uncanny resemblance to the murder of an old Indian healing woman, and the only motive Maddie can find involves the death of Lavina's friend, Julia Carson. The cause of Miss Carson's death is not the sort of thing one talks about, and Lavina's unmentionables are missing.

How does a proper lady get the answers she needs to stop a killer determined to stop her first?

And don't forget the first three books in the series:
Death of the Zanjero
Death of the City Marshal and
Death of the Chinese Field Hands

Other books by Anne Louise Bannon

'm so glad you liked this book! Check out my other novels, available in print or ebook at your favorite retailer:

Freddie and Kathy Series:
Fascinating Rhythm
Bring Into Bondage
The Last Witnesses
Blood Red

Operation Quickline Series
That Old Cloak and Dagger Routine
Stopleak
Deceptive Appearances
Fugue in a Minor Key
Sad Lisa
These Hallowed Halls

Old Los Angeles
Death of the Zanjero
Death of the City Marshal
Death of the Chinese Field Hands

Daria Barnes
Rage Issues

Mrs. Sperling
A Nose for a Niedeman

Brenda Finnegan
Tyger, Tyger

Romantic Fiction
White House Rhapsody, Book One and Two

Fantasy and Science Fiction
A Ring for a Second Chance
But World Enough and Time

And I would be honored if you left a review for this and any of my books on GoodReads or any other retail site. It really helps.

Connect with Anne Louise Bannon

Thank you for sticking it out this long! Please join my newsletter. It's the best way to stay up-to-date on my upcoming projects, blog posts and even games and giveaways.

Sign up here: http://eepurl.com/zH0Ab

Or connect with me on your favorite social media platforms:

Visit my website: http://annelouisebannon.com
Friend me on Facebook: http://facebook.com/RobinGoodfellowEnt
Follow me on Twitter: http://twitter.com/ALBannon
Favorite my Smashwords author page: https://www.smashwords.com/profile/view/MsBriscow
Connect on LinkedIn: http://www.linkedin.com/in/annelouisebannon
Follow me on Pinterest: http://pinterest.com/msbriscow

About Anne Louise Bannon

Anne Louise Bannon is an author and journalist who wrote her first novel at age 15. Her journalistic work has appeared in Ladies' Home Journal, the Los Angeles Times, Wines and Vines, and in newspapers across the country. She was a TV critic for over 10 years, founded the YourFamilyViewer blog, and created the OddBallGrape.com wine education blog with her husband, Michael Holland. She is the co-author of Howdunit: Book of Poisons, with Serita Stevens, as well as author of the Freddie and Kathy mystery series, set in the 1920s, the Old Los Angeles series, set in 1870, and the Operation Quickline series, plus several stand alones. She and her husband live in Southern California with an assortment of critters.